MURDER TAKES A TURN

*The Langham and Dupré Mysteries by Eric Brown
from Severn House*

MURDER BY THE BOOK
MURDER AT THE CHASE
MURDER AT THE LOCH
MURDER TAKE THREE

MURDER TAKES A TURN

A Langham and Dupré mystery

Eric Brown

This first world edition published 2018
in Great Britain and the USA by
SEVERN HOUSE PUBLISHERS LTD of
Eardley House, 4 Uxbridge Street, London W8 7SY.
Trade paperback edition first published
in Great Britain and the USA 2018 by
SEVERN HOUSE PUBLISHERS LTD

British Library Cataloguing in Publication Data
A CIP catalogue record for this title is available from the British Library.

ISBN-13: 978-0-7278-8781-8 (cased)
ISBN-13: 978-1-84751-904-7 (trade paper)
ISBN-13: 978-1-78010-959-6 (e-book)

This is a work of fiction. Names, characters, places and incidents are either the
product of the author's imagination or are used fictitiously. Except where actual
historical events and characters are being described for the storyline of this novel,
all situations in this publication are fictitious and any resemblance to actual persons,
living or dead, business establishments, events or locales is purely coincidental.

All Severn House titles are printed on acid-free paper.

Severn House Publishers support the Forest Stewardship Council™ [FSC™],
the leading international forest certification organisation.
All our titles that are printed on FSC certified paper carry the FSC logo.

ONE

I n his *pied-à-terre* above the Elder and Dupré literary agency, Charles Elder was tucking into his favourite breakfast: devilled kidneys with toast and coffee. It was a meal fit for a king and set him up nicely for the day; sometimes, after such a breakfast, he had been known to forego lunch . . . though not often. Meals, for Charles Elder, were one of the delights of life, together with the very best novels and poetry. Fine meals and good books, and friends with whom to share these, were the necessities of life – which, all things considered, had been kind to him of late.

In Albert he had a faithful and considerate companion, and in Maria Dupré not only a brilliant colleague but a trusted friend. The agency was ticking over very nicely, with fifty authors whose books, both novels and non-fiction, ameliorated the cultural climate of the land. At fifty-six he was in tolerable health, though his doctor had recently suggested that he shed a few pounds. He was, he admitted, rather on the large side. Over lunch last week, one of his authors had commented that the size of his girth made his feet appear so tiny that he resembled a spinning top.

A spinning top, indeed!

His housemaid bustled into the room. 'That's me, Mr Elder. I'll be back at six. Sirloin with potato dauphinoise and honey-glazed carrots for dinner.'

'And dessert?'

'Sherry trifle suit you?'

'That sounds a delight, Mrs F.'

'Ta-ta for now, then.'

'*Au revoir.*'

Not that life was *all* blissful contentment at the moment. There was always a fly in the ointment, and this particular fly was sorely vexing him. Last week, he'd received an unwelcome letter from an old school friend, the novelist Denbigh Connaught. The writer had sacked his agent and wished to appoint Charles to look after his literary affairs. Moreover – and this was what pained Charles

– Connaught wished to apologize for something that had occurred during their schooldays almost forty years ago.

Charles had not deigned to reply. The missive had brought back a slew of painful memories. Almost as bad as those memories, however, was the niggling voice in the back of his head which insisted that he ought to accept the novelist's apology and agree to represent him.

He finished his coffee and gazed through the window overlooking the lawn at the rear of the premises. It was a fortnight until his annual garden party, and he must really draw up a guest list. His mind whirring over whom to invite, and whom not to, he moved to the bathroom, attended to his *toilette*, then descended to the agency. It was ten thirty, and his working day was under way.

Molly was tapping away at her typewriter in the reception area and smiled as he appeared. 'Morning, Mr Elder.'

'Good morning to you, my dear – and a fine one it is, too. The sun shines and all is well with the world. Post?'

She indicated two piles on the desk beside her, a tottering tower of manuscripts and a smaller stack of letters.

'Would you be a darling and go through the manuscripts? Unsolicited in one pile, agency authors in the other. I'll take the letters now.'

He picked up the letters and moved to his office.

'Oh,' Molly said, 'Albert rang. He took the car into the garage yesterday, and it's bad news. It's something to do with the carburettor, and they won't be able to supply a replacement until next week.'

'Botheration! Very well, I'll phone Albert later.'

All weekend, Albert, sweating and covered in grease, had toiled like a trooper beneath the Bentley, before admitting defeat and calling the garage. That was one of the many things he admired about the young man: he could turn his hand to anything, and more often than not was successful. That he occasionally admitted his limitations was only, as far as Charles was concerned, an admirable trait.

He had hoped to drive to the coast with Albert on Saturday, but now they would have to entertain themselves at home.

The door to Maria's office stood open, and Charles paused. She sat at her desk, her red lips skewed into an amused pout as she read a manuscript. Oh, how his heart surged when he regarded her like this, in her unguarded, unselfconscious moments. Charles thought of Maria as the daughter he had never had, and was fuelled by the foolish but heartfelt desire to cherish and protect the woman.

She looked up and blessed him with her heart-warming smile. 'Charles . . . You're looking well.'

'Never better, my dear. Something amuses you?'

'Nevinson's latest. He really gives Wodehouse a run for his money.'

'Excellent. I look forward to reading it in due course.'

'Donald sends his regards,' she said.

'I really must take you both out for dinner. It must be at least two weeks since I had a good heart-to-heart with Donald.'

'That would be lovely. He's putting the finishing touches to his latest.'

'Excellent news. I shall look forward to reading that one, too.'

He was crossing to his office, leafing through the correspondence, when his gaze alighted on the return address of the uppermost envelope. He stopped in his tracks, feeling suddenly dizzy.

'Charles?' Molly said from her desk.

His hand trembled as he ripped open the letter. He read the single sheet of notepaper, felt decidedly ill, and gave Molly a wan smile.

'That dreadful man Connaught again,' he murmured.

'Perhaps Maria or I should write to him . . .' Molly began tentatively.

'I wouldn't dream of it, my dear. I shall deal with him myself.' He crossed to the staircase. 'I think I'll go and lie down, Molly. I do not wish to be disturbed, there's a good girl.'

Clutching the letter and murmuring imprecations, Charles hurried up the stairs.

Two miles across London, in Knightsbridge, Lady Cecelia Albrighton was taking her daily constitutional.

It was her habit to take a turn around the park every day after breakfast, come rain or shine, buy a *Daily Mail* from old Billy on the corner, then return to her apartment and peruse the news over a cup of lapsang souchong. Today, however, such was the state of her thoughts that she sailed right past Billy, halted only by his cry of, 'Here! Lady Cee! Wot's up, luv? Somethin' I said, is it?'

'Why, Billy . . . How remiss of me. I was miles away.'

She retraced her steps, bought a paper, and turned to go.

'Here, you OK, luv?'

She forced a smile. 'I am very well, thank you, Billy.'

The old newspaper vendor nodded, unsure, and Lady Cecelia hurried away.

Back at her tiny apartment overlooking Hyde Park, she made herself a cup of tea and sat at her escritoire beside the window.

For perhaps the tenth time, she reread the letter she had received that morning – the second from Connaught in two weeks. Then she laid it aside and stared around the spartan but impeccably furnished room.

She led, in the circumstances, a satisfactory life; she had her little routines and a select circle of friends, and she enjoyed living in London. A little more money would have eased her circumstances somewhat, but she could not complain. There were many people in more reduced circumstances than her. She had made it a rule of life never to succumb to self-pity, and never, ever, to regret what might have been.

The letters, however, had thrown her into such a state of confusion that she had found herself not only looking back but pitying the woman she had become.

She was sixty, though sometimes she felt older, and she was lonely. Friends were all very well, but what a woman of her age needed was a life companion: a husband, preferably, but a lover if a husband was not to be found – at any rate, a strong man on whom to unburden oneself from time to time, and with whom she could share the trials and tribulations of existence in this uncertain age.

She shook her head, remonstrating with herself: she really must not slip into the slough of self-pity.

Phrases from the letter surfaced unbidden in her mind.

I am deeply sorry for what occurred all those years ago . . .

I was a fool, and only now, with age and experience, can I admit as much . . .

I would very much like to make reparations, if that would be at all possible, and therefore extend this invitation: Please, Cecelia, do me the honour of being my guest at Connaught House . . .

Along with the pain provoked by the letter, however, Lady Cecelia admitted that she felt also not a little frisson of excitement.

She picked up her pen, pulled a sheet of Basildon Bond towards her, and began to write.

Dear Denbigh, I would be delighted to accept your invitation . . .

* * *

Fifty miles from London in the sleepy Hampshire village of Coombe Lacey, Colonel Haxby set off from his thatched cottage on the stroke of eleven, bound for the Horse and Hounds.

He was nothing if not a creature of habit. His all-too-brief enlistment in the 11th Hussars had instilled in him a military discipline, a respect for order and the acceptance that one must abide by the rules. Rommel might have put an end to his army days in 1941, but in the fifteen years since then he'd prospered by living life on strictly martial lines.

He rose every day at seven, bathed and shaved, and breakfasted at seven thirty. At eight he spent an hour reading the *Express,* and at nine attended to his correspondence. At ten he read a volume of military history. At eleven, the Horse and Hounds opened its hallowed portals and he arrived on the dot of five past for two pints of Mackeson with whisky chasers, followed by lunch, which set him up nicely for his afternoon nap at three. At five thirty, he tucked into whatever his housemaid, Edna, had rustled up, and at seven it was back to the Horse and Hounds for an evening session. However fine the whisky, and however good the company, it was his rule to be back home by ten. It didn't do to burn the candle at both ends, and after all he had to be up at the stroke of seven every morn.

His Mackeson and whisky chaser was waiting for him on the bar, as ever, and he ferried the drinks to his armchair before the mullioned window.

'How are we this morning, Colonel?' Lilly the barmaid called out.

He imbibed the milk stout, smacked his lips, and stretched out his artificial leg beneath the table. 'Terrible, if y'must know.'

She blinked. His usual response to her greeting was, 'Fine, fine. And all the better for seeing your smiling face, Lilly.'

'Oh, and why's that, Colonel?'

'Spectre from the past.'

'Say again.'

'Y'know how it is. You fight the battle and forget about it, hmm? Put it behind you and get on with life. Don't blubber over spilt milk.'

'Ye–es,' she said.

'Nothing worse than an old soldier who bores people with talk of past battles, what?'

'Quite.'

'Then something like this comes out of the blue – a spectre from the past.'

He took his first mouthful of Scotch and closed his eyes. Oh, bliss . . . *Heaven!*

Lilly leaned over the bar. 'What happened, Colonel?'

'Fell in with a rogue in 'thirty-three. Should've known better. I was a bloody fool.' He fell silent.

'Who was that, then?'

'Nasty piece of work – not that I knew it at the time. Only later, a year later. Cad did the dirty. Left me high and dry.'

'I'm sorry, Colonel. Best to forgive and forget, though?'

'Forgive?' he grunted. 'Never! Especially . . .'

'Yes?'

'Chap's written to me – twice, would you believe? After all these years. Bold as brass. And what's more, he claims he's sorry. Sorry? After what he did? As if mere words might atone . . . Wants me to pay him a call, stay for a weekend, so that he can apologize face-to-face.'

'Well,' Lilly said, 'are you going to go?'

The colonel didn't hear the question. He chewed his moustache, rearranged his false leg and finished the Scotch.

'Same again, Lilly, there's a good girl. And make it a double whisky this time.'

She poured the drinks and carried them across to his table. 'Well, are you going to visit him, or what?'

He thought about it, then said, 'Yes, Lilly, I am.'

He'd go down to Cornwall, he decided, and shoot Denbigh Connaught through the ruddy heart.

Back in London, Pandora Jade was in the throes of creation.

She regarded the naked girl who was lying on the bed with her bottom in the air. 'Head a little further up. Stop! Wonderful, darling. Hold it there.'

'But it's uncomfortable!' Nancy protested.

'Almost done, darling. Two minutes.'

With a palette knife she applied impasto daubs of sienna acrylic to the canvas and smeared it in an impressionistic approximation of her lover's perfect body. She worked fast, her eyes shuttling between the girl and the canvas. As ever, when painting, she felt as if she were on another plane, the cares and concerns of daily life temporarily forgotten.

She stepped back and regarded the painting. Another session

tomorrow and it would be finished. She was excited, as ever at this stage of creation; the image before her caught the essence, she thought, of Nancy Carter.

'There. You can relax now, darling.'

'Phew! What I do for art,' the girl said, swinging her legs off the bed and massaging the feeling back into her arms. 'Can I look now?'

'Come on, then.'

The naked girl padded around the easel and stood beside Pandora, staring at the canvas.

'And that's supposed to be me?' Nancy said, indignant.

'Well, an abstract representation of you.'

'And what's that mean in plain English?'

'It means, it represents what I feel is the essential you.'

'But . . .' Nancy pulled a sulky face. 'I mean, my bum doesn't look like a cardboard box, does it? And why is my head so big? You've made me look ugly!'

Pandora slipped her arm around Nancy's waist and kissed her cheek. 'Cubist convention,' she whispered. 'It's meant to represent not so much your physical beauty as your inner strength, your determination.'

'My strength?' the girl said dubiously.

'That's right, your indomitable spirit.'

Nancy turned to her and grinned. 'You and your big words!' she laughed, then fell silent. At last, wonderfully demure, she asked in a small voice, 'Do you love me, Dora?'

Pandora had been smitten by Nancy ever since she'd clapped eyes on the girl over the counter of the butcher's shop in Bow three months ago. Nancy's blonde curls, her china doll face, her fetching shyness . . . Over her purchase of half a pound of chopped liver, Pandora had dreamed. On her next visit, she'd given Nancy her card and asked if she would care to earn a 'little extra' as an artist's model.

She kissed the girl again. 'Climb into bed, my darling, and I'll show you how much I love you. Just give me a minute to get cleaned up.'

Pandora crossed to the screened-off area of the studio and scrubbed her hands with turpentine.

She was about to rejoin Nancy when her gaze fell on the letter she'd flung aside that morning.

She picked up the single sheet of notepaper and reread the missive. The infernal cheek of the man – three importuning letters in a fortnight, and after all these years! And what the hell did he mean when he said that he wanted to apologize? She sighed, torn between ignoring this summons, as she had the first two, and satisfying her curiosity by accepting the invitation to spend a weekend at his pile in Cornwall.

She wondered if Annabelle might still be living with him.

If so, did she really want to see the girl? Come to that, did she want to renew her acquaintance with the egotistical Denbigh Connaught? She detested the man – though, she allowed, he had done her a favour all those years ago: their brief fling had put Pandora off men for life.

'Dora!' Nancy called out. 'Are you coming, or what?'

Pandora returned to the studio, undressed, and climbed into bed with the girl.

Monty Connaught came to London as infrequently as possible, but when he did so, he invariably stayed at the Travellers Club on Pall Mall. It was one of the few oases of civilization in this metropolitan hellhole; the food was above average for a country that had emerged from rationing just two years ago, and the wine cellar was excellent. This evening found him enjoying a postprandial port in the library, wondering whether to push off first thing in the morning or spend another day in London visiting friends.

Yesterday he had delivered the manuscript of his latest travel book, *White Sails in the Sunset*, and in order to kill two birds with one stone had mooted a couple of future titles to his editor: *Blue Sea, White Sands*, an exploration of the Adriatic islands, and *By the Caves of Hercules*, a voyage along the coast of Morocco. Old Gilby had jumped at the latter and offered a three-hundred-pound advance. Connaught was delighted. In a day or so he would put this dreary city in his wake and head for the sunny climes of the Mediterranean.

He was contemplating a second glass of port when the waiter ghosted up to his chair. 'A telegram, sir.'

He ripped it open and read the brief missive.

Heard you were back in Blighty. Need to see you. Urgent. Come down this weekend. Denbigh.

Trust his brother to be so maddeningly vague! And what the hell did he mean by 'urgent'? What matter could be so urgent that it required his presence at Connaught House after an absence of ten years?

'Do you wish to send a reply, sir?'

He regarded the telegram, lost in thought.

He could ring his deckhands, Sam and Ginger, tonight and tell them to provision the ketch, presently moored down at Brighton, and be ready to sail at noon tomorrow. He'd catch a train down to the coast first thing in the morning, and they could putter along the channel at their leisure and take a day to reach Cornwall. It was on the way to the Med, after all.

'Yes. Take this down: *Leaving London Thursday noon. See you Friday.*'

'Very good, sir,' the waiter said, and departed.

What might the old rogue want with him all of a sudden?

He was intrigued.

He decided that he would, after all, have that second glass of port.

TWO

'Hello, Ryland and Langham Detective Agency.'

'Is that Mr Langham? Donald Langham?'

'Speaking. How can I help?'

'I wonder if I might make an appointment to see you?'

Langham leaned back in his chair and lodged his feet on the desk. He judged the woman to be in her thirties; she had a light, pleasant voice, with the precise consonants and extended vowels of an aristocrat.

'By all means. I'm free for the rest of the afternoon, all Thursday and Friday. Can I take your name?'

'Annabelle Connaught,' she said. 'I was wondering . . . When I said I'd like to see you, I really meant to ask if you would be free to come and see me.'

Langham smiled to himself. He wondered if this were another case of a potential client being put off by the agency's location on Wandsworth High Street. Some people turned up their noses at the very idea of travelling south of the Thames.

'I'm free for the next couple of hours,' he said. 'If you're in London, that is.'

She sounded relieved. 'That's wonderful. I'm staying at the Grosvenor in Victoria. Perhaps we could meet for tea at four?'

He looked at his watch. It was almost three thirty. 'By all means.'

'I will be in the Queen Anne tearoom, on the ground floor.'

'Might I ask why you'd like to see me, Mrs Connaught?'

'Doctor. And . . .' She hesitated. 'I wonder if we might leave that until we meet?'

'Right you are. The Grosvenor at four. I'll see you then.'

She thanked him and hung up.

He wondered, as he swung his legs from the desk and unhooked his suit jacket from the back of the door, whether the meeting would come to anything. If not, then there was nothing lost. Victoria was only a stone's throw from where he was now living in Kensington. He'd interview Dr Connaught, knock off early and take Maria for a drink before dinner.

My wife . . . he thought.

The fact still brought him up short, a month after their marriage. He sometimes caught himself wallowing in a metaphorical bathtub of blissful contentment, no doubt with a fatuous grin on his face. In fact, Ralph had caught him at it in the office last week. 'You're still on your honeymoon, by the look on your mush, Don.'

Their honeymoon, a week in Paris, had been idyllic, and the weeks following it a continuation of that happy state: even the affairs of the world, with the US and Russia ramping up tensions in the so-called Cold War, and the brewing trouble in Suez, did little to tarnish the patina of his euphoria.

He scribbled a quick note to Ralph in case his partner returned to the office today: *Interviewing a Dr Connaught in Victoria. See you in the morning.*

He locked the office door, hurried down the steps and crossed the busy pavement to his racing green Rover 90. His beloved Austin Healey had recently, after five years' loyal service, succumbed to engine failure. Maria had insisted that she buy him a bigger vehicle as a wedding present, and he'd regretfully consigned his Austin to the scrapheap.

It was a mild day, the air humid with the threat of thunder. To the north, slate-grey clouds were gathering in preparation to inundate the capital. That evening he was due to take Maria out for dinner at the Moulin Bleu in Highgate. He smiled: let it rain.

He tooled north through the busy streets, crossed the Thames on Wandsworth Bridge, and made his way into central London.

'Connaught, Connaught . . .' he said to himself. It wasn't that common a surname, and it came to him that he'd heard it somewhere else of late.

As he approached Victoria, big raindrops spattered the windscreen, and over the grey buildings of central London even greyer clouds massed, shot through with probing searchlights of late-afternoon sun.

He parked in a side street around the corner from the hotel, waited five minutes until a minute before four, then hurried through the rain to the Grosvenor.

A sign on a polished walnut pedestal in the foyer directed him to the Queen Anne tearoom, and he paused for a few seconds to take stock of his reflection in a floor-to-ceiling mirror beside a stand of ferns. He wondered if he would ever shake the feeling of social inferiority in places like this, where men in dress suits and women in fox stoles strolled around as if they owned the world. Which they probably did, he thought. It didn't help that his jacket was frayed and his shoes scuffed. Maria had suggested she buy him a new wardrobe for work, but he'd explained that it was all part of the calculated effect. According to Ralph, punters didn't trust private detectives who were too well dressed. 'You see, Don, we're like servants, and clients like to feel superior to servants, geddit?'

Langham had declined to debate the contention, and anyway he was happy with his worn threads most of the time.

He straightened his tie, slicked a hand through his hair, and strode into the tearoom.

Only three tables were occupied: one by a pair of elderly dowagers, another by a middle-aged couple and the third by a silver-haired woman in her fifties. By a process of elimination, Langham made his way across to the woman and smiled in greeting. 'Doctor Connaught . . .' He held out his hand.

The woman scowled up at him. 'Doctor? Did you say "Doctor"? I think you have the wrong person, young man.'

He was muttering an apology when he heard a voice behind him. 'Mr Langham?' She sounded breathless. 'I'm sorry, I was delayed. I had to make an important phone call.'

He turned to see a Pre-Raphaelite beauty in her early thirties with a tumble of auburn hair and a flawless oval face whose full lips were pursed with ill-concealed amusement at his *faux pas*. She wore a well-tailored two-piece suit in light green twill and carried a tiny matching handbag.

She crossed the room to a spare table and smiled as she sat down. 'Did you really think,' she said, 'that I sounded *that* old? Why, she's sixty if a day!'

Flustered, Langham took his seat. 'I had little choice,' he said. 'At least I didn't approach . . .' He gestured to the dowagers by the window.

She laughed. 'I should hope not! Now, will you have tea, Mr Langham?'

They ordered Earl Grey from a waiter, declined the offer of cakes, and Langham sat back and regarded the woman.

He had to admit that she was a cut above the usual run of clients who brought their woes to the Ryland and Langham Detective Agency. In the past month he'd dealt with a Brixton market-trader who suspected his accountant of diddling him out of fifty guineas a quarter, an ex-Fulham footballer who was being blackmailed for certain sexual indiscretions, and the usual bevy of spouses seeking the surveillance of unfaithful better halves.

He was curious how he might be able to help Dr Annabelle Connaught.

The tea arrived; she poured. He took his cup and crossed his legs. 'It isn't every day I interview clients in such plush surroundings.'

'I would have come down to Wandsworth, Mr Langham, but time is pressing. I really must catch the five-thirty train back to Cornwall.'

He wondered if that was an excuse. 'If I might ask how you came by our number?'

She drew a silver cigarette case from her handbag and offered him one, which he declined. She lit a Chesterfield with a pearl-inlaid lighter and lifted her head to blow smoke to her right.

'I'm not in the habit of employing private detectives, Mr Langham, and when I came to do so, I wanted the assurance that I was approaching the . . . the right people.'

He sipped his tea. 'And how can you be assured of that?' he asked, intrigued.

'I came upon your name quite fortuitously. You see, my father is the novelist Denbigh Connaught.'

The penny dropped. That's where he'd heard the surname recently. Just last week Maria had mentioned that her partner at the literary agency, Charles Elder, had received a letter from Denbigh Connaught: the writer had sacked his agent and wanted Elder and Dupré to represent his interests.

Langham knew of Connaught by reputation only: a gifted novelist whose books sold well and pleased the critics, but who was, by all accounts, a cantankerous bully with few friends in literary London and none at all in Cornwall where he lived the life of a hermit. He frowned. 'I see . . . But I don't quite get the connection.'

Dr Connaught regarded him over the rim of her cup, her cigarette smouldering in the same hand. 'I like to keep abreast of what my father is doing. When he sacked his agent and told me he was considering Elder and Dupré, I made enquiries. I learned that they represented you, and when I read on the back-flap of one of your thrillers that you worked part-time as a private detective, and were engaged to the daughter of the French cultural attaché here in London . . . I was in need of a private detective, and you seemed to fit the bill admirably.'

Langham smiled. 'This is the first time my agent has ever, however indirectly, landed me detective work,' he said. 'How can I help?'

She sat back, regarding him. 'Last year my father hired a young man by the name of Wilson Royce to act as his business manager. He'd muddled along quite adequately by himself for years but wanted more time to devote to his writing.'

Sensing her displeasure at the arrangement, Langham asked, 'And how did you feel about this fellow's appointment?'

'At the time, it didn't concern me in the slightest.'

'But since then?'

Annabelle Connaught sipped her tea, her green eyes distant. 'I'll be perfectly frank and admit that I don't like the man one bit, and I'll be even more candid and admit that I have no palpable grounds for my prejudice. But I set great store by my intuition, and something tells me that Wilson Royce is . . . I was about to say *evil*, but I'm not sure I believe in evil. Let me just say that Royce is corrupt.'

She withdrew a black-and-white photograph from her handbag and slid it across the linen tablecloth. The picture showed two men. One he recognized as the novelist Denbigh Connaught, a huge ursine figure scowling at the camera. The other was a tall youth in flannels, with a hatchet face and a glint in his eyes which, even reproduced in the unreliable medium of the grainy monochrome snapshot, struck Langham as untrustworthy.

'Royce comes up to London once a week, on a Wednesday, usually returning on a Friday. He has a mews flat in Chelsea – you'll find the address on the back of the photograph. I'd like you to follow him, find out what exactly he is up to here.'

'Does he come up by car?'

'That's right. He drives a rather sleek Morgan, in keeping with the "flash" image he likes to project.'

'And the ostensible reason for his trips?'

Annabelle Connaught shrugged her slim shoulders. 'Literary and financial business on my father's behalf, meetings with my father's agent and publisher.'

'You do realize that I might find nothing . . . and that my services don't come cheaply.'

Her lips essayed a superior smile. 'I think my funds will cover whatever your fees might be.'

Langham held her gaze as he said, 'Three guineas an hour, plus expenses.'

She didn't flinch. 'That's perfectly acceptable,' she said. 'I will hire you initially for one week, and then I shall assess your findings, if any.' She took a card from her handbag. 'This is my address and phone number. I would like you to report to me every day, between eight and nine in the evening. If you could begin in the morning . . .'

He slipped her card, along with the photograph, into an inner pocket of his jacket. 'I'll do that.'

Annabelle Connaught finished her tea, pushed up the cuff of her sleeve with her little finger, and peered at a tiny gold watch. 'It's been a pleasure meeting you, Mr Langham. Now I really must dash if I'm to catch my train.'

He rose with her, shook her delicate hand, and watched her walk quickly from the tearoom.

THREE

The thunderstorm had broken over London last night, treating the inhabitants of the city to a spectacular display of forked lightning across the northern skyline. This morning the air was clear and the sun was shining brilliantly.

It was ten o'clock and Langham had been waiting in his Rover for the past hour, dividing his attention between the *Daily Herald* spread across the steering wheel and number ten Saddler's Way, where Wilson Royce had his London home. Royce's car, the silver-grey Morgan two-seater that Annabelle Connaught had mentioned, was parked outside.

Langham wished that Royce would make a move, then reminded himself that Dr Connaught was paying him well to sit on his backside.

Last night over dinner at the Moulin Bleu, Langham had told Maria about Annabelle Connaught's request that he tail Royce, and asked her about the novelist Denbigh Connaught. It turned out that she knew very little about him, other than what was reported in the literary journals, and that just last week Connaught had contacted Charles Elder with a view to being represented by the agency.

'And I take it that Charles agreed?'

'For some strange reason, he refused to discuss the matter,' Maria had replied. 'I was surprised. Connaught is a big name; not only does he sell well, but he's feted as a great novelist by those in the know. It would be a feather in the agency's cap. I said that we should meet him and discuss terms.'

'And what did Charles say?'

'Very little. He said he'd think it over, then changed the subject whenever I brought it up.'

'Strange.'

'I suspect there is – how do you say? – bad blood between the two. They were at school together, many moons ago.'

'Hmm . . . That might explain it. Indiscretions in the dorm, perhaps?'

'Oh, you're a naughty man, Donald!'

Langham wound down the side window and read a report on the Egyptian nationalization of the Suez Canal, hoping that the British government would have more sense than to get drawn into that political quagmire. He turned, for relief, to the sports pages, and was reading about the forthcoming test match against Australia when the front door of number ten opened and a tall young man tapped down the steps with all the grace of the lead in a Busby Berkeley musical. He was dressed in honey-coloured tweeds and sported a canary-yellow cravat.

He slipped in behind the wheel of his Morgan and raced off along the mews.

Langham gave him ten seconds, started the engine and set off in pursuit.

Royce turned left along Fulham Road and headed east, then took a right down Beaufort Street. Langham followed at a distance. The traffic was light this Thursday morning, and Langham had no difficulty keeping the Morgan in sight. The young man turned left along the King's Road; Langham did likewise.

Half a mile further on, Royce turned right and drew up outside a row of plush town houses. Langham overtook the stationary car and pulled into the side of the road a little further on. He turned in his seat and watched as the young man ran up the steps of number twenty-two.

Langham reversed, stopped just in front of the Morgan, and peered up at the house. A young woman with peroxide-blonde hair appeared at a bedroom window, looked right and left along the street, then briskly drew the curtains.

So Royce had come up to London to visit a lady friend; he wondered if Annabelle Connaught would want to know the identity of the young woman.

An hour later, the door opened and Wilson Royce appeared on the threshold. He turned to embrace the blonde, gave her a farewell kiss, and hurried down the steps.

Instead of ducking into his Morgan, he sauntered along the street past Langham's car, whistling a spirited ditty as he went. Langham kept him in sight and, when Royce was a hundred yards ahead, rolled up his newspaper and followed.

He'd lost count of the number of times he'd had the hero of his novels, Sam Brooke, tail villains down the mean streets of the capital. In fiction, Brooke had more at stake from being caught in the act: as a matter of course, he dealt with hardened criminals and psychotic thugs who would think nothing of breaking a nosy PI's legs for the sheer sadistic fun of it. He doubted if the willowy Wilson Royce could break a pretzel in anger.

The young man turned the corner and Langham increased his pace; when he came to the end of the street, he was in time to see Royce cross the road and push through the door of a public house.

He glanced at his watch. It was almost midday. He crossed the road and entered the public bar.

Wilson Royce was chatting to the blonde barmaid, who was laughing and pouring him a whisky and soda. Langham stationed himself at the end of the bar and ordered a pint of Fuller's bitter and a pork pie from the publican, then moved to a nearby table from where he could command a view of wherever the young man elected to drink.

Royce remained at the bar, chatting up the barmaid who seemed flattered by his attention. He paid for his drink, ostentatiously pulling a fat wallet from an inner pocket and flashing a bundle of tenners.

Langham chewed on his pie, read a preview of the Arsenal's game against Cardiff City the next day, and bent an ear towards the youth's witless blather.

'Have you worked here long?' His tone was Eton-posh, modulated to impress the likes of the barmaid.

'Me? Seems like years.'

Royce spoke again, his words lost as three businessmen pushed through the door, conversing loudly.

The barmaid laughed. 'What do I do for entertainment? I can tell you where I don't go – pubs like this. I like the flicks, me.'

She moved off to serve the new customers, and when she returned, Royce said, 'Have one on me, go on. Make it a double. I'm celebrating, after all.'

'Celebrating? What're you celebrating, then?'

Langham would have liked to hear the reply, but one of the businessmen came to the punchline of a joke and the others guffawed.

Whatever Royce told her, the barmaid looked impressed and poured herself a gin and tonic.

Royce finished his drink and ordered another, chatting with the blonde between customers as the pub filled up with lunchtime trade.

This set the trend for the next couple of hours. Royce wooed the woman, made his way through another three whiskies, and even stood drinks for Johnny-come-latelys at the bar.

Towards two o'clock, with Royce showing distinct signs of inebriation, Langham moved to the bar and ordered a half of bitter. Royce was bragging to the barmaid about 'pranging' his last car, a Jaguar, and walking away without a scratch.

Langham thought he had the young man's measure: he was the cosseted product of a minor public school who spent all pater's allowance on nightclubs, fast cars and impressionable young women.

'You were lucky to get out in one piece,' Langham said when Royce repeated his pranging escapade to whoever would listen.

He turned and peered at Langham. He reeked of eau de cologne and his cravat was soaked with spilt whisky. 'Dashed lucky! One second there I was, whizzing along at sixty, and the next thing I knew, this blighter pulled out right in front of me. Totalled the old Jag and almost bought it myself – but I'm nothing if not lucky.'

Langham raised his empty pint glass. 'To your luck. Let me buy you a drink.'

'No . . . No! I insist. My round. Stroke of luck with a little investment.'

Langham accepted a half and drank it slowly. 'Stocks and shares?'

The young man brayed like a stallion. He showed a lot of teeth when he laughed, and Langham saw that his left eye-tooth was embedded slightly higher than the rest of his teeth, giving his face a wolfish cast. 'Stocks and shares? Beggar stocks and shares. Art's where the money is, these days.'

'Art?'

'Mark my word. Solid investment. If you know what you're doing, then art's where the money is.' He tapped the side of his nose with a long forefinger. 'Know what I mean?'

For the next hour, Langham plied Royce with spirits and tried to learn more about his recent 'investment', but the young man was more interested in boasting about the various cars he'd owned.

At three thirty, with last orders long ago called, the barmaid made her escape, quickly pulling on her coat and hurrying through a back door. Royce made to follow, but the portly publican barred his way and turned him one hundred and eighty degrees with a meaty hand and a couple of well-chosen words.

'Tell you what,' Royce said when he returned to Langham's side. 'Tell you what, I . . . I know a little club. Member there. I'll get you in as my guest. What say we tootle up to Soho? I'll drive.'

Langham assisted the young man from the pub and along the pavement. 'I think you're in no condition to drive,' Langham said. 'We don't want another accident, do we? It might be wise if we forgot all about private clubs and I took you home.'

Royce stood swaying in the centre of the pavement, hiccupping. 'You would? You'd do that for me? Drive young Roycey home in his cups? Why, that's dashed decent of you, sir.'

'This way,' Langham said, and he led Royce around the corner to his Rover.

*   *   *

As they drove along the King's Road and turned left, Langham glanced at his passenger. Royce sprawled in the seat as if it were a chaise longue. 'So you're in the art business. Sold anything of any value recently?'

'I'll say. Nice little piece. Eighteenth century. John Varley. Heard of him?'

'Afraid that's not my line,' Langham admitted. 'How long have you been a dealer?'

'Technically,' Royce said, '*technically*, I'm not. It's just something . . . something I dabble in. A little sideline.'

'Oh . . . and what do you do the rest of the time?'

Royce sighed, laid his head back, and closed his eyes. 'I . . . I work for a bastard.'

Langham laughed. 'We've all done that in our time.'

'But I,' Royce said, 'I work for the *biggest* bastard in Christendom.'

'And who might that be?'

'One Denbigh Connaught. Soon to be *Sir* Denbigh Connaught, if the old bastard's to be believed. A scribbler.'

'A scribbler?'

'Or, to put it more grandly . . . as he likes to be known . . . a Man of Letters. He writes big, fat, eru . . . *erudite* novels. I run the business side of things for him, for all the thanks I get. The man's' – Royce reached out and gripped Langham's forearm – 'the man's a monster of ego . . . egocentricity. A veritable monster. But I'll say this for him, he has a rather beautiful daughter.'

'He does?'

'A corker. Annabelle. Beauty *and* brains.'

'I see,' Langham said. 'And have you tried your luck with her?'

'Tried . . . and failed. My charms didn't work on that . . . that particular snake.'

'Snake?' Langham said.

Royce laughed. 'Vicious and cold-blooded,' he said.

Langham turned on to Fulham Road. 'Tell me. How did you get the job as his business manager?'

It was some time before Royce replied. Langham wondered if he was asleep; then the young man said, 'Was working in publishing, but getting a bit restless. I admired Connaught's books, so . . . so one day last year' – he hiccupped – 'I wrote to him on the off-chance . . . asked if he needed a business manager. Went for an interview and – hey presto – got the job.'

He closed his eyes again and two minutes later was snoring.

Langham turned into Saddler's Way and pulled up outside number ten. He shook Royce's shoulder. 'Here we are.'

'Don't want to . . .' Royce mumbled. 'Fine here.'

Langham moved around to the passenger side and took Royce under the arm. 'Up we get. We'll get you nicely tucked up and you can sleep it off.'

He swivelled the young man in his seat, pulled his legs out and assisted him to his feet. Half-carrying Royce, he staggered up the short flight of stairs to the front door.

'Key in my pocket . . .' Royce supplied helpfully.

Langham found a bunch of keys and tried three in the lock before the door swung open on to a small sitting room. A flight of stairs rose to the right, and Langham propelled the young man to the top by main force. On the small landing, he applied his foot to a door and entered a bedroom.

'Owe you one, sir,' Royce said as Langham laid him out on his side on the double bed.

The young man reached out as Langham made to leave. 'One thing! One thing – don't know your name . . .'

Langham smiled. 'Call me Sam,' he said.

'Well, you're a fine fellow, Sam!' Royce said. He buried his head in the pillow and was soon dead to the world.

After ensuring that the young man was indeed out for the count, Langham left the bedroom and paused on the landing. A second door gave on to a small bedroom, bare but for a single bed. He made his way downstairs and looked around the sitting room.

The room was sparsely furnished but for a couple of overstuffed sofas and three small bookshelves. He examined the titles and found a dozen literary novels and a handful of books on art – mainly on the subject of seventeenth- and eighteenth-century watercolours.

On a small desk in one corner stood a portable typewriter with a sheet of foolscap lolling in the platen. Langham crossed to the desk and read what Royce had typed: *Dear Beatrice, please forgive me for the contretemps the other evening.*

Which was the extent of the apologetic missive.

He found an address book next to the typewriter, the entries going back years by the evidence of the many crossed-out addresses. Royce listed his contacts by their first names, and Langham soon found Beatrice: it was the woman Royce had visited that morning on Smith

Street, Chelsea. Perhaps he'd decided to make it up to Beatrice in person . . . He copied the telephone number into his notebook.

He was about to replace the address book when a name jumped out at him: Bernard Radley, Brewer's Yard, Hanover Street, Rotherhithe.

'Interesting,' he murmured.

He found Royce's telephone, sat down and called Ralph at the office, hoping his colleague was not out on a case.

Ralph answered almost immediately. 'Ryland and Langham—'

'Ralph, Donald here.'

'How's it going?'

He explained the situation, then went on, 'Ralph, recall the Sudbury diamond haul a few years back?'

'How could I forget it? Earned meself a nice cosh on the head for me troubles.'

'Now, what was the name of that old codger in Rotherhithe who—'

'Radley. Bernard Radley. Best fence in the business, if you believe his self-publicity.'

'Bingo!'

'Why?'

'He's down here in Wilson Royce's address book.'

'Good work, Don. What do you think he's up to?'

Langham relayed Royce's boasts about buying and selling works of art. 'I thought he might be doing it legit, but after finding Radley's name . . . I'm not too sure.'

'You want me to drop by old Bernie's place and have a word? I'm just about to pop out, but I could pootle over to Rotherhithe tomorrow.'

'That might be an idea,' Langham said. 'Look, I'd better skedaddle. Royce's sleeping off a bender upstairs and I don't want to be around if he wakes up.'

He replaced the receiver, looked around the room, and saw the keys where he'd left them on the bottom step of the stairs.

He would not normally stoop to what he was about to do, but the Bernard Radley connection convinced him that Royce was up to something. He took the keys into the small scullery, found an old tablet of Fairy soap beside the Bristol sink, and pressed the front-door key into the block. Ralph had contacts who could knock up a facsimile key in no time.

He wrapped the soap in his handkerchief, locked the door behind him, and posted the keys through the letter box.

FOUR

M aria sat at her desk and tried to concentrate on the manuscript by a first-time novelist that her agency was about to
take on. Her attention wandered, and she glanced at the
pile of letters on the desk and smiled. Most were addressed to Maria
Dupré, but one or two carried her new name: Maria Langham.

It would take some getting accustomed to. She had been proud
of her French surname, but adopting her new name felt like leaving
behind her old life – with its failed love affairs and doubts about
her profession – and starting afresh.

A tap at the door broke into her reverie.

Molly popped her head into the room and said, 'I wonder if I
might have a word, Maria, if you're not too busy?'

'Of course. Come in.'

Molly was twenty-three, small and ginger-haired with green eyes
and a pretty constellation of freckles across her nose and cheeks.
She was ferociously intelligent and – much to Maria's chagrin –
constitutionally under-confident. She perched on the edge of the
chair across from Maria and grinned.

'I saw Gerry last night.'

Maria smiled. 'And how did it go?'

'I had a lovely time. We went to see *The King and I*, and then
had a drink at his local.'

'You see – and there you were, going on about how no boy would
find you attractive.'

Molly blushed to the roots of her hair.

Maria looked at her watch. 'Look, it's almost lunchtime. Shall
we pop out to the Lyons'? You can tell me about your date, and
then I'll tell you all about Paris.'

The girl's eyes widened. 'That would be super. Oh – I almost
forgot. I came to see you about Charles. I think you should have a
word with him.'

'Charles? Why, is something wrong?'

'He had another letter yesterday, from you-know-who.'

'Ah . . .'

'He positively blanched when he read the letter. I thought he was going to faint.' Molly shook her head. 'Maria, what is it all about?'

'I wish I knew. How is he today?'

'I don't know. He hasn't come down yet.'

'Perhaps I should pop up and have a word,' Maria said. 'I won't be long. And then we'll go for lunch, *oui*?'

'That would be lovely.'

They left the office and Maria opened the door leading to Charles's upstairs flat.

'Charles?' she called out. 'Can I come up?'

His fruity tones rang down the staircase. 'Ascend, my dear. Ascend!'

She hurried up the stairs and peered around the door at the top. The luxuriously appointed room, with its thick cream carpet, Regency furniture and an ancient grandfather clock ticking in the far corner, appeared uninhabited. 'Charles?'

'Here, my dear. Taking my rest.'

A plump hand appeared over the back of the settee, waving at her.

Maria pulled up a footstool and sat before her partner. Charles presented a woebegone sight, stretched out with a cold compress covering his forehead.

She took his hand. 'Molly told me you had another letter.'

He mopped his vast expanse of face, the vigour with which he did so setting the flesh of his cheeks and triple chins juddering.

'Will you tell me what the problem is?' she murmured.

'The man is an ogre,' he said.

'I know. I've heard the stories. Foster at Gollancz once told me he had dealings with Connaught over a short story of his they wanted to anthologize. Connaught asked about the other writers in the volume, and when he found out that Durrell was one, he refused point blank to have anything to do with the editor.'

'I've heard the same story. Durrell and Connaught. Now there are two egotists for you.'

'But . . .' Maria said tentatively, 'he's a respected novelist, despite what you might think of him personally. You can't deny that he would be an asset to our list.'

'My child, do you think I am not aware of the fact? The thought of missing out on the kudos that would accrue to the agency sorely troubles me.'

Maria squeezed his hand. 'I have an idea, Charles. If we were to take him on, then *I* would deal with him. You needn't even meet the man, still less enter into negotiations with him. I'd handle everything.'

'You are goodness personified, my child. You don't know how much I appreciate the offer, but—'

'Yes?'

'But such an arrangement would not work. I think Connaught would not be fobbed off by being attended to by – as he would see it – a "mere" woman. He would insist on dealing with me and no one else. *Insist!*'

She nodded. 'I see.'

Charles pointed to the dining table. 'There is the missive in question. Pray, bring it to me, my dear.'

She did so and passed him the single sheet of notepaper.

He read it once, winced, and passed it to her.

> *Charles,*
>
> *I haven't heard from you. Did you get my last? As I mentioned, I've sacked Pritchard and Pryce – tell you all about it when you come down. Here's the deal – I've just finished a new one. The bods at Cape've seen it and made an offer. But I want more – and I need a good agent to fight my corner.*
>
> *It's time to let bygones be bygones. Water under the bridge, right? What happened was a hell of a long time ago. I'm prepared to apologize, and I don't do that too often.*
>
> *What do you say?*
>
> *Come down this weekend. Open house. We can talk.*
>
> *Yours, Denbigh Connaught.*

She looked up from the letter. 'What *did* happen, Charles?'

She was shocked to see that he was weeping. He fumbled with a kerchief and dabbed at his eyes. 'As he said, a long time ago. A very long time ago. But . . .' He reached out and grasped her hand. 'But it brings back so many memories, so many *terrible* memories.' He sniffed. 'The thing is, I know I should go down to Cornwall, and accept his apology – if he really means it, and it isn't part of some nasty ploy of his to hurt me even more – and, as he says, let bygones be bygones. But' – he smiled at her – 'but I do not know, Maria, if I am strong enough to do so.'

She raised his plump hand and kissed his knuckles. 'If it will make it any easier, I'll come with you.'

He brightened. 'Would you, my child? Would you really? That would be . . .' He trailed off.

'Charles?'

'I wonder . . . Would it be terrible of me to ask that Donald come, too? He's such a reassuring presence to have on hand in times of need.'

She smiled. 'I'm sure he'd be delighted.'

'Capital! I feel a little better already.'

Maria smiled. 'That's the ticket.'

He murmured, 'He hurt me grievously, Maria. What Denbigh Connaught did, back then . . . I swore that I would have nothing more to do with him. But . . . but perhaps what I am about to do is necessary: I will no longer be running away.'

She patted his hand. 'I think it would be a wise move.' She stood, a sudden thought occurring to her. 'Charles, would you like to lunch with Molly and me? We're popping around the corner.'

'To the Lyons'?' The fleshy acreage of his face arranged itself in lineaments of horror at the very notion of being seen anywhere as *infra dig* as a Lyons' tearoom. 'I couldn't possibly, Maria – their tea is positively vile. But I have a better idea. I will take you and Molly for lunch at the Beeches, as a token of gratitude for your kindness.'

'The Beeches? Are you absolutely sure?'

'I insist, my child.'

'Then I'd be delighted, and I'm sure Molly would be, too. I was going to tell her all about gay *Paree*.'

Charles struggled to his feet. 'Then to the Beeches it is!'

Smiling at his rejuvenated spirits, she followed him from the room.

It was almost four, and Maria was thinking of packing up and calling it a day, when a knock sounded on the door.

'Come in!' she called, and Donald poked his head into the office. 'Surprise,' he said.

She hurried to greet him with a kiss.

'I thought,' he said, 'I'd take you home and cook something while you put your feet up with a glass of wine and tell me all about your busy day.'

She laughed. '*You?* Cook? And what do you suggest you cook, Donald – cheese on toast?'

'Garnished with the finest grilled tomatoes.'

'No, *I* will do the cooking tonight. Ratatouille?'

'That'll be wonderful,' he said. 'Oh, I don't suppose the Hollywood bods have stumped up the dosh yet?'

A week before their wedding, Donald had agreed a deal with an agent in Los Angeles for the option on one of his Sam Brooke thrillers. He'd told Maria that the cash they were offering – two thousand pounds – was almost obscene: five times what he'd normally be paid for a single novel. She'd replied that he could always make a donation to charity – once, that is, he'd bought her a cottage in the country.

'These things take time, Donald,' she said. 'Now, tell me all about your day following Mr Royce.'

He sat on the corner of the desk and gave her a brief résumé of Wilson Royce's exploits. 'And considering his connection with the fence in Rotherhithe,' he finished, 'I think he's up to something. No smoke without fire, as they say.'

Maria regarded him, tapping her teeth with a fingernail. 'Donald, how would you like to go down to Cornwall and stay at Connaught House this weekend?'

'Oh – so Charles has decided to take on Denbigh Connaught?'

She rocked her head. 'He's undecided. There's something very much troubling him, but he won't tell me what it is.' She paused. 'I think he'd like your opinion of Denbigh Connaught. And he would feel safer with you around.'

'Safer?'

'I think that, for some reason, Connaught frightens him.'

'Well, Wilson Royce did describe him as an egotistical monster. I'm intrigued to see if the ogre is as black as he's painted. Very well, let's go.'

'You don't mind?' she said. 'You did say you wanted a quiet weekend.'

'I'll be with you, so I don't mind what I do. And, you never know, it might prove interesting. I might find out a little more about our friend Royce.'

'But what if he turns up, Donald, and recognizes you?'

'Then I'll pass it off as a big coincidence,' he said. 'Ralph can look into Royce's dealings in London while we're away. Oh, I'd better pop into the office first thing in the morning. I have a bar of soap for him.'

She laughed. 'A bar of soap?'

'How about I explain over a quick drink?'

'That would be wonderful, *mon cheri*.'

FIVE

On Friday morning Ralph Ryland unwrapped the bar of soap from its nest of tissue paper. Donald had done a good job. The impression of the key was deep and sharp. He took his last two Woodbines from their packet, wedged one behind his right ear and lit the second, then slipped the soap into the empty packet for protection. It was only a short drive to Harry the key-cutter up in Brixton, but he didn't want the soap to get battered on the way.

He sat back in his chair, lodged his winklepickers on the desk and enjoyed his smoke.

It was good to have Don working with him again. They made a good team. Ryland had been at this lark for more than ten years and he knew the underworld and all its quirks like the back of his hand. Don had a cunning brain when it came to psychology and motivation, experience he'd gained from churning out all those books about criminals.

They were like chalk and cheese, really, him and Don. He liked a night at the dogs while Don preferred the theatre and good restaurants, even more so since he'd hitched himself to Maria – a high-class girl if ever there was one. Don read novels, while all Ryland read these days was racing form. And just the other day Don told him that he was beginning to appreciate classical music, while Ryland's idea of a good sing-song was a night round the piano at the Grapes.

But for all their differences, they were as close as brothers, and all because of what had happened on Madagascar back in 1942.

The phone shrilled on the desk, and reluctantly Ryland tipped his chair forward and picked up the receiver.

It was the landlord, whingeing about the non-payment of last month's rent. 'Like I told you, mate,' Ryland said past his fag end, 'you'll get the dosh when you've fixed the ruddy window. Like Niagara Falls in here every time it rains.'

He slammed the phone down and stared around at the down-at-heel office. When a client came here for the first time, Ryland saw the place through their eyes, and he didn't like what he saw: cracked linoleum the colour of excrement, walls daubed a shade of mouldy green, and rotting window frames. And the smell from the chippy down below! To make matters worse, the landlord had recently upped the rent to twenty guineas a month. Daylight robbery, it was. He'd have a word with Don, go through their takings and see if they could afford somewhere a bit more upmarket. He'd like to see the look on their landlord's mug when he told him they were flitting.

He checked his address book for Bernard Radley's details, then picked up the fag packet from the desk and left the office.

He turned up the collar of his jacket against the chilly wind and crossed the pavement to his Morris Minor. Like the office, it had seen better days. The engine was sound enough, but the bodywork was rusted through in places. He reckoned he'd get another year out of the old girl before she clapped out completely. And then more bleeding expenses.

The rain started as he drove to Brixton. He found himself behind a slow double-decker and lit his last cigarette.

He still had nightmares about Madagascar. He'd wake in the early hours, shouting and sweating, until he realized he was at home in Lewisham and Annie had her arms around him, reassuring him that he was safe. What was really frightening, he thought, was not so much what had happened – though that had been bad enough – but what *might* have happened if Don hadn't saved him. In the advance on the port town of Diego Suarez, he'd got himself pinned down in a ditch just below a Vichy machine-gun post. To make matters worse, his Enfield had jammed just as a French goon appeared at the top of the hill, about to throw a hand grenade.

What happened next would live in Ryland's memory until his dying day.

He'd heard the rattle of machine-gun fire in the ditch behind him, and the soldier fell backwards, ripped to shreds. Then he'd felt someone gripping him, dragging him along the ditch and into cover.

He'd stared at the soldier's sweat-soaked face in the moonlight, saw the fear in his eyes – and the fact that both men had seen and understood the other's fear had in some strange way cemented what would become a long-lasting friendship. Donald had been mentioned in despatches for his bravery. As far as Ryland was concerned, he deserved a ruddy VC.

The bus turned right at the traffic lights, and Ryland continued straight on to Brixton High Street.

Donald didn't like to talk about that night – and hated it when Ryland brought it up in conversation – and Ryland knew that Don still had nightmares about killing the man. 'I know it's irrational, Ralph. It was him or us, and I know I did the right thing. But even so, I can't forget the fact that I killed someone . . . And it's even worse because I saw the look on his face before he died.'

When they were demobbed, Don had gone through a tough year finding a publisher, and Ryland suggested he work part-time at the agency. To his delight, Don had agreed, and they'd worked well together for a couple of years before the novel commissions came in and Don returned to full-time authorship. More recently, with marriage on the cards and a move to an expensive apartment in Kensington in the offing, Ryland had suggested Don rejoin the agency and put in a two-day shift.

It was like the good old days all over again.

He parked on the High Street and made his way to Harry's cramped premises squeezed in between the Lyons' tearoom and Woolworth's.

Harry Beckett was a huge bald-headed geezer who wore a stained apron and a printer's eye-shade. Like his shop, he exuded the pungent odour of metal shavings and lathe lubricant.

Ryland pushed the cigarette packet across the counter. Harry grunted a laugh. 'You know I only smoke roll-ups, Ralph.'

'Little present.'

Harry opened the packet and tipped out the soap. 'You trying to tell me I need a wash?' He examined the impression. 'Chubb. Latch key. Pre-war. Don't keep 'em in stock – I'll have to send out for a blank. Won't be ready today. Maybe tomorrow, but I'm going to the match, so I don't know. Look, I'll certainly have it done Monday morning, OK? I'll give you a bell when it's ready. And I'll only charge you two and six.'

'You're a scholar and a gent, Harry, and there's not many of us left.'

'You off to the match?'

It was the first game of the season tomorrow, and Millwall were at home to Walsall. 'You bet. Taking the boys.'

They chatted for five minutes about Millwall's prospects after their lowly finish the previous season, and then Ryland thanked Harry and made his way back to the car.

He drove north-east to Rotherhithe and turned off the main road into the warren of slums that clung to the bank of the Thames. The Luftwaffe had done its best to demolish the area, and even now, years later, rows of back-to-back terraces were interrupted by gaping holes, piles of red bricks and shattered timber.

Bernard Radley ran his rag-and-bone business from the cobbled yard of an old brewery – a convenient front for his real money-maker: the receiving and selling of stolen goods. His idiot son ran the rag-and-bone side of things, while Bernard – an embittered, raddled old alcoholic – led the local constabulary a merry dance with his wheeling and dealing.

Ryland ducked through a tiny door in the huge wooden gate and found himself in a cut-price Aladdin's cave full of every conceivable kind of junk known to humanity: piles of brass bedsteads and bath-tubs, kitchen sinks and cast-iron radiators, a tottering pile of car doors and windscreens. There might have been order in the chaos, but Ryland was beggared if he could see it.

'Wot you want, mister?'

Across the yard Radley's son Len, a lanky youth with a slack expression, was grooming a huge Shire horse, its muscled splendour and shining coat out of place in the insalubrious environment of the junk yard.

Len stared at Ryland with a blank, gormless expression. 'I said, wot you want, mister?'

'Bernie about?'

'You a rozzer?'

'Yeah, the ruddy Chief Constable,' Ryland said, crossing the yard to the green-painted lean-to that Radley used as an office when he wasn't out and about on nefarious errands in his Morris Commercial.

A stooped, grey-haired old man opened the door and gave Ryland a quick once-over. 'Oh, it's you.'

'Come to pay me respects,' Ryland said, following Radley into the office.

A gas fire belted out a furnace heat and a classical record revolved on the turntable of a huge, pre-war radiogram. The music finished and Radley lifted the needle off the spinning disc. He sat behind a desk piled with ledgers and poured a shot of whisky into a chipped mug celebrating Queen Elizabeth II's coronation. That, like the opera, was another oddity: Bernie Radley was a staunch monarchist.

'You won't be drinking on duty?' Radley said.

'What makes you think I'm working, Bernie?'

'You ever come here when you're not?'

Radley was as grey as a corpse that had been dug up a day after burial and brought back to a semblance of shuffling life. His first wife had died of lung cancer in the thirties, and his second had been killed in an air raid back in 1941. His only son was retarded and, perhaps not surprisingly, Bernard sought solace in drink. Ryland pitied the old man, but never left the junk yard without feeling that he was escaping.

'So what is it you're wanting?' Radley asked.

Ryland remained standing and leaned back against a filing cabinet. 'You heard of a young fellow called Wilson Royce?'

Although Radley turned his head in Ryland's direction, he couldn't bring himself to establish eye contact. His defeated grey eyes gazed at something over his visitor's right shoulder. 'Should I have?'

'Your name was in his address book.'

From his breast pocket Ryland took the photograph that Don had given him that morning. 'Young chap on the right.'

Radley glanced at the picture and passed it back. 'What's it to you?'

'I'm looking into his activities.'

'What's he been doing?'

'That's what I'm trying to find out.'

Radley took a drink of whisky. His gaze switched to something on Ryland's left. 'Came here a while back. Odd fellah, well spoken. Bit of a toff. I asked him if he'd met Her Majesty.'

'And had he?'

'Funny you should ask. Said he'd just been to a garden party at the Palace. He were introduced to Her Majesty, he said. So I shook his hand. Fancy that, eh? I shook a hand that'd shook the hand of Her Majesty.' He raised his right hand, as white as a fillet of Dover sole, and stared at it incredulously.

'Can you credit it?' Ryland said. 'So when was it you saw this Wilson Royce?'

Radley sniffed. 'About a year back. He had a painting. I told him I don't deal in art. Put him on to this bloke up Belsize Park way.'

'What was his name, this Belsize Park chap?'

Radley leaned back in his chair. 'What's it worth?'

'Five bob,' Ryland said.

'A quid?'

'Ten bob, then.'

'Right-o, ten bob.' He reached for a ledger, leafed through the dog-eared pages, then looked up.

Ryland took a ten-shilling note from his wallet and held it ready. 'Go on.'

'Geezer by the name of William Harker.'

'Address?'

'The note,' Radley said, 'in my palm.'

Sighing, Ryland passed the money to the old man.

Radley examined the note, folded it into quarters, and slipped it into his shirt pocket. 'William Harker, he owns a place called Harker Fine Arts on Beverly Road.'

'This Harker a friend of yours?'

'Wouldn't call him that.'

Ryland pushed himself away from the filing cabinet and saluted. 'It's been a pleasure doing business with you, Bernie. Cheerio.'

'Pleasure's all mine,' Radley said, replacing the needle at the start of the record and pouring himself another whisky.

Ryland stepped from the claustrophobic warmth of the lean-to and crossed the cobbled yard.

'Wot you want, mister?' Len called out as Ryland ducked through the door and escaped into the street. 'You a rozzer?'

He decided to call it a day. He didn't feel like tooling all the way up to Belsize Park. If he knocked off now, he could have a couple of pints and a pork pie at the Grapes and surprise Annie by coming home early. He'd spend a nice, quiet afternoon studying form for the races at Haydock tomorrow.

He'd pay his respects to William Harker in the morning.

SIX

They came to the crest of the road and Charles leaned forward and touched Langham's shoulder. 'I wonder if you could halt here, my boy, so that we might admire the view?'

Langham pulled on to the grass verge and Charles sighed.

Maria said, 'I never realized Cornwall was so beautiful.'

'The coastline is famed for its spectacular scenery,' Charles said. 'And look, that must be Trennor Pendennis.' He pointed a stubby finger at a distant village.

The grey skies had lifted as they'd motored from London and, after lunch at a roadside inn just outside Andover, the sun had emerged from behind a caul of piled cumulus. Now the sunlight scintillated on the bright blue sea and picked out the nooks and crannies of the coast.

The village nestled in a cove far below, a collection of stone-built cottages climbing the hillside above a small harbour.

'And there is Connaught House,' Charles said.

The bay was enclosed by two headlands, and high up on the furthest was a rambling house set amid lawned gardens. Connaught House was severely Gothic, with numerous belvederes, peaked gables and high, narrow windows.

'I recall the place from a feature about Connaught in the *Telegraph*,' Charles said. 'The photograph was black and white, of course, and the house seemed a bleak and austere pile. But it seems even bleaker, bathed as it is in sunlight, don't you think?'

'A suitable abode for a curmudgeonly, reclusive scribe,' Langham said.

'"Curmudgeonly",' Charles laughed, 'is being generous.' He leaned forward between the front seats, staring at the house. 'Did I tell you that Connaught and I were once close?' he murmured.

Langham said, 'I don't think I've heard you mention him before.'

'We were at school together. I met him when I was thirteen, an impressionable age. He was the same age as me, and I must admit that I rather took to him.' He smiled. 'A "pash", as they called it then. You would hardly believe it now, but he was a handsome youth. We shared a passion for the Greeks. But he discovered Catullus, and let it turn his head. He declared Christianity dead and became somewhat . . . libertine. But he made it obvious that he felt nothing for me . . . in *that* respect. We went our separate ways, philosophically. I moved on to the Romantics, fell under the spell of Coleridge and that set, and then I met Daniel . . .' He fell silent, staring blankly down at the sea. Langham glanced at his agent and was surprised to see incipient tears welling in his eyes.

Beside Langham, Maria made a discreet gesture for him to drive on, and he let out the clutch and rolled the Rover down the road.

They passed through Trennor Pendennis, with its picturesque harbour and cottages, then took the road around the bay and climbed to the promontory on the far end of which perched the novelist's residence.

To their right was a plantation of fir trees, to their left a long drop to a tumble of rocks where the surf crashed. The road became a narrow lane and turned inland, through the firs, and minutes later they arrived at the gates of Connaught House.

The gates stood open – permanently, Langham thought, as they were rusted and overgrown with ivy. To the right was a small lodge, its windows shattered and its window frames and front door long given over to dry rot.

He wondered in what state they might find the house itself.

He eased the Rover between the mossy stone pillars and proceeded up the weed-choked gravelled drive. Beyond a stand of dowdy rhododendron, the house came into view, and Charles reached forward and squeezed his shoulder. 'Stop!'

Langham braked suddenly.

'I'm sorry, my boy. Forgive me.' Charles took deep breaths.

Maria murmured, 'We're with you, Charles. There's nothing to fear.'

Charles smiled, a kindly glint in his eyes. 'Your words are well meant, child. But I have everything to fear: the ghosts of the past, my treacherous cowardice, and not least the unknown – and by that I mean the person Denbigh Connaught has become. It is, after all, forty years since we last met.'

'You might be pleasantly surprised by how he's changed,' Maria said. 'In his letter he did offer to apologize, after all.'

'And I castigate myself for casting suspicion on his fine words, Maria. He might very well have changed, and meant every word in his missive, but I have only my memories of him as a youth on which to base my . . . my fears.' He tapped Langham's shoulder. 'Onward.'

Langham released the handbrake and rounded the rhododendrons. A lone car was parked before the house – Wilson Royce's silver-grey Morgan. So the young man must have slept off his hangover, recalled where he'd left the car and retrieved it for the drive down to Cornwall.

He parked beside the sports car and hauled their cases from the boot. Charles struggled from the rear of the vehicle, emerging with all the gargantuan improbability of a genie from a magic lamp.

'Hello there!' a familiar voice called out.

Langham turned to see the loose, lank figure of Wilson Royce, garbed in blazer and cricket whites, waving a languid hand from the top of the steps. Maria glanced at Langham, who nodded minimally and murmured, 'That's the fellow.'

'Do you think he recognizes you?'

'We'll soon see.'

Royce tapped down the steps and approached them, his hand outstretched. 'Royce. Wilson Royce. Call me either Wilson or Royce. It's all the same to me.'

He shook Maria's hand first, murmuring, 'Enchanted,' then Charles's, then moved on to Langham and smiled without the slightest hint of recognition.

'I look after Connaught's business interests, and I'm on hand to meet everyone today. Old Watkins, the butler, is taking the afternoon off – touch of the ague. Fortunately, cook's fighting fit, so we'll be eating tonight.'

Maria said, '"Everyone"?'

Royce smiled at her. 'You didn't know? It's full house for the weekend. Here, allow me to take that,' he went on, lifting Maria's case.

Langham picked up his own case and Charles's and followed Royce towards the house which appeared, on cursory inspection, to be in far better upkeep than the lodge.

'I must say,' Royce addressed Langham as they climbed the steps, 'your face is rather familiar. Have we met, by any chance?'

'I think not – but people often make the same mistake.'

Charles carolled, 'It's his film-star good looks. Donald is a dead ringer for Robert Donat.'

Royce laughed. 'That must be it. I'll show you to your rooms. If you'd like to refresh yourselves, then come down for drinks in the drawing room. First on the right at the foot of the stairs. The others should be arriving in due course.'

They processed up a wide oak staircase and Royce escorted them along a panelled corridor to the east wing overlooking the sea.

Beside Langham, Charles danced along in agitation, his plump fingers worrying his bow-tie. 'I was wondering, Mr Royce, is Connaught . . .?'

'Never makes an appearance before six o'clock, Mr Elder. Locks himself away in his study – working, or so he claims. He'll emerge for drinks before dinner.'

'Ah,' Charles said, a shadow falling across his features. 'Capital.'

Royce opened the door to a room with a view across the rear lawn. 'Your room, Mr Elder. And you, Mr and Mrs Langham, are next door. This way.'

They followed the young man to their room.

'See you downstairs when you're ready,' Royce said.

When the door had closed, Maria said, 'Well, he's not quite what I was expecting.'

'And what was that?'

'From your description of him yesterday, I thought he'd be good-looking and – what is the word? – *louche*. In reality, he appears younger than I expected, even immature, and somewhat nervous.'

'Well, I did see him the worse for drink.'

They took turns to wash in the en-suite bathroom, then Langham changed into a casual shirt and Maria swapped her two-piece for a gingham summer frock and sprayed eau de cologne behind her ears. 'There.'

'You look divine,' he said.

They left their room and Langham tapped on Charles's door. 'You decent?'

'Come.'

He opened the door and found Charles seated upon the bed, his weight creating a deep vale in the mattress. He looked like a disconsolate Buddha.

'Are you joining us?'

'Far be it from me to decline the offer of alcohol,' Charles said, 'but would you mind awfully if I joined you a little later? I need, I think, a period in which to reflect.'

'Are you sure you're all right?' Maria asked.

Charles smiled. 'I feel a good deal better than if I were facing this ordeal alone, my child. Now, off you go and enjoy yourselves. I shall be down presently.'

They closed the door and made their way along the landing. 'Do you know, Donald, I am beginning to wonder at Connaught's motives . . . and beginning to feel a little guilty at encouraging Charles to come down here.'

'Don't,' he said. 'Didn't you tell me Charles himself said he must gird his loins and face his demons, or some such?'

Maria sighed. 'He did, but I just hope he's strong enough, and that Connaught isn't planning something . . . horrible.'

'Aren't you over-dramatizing things a bit, my girl? I thought he'd summoned Charles to apologize, and to offer him his latest magnum opus?'

'He did, and perhaps I am.'

Langham took her arm as they descended, crossed the hall and entered the drawing room.

Wilson Royce stood before a bar at the far end of the room, pouring himself a drink. He turned as they entered. 'What's your poison?'

Maria said, 'Just a tonic water, please.'

'And you, Mr Langham?'

'A Scotch and soda would be wonderful.'

'Coming up.'

They moved, with their drinks, to the French windows overlooking a long lawn and the hazy horizon, where the sea merged impercep-tibly with the sky.

Royce said, glancing at Langham, 'So you both work for the literary agency the old man is thinking of switching to?'

Langham wondered why, as Royce was Connaught's business manager, he was making the enquiry, unless it was merely to break the ice.

Maria replied, 'I'm a partner in the agency. Donald is a writer.'

Royce sipped his Scotch. 'The old man's playing his cards close to his chest with this particular hand. His sacking of Pritchard and Pryce came out of the blue – he didn't so much as mention it to me. Left me with egg on my face, I can tell you.'

'Do you have any idea why he should select Elder and Dupré?' Maria asked.

'Other than the fact that he and Mr Elder were at Winchester?'
He shook his head. 'No, none at all. I mean, you're known to be
efficient, but you are a rather small concern, after all.'

Maria bridled. 'And growing,' she said.

'Quite,' Royce said, smiling his wolfish smile.

Langham said, 'And the other guests arriving today?'

Royce frowned into his drink. 'Odd bunch. Old acquaintances of
Connaught's. Some of them he hasn't seen for decades. Must say
I had to do a bit of detective work to dig up their whereabouts.'

Langham looked at the young man sharply at the word 'detective',
but it appeared he'd said it without irony.

'I wonder why he's gathered them together for the weekend?'
Maria said.

Royce smiled, and sunlight glinted on the saliva of his misplaced
eye-tooth. 'No doubt we shall find out in the fullness of time,' he
said. 'Oh, before I forget,' he went on, withdrawing a small envelope
from his blazer pocket, 'the delightful Annabelle dropped by earlier
and gave me this.'

He passed Langham the envelope, watching him closely as he
opened it.

Langham read the handwritten note, then told Maria, 'Annabelle
would like to see us for tea or drinks at five, at her place in
the village.'

Royce sipped his Scotch. 'Acquainted, are you?'

Langham said, 'She's read my thrillers,' and left it at that.

'Yes, Annabelle likes to lose herself in books like that,' the young
man said, not without a note of condescension.

Maria looked up at the sound of a car engine as the sleek nose
of a 1940 electric-blue Lagonda coupé appeared before the window.

Royce said, 'I say, what have we here? They certainly don't make
'em like that any more. Excuse me while I play host.'

He hurried from the room.

'What a conceited young man,' Maria said.

'Compared with yesterday, my darling, he's on his best
behaviour.'

Only the long bonnet of the Lagonda was visible through the
open window of the drawing room, so Langham could not see
the driver as she alighted and addressed Wilson Royce.

'The drive down was appalling,' she shrilled, 'and the roads
around here are obviously made for hay wains. I stopped counting

the potholes after the first fifty.' The rest was lost as Royce escorted her around the house to the entrance.

She pushed open the drawing-room door and entered, Royce skipping along in her wake. 'No, I don't want to refresh myself before a drink,' she was saying. 'I want a bloody large G and T.'

Langham had envisaged, judging by her soprano, a tall woman in formal dress, heavily mascaraed and smoking a Turkish cigarette in a long holder.

Nothing, in the event, could have been further from the mark. She was a small, plump woman in her fifties, dressed in baggy brown corduroy trousers and a man's white shirt. Her round face had the pallor of icing sugar, which was accentuated by her crimson lips and a helmet of jet-black hair.

While Royce was at the bar mixing her drink, she approached Langham and Maria with an outstretched hand. 'Pandora Jade,' she said. 'Artist. I paint abstracts.'

Langham made the introductions.

Pandora Jade laughed. 'Ah, a writer *and* his agent. Often seen in pairs – less often married.'

Royce returned with her drink.

'Here's to you both,' Pandora said. 'And perhaps you can tell me, young Wilson, what the hell's going on here?'

'Sorry, no can do. I'm as much in the dark as you are.'

'Balderdash! Supposed to be his business guru, aren't you? Surely you know what the old goat's up to?'

'As I told Donald and Maria,' Royce said, 'the old man's playing his cards close to his chest.'

Outside, another car drew up beside Pandora's Lagonda – this one a decrepit maroon-coloured Vauxhall. Its driver, a thin, stooping man, limped around the car and bent to examine the offside headlight.

'Excuse me while I . . .' Royce said, gesturing towards the new arrival, and made his escape.

Pandora drained her glass. 'That one didn't touch the sides. Care for another?'

They declined, and she stumped off across the room and helped herself from the bar. Langham smiled to himself. Despite the woman's eccentric appearance and brusque manner, he warmed to her.

'Do *you* have any idea why the old bastard summoned us?' she asked on her return.

'Well,' Maria said, 'in our case, he might be joining my agency.'

'Rum job, as far as I'm concerned. Haven't seen the reprobate for thirty years, and then a couple of weeks ago I received the first of three letters. "Hie yourself to Cornwall pronto, and here's twenty quid for the petrol." I'm a bloody artist – ergo, perpetually skint. He called, waving spondulics, and I came. Expecting fireworks. He's up to something, mark my word.'

'You mentioned you knew Connaught years ago . . .' Maria said.

'Met him at a party in London. This was in the mid-twenties. Long and short of it, we had a fling.' She snorted. 'Upshot: he put me off men for life. I could tell you more, but I'm not drunk enough.'

Langham laughed. 'I look forward to when you are.'

The door opened and Charles Elder entered and joined them, smiling as Langham made the introductions.

'Would you care for a drink, Charles?' Maria asked.

Pandora knocked back her G and T and said, 'No, let me play the tar-bender. What'll it be?'

'That's so kind of you,' Charles said. 'Do you think they would run to a vermouth with ice?'

'If Connaught still likes his drink as he did thirty years ago, I don't doubt it,' Pandora said, and crossed to the bar.

'What a very strange lady,' Charles said as he watched her upend a bottle over a glass at the bar.

'I quite like her,' Maria said.

'Me, too,' Langham said. 'She certainly calls a spade a spade.'

Pandora returned. 'Here's mud in your eye. Vermouth, straight, with ice.'

'You're a lifesaver, my dear.'

The door opened and a man in his early fifties limped into the room, escorted by Wilson Royce. 'And this is Colonel James Haxby,' Royce said.

He made the round of introductions, then moved to the bar and poured Haxby a whisky.

The colonel was tall and emaciated, with the complexion of a seasoned alcoholic: his flesh was deathly pale, but shot through with a network of broken veins. His rheumy green eyes regarded the group with bleak melancholy, like pale garnets swimming in catarrh.

He wore a black blazer and a regimental tie, both threadbare, and leaned heavily on a stick, gripping his whisky in his left hand.

'Eleventh Hussars,' he barked to all and sundry, apropos of nothing. 'Lost me leg in Egypt fighting Rommel's mob.'

'What terribly rotten luck, Colonel,' Charles said.

'Landmine. Chappie next to me wasn't so lucky. Blown to bits. I ended up with his head in me lap. You don't know you've been in a war till you've had your pal's head land smack-dab in your lap.'

'I'm sure you don't,' Royce said, smiling weakly at the guests as if in apology.

The colonel fixed Royce with his strange eyes. 'You served?'

'National Service in 'fifty-three,' the young man said.

Haxby grunted and swung his gaze to Langham. 'You?'

'Captain, Field Security. Madagascar and India.'

'Saw action at Diego Suarez, by any chance?'

'In the thick of it, sir.'

'Good man.'

Pandora cleared her throat. 'And I flew Spits and Hurricanes for the Air Transport Auxiliary,' she said.

Colonel Haxby looked taken aback. 'Flew? You say you *flew*?'

'Don't sound so shocked, Colonel. Women can fly kites, you know. Started off as a mechanic, then took flying lessons. Might not've seen active service, but I delivered the damned things to squadrons up and down the land.'

'Well, you live and learn,' the colonel declared, draining his Scotch. 'Top this up, would you, laddie?' he said, thrusting his glass at Royce. 'And you,' he said to Maria. 'No doubt you were still in nappies?'

She regarded him neutrally. 'I was still at school when the war started, Colonel.'

Haxby turned to Charles. 'And you, Elder?'

Charles beamed at his interlocutor. 'Sadly, I was exempted military service on, ah . . . health grounds, and pushed papers across a desk for the Department of Information.'

Colonel Haxby chuntered, 'Well, someone had to do it.'

Royce returned with the old soldier's Scotch.

Having determined everyone's service record to his satisfaction, if not approval, Haxby declared, 'It's all very well standing around shooting the breeze, but what I'd like to know is, where is he?'

'"He"?' Pandora asked impishly.

'Who else?' the colonel brayed. 'Ruddy Connaught.'

'Ah . . .' Royce said, 'he'll join us for drinks at six.'

'He will, will he? Hard bird to flush from cover? Always was a bit of a coward, old Connaught. Know what *he* did in the war?'

When no one obliged him with a reply, he said, 'Sweet bugger all. Bloody conchie. Pulled up spuds in the shires. That's the measure of the man.'

He opened the flap of his blazer, and Langham was surprised to see a leather holster equipped with a service revolver strapped to his thin torso. 'Well, I'll give you notice. I've come to shoot the yellow belly.' He knocked back his Scotch and almost hit Royce in the chest with his glass. 'If you please, waiter.'

While the young man scampered off to the bar, the guests stared in shock at Colonel Haxby.

'Shoot the great man?' Pandora said with relish. 'Well, we might not love D.C., but that's going a bit far, isn't it?'

'Great Man, my *derrière!*' the colonel expostulated. 'The man's a coward. Asked me down here so he could apologize, he did. Only way he can apologize is to accept my challenge to a duel, and when he's laid out dead, I'll rejoice.'

'Apologize?' Maria enquired.

'Not for the ears of the fairer sex, my dear.'

Royce returned with the old soldier's Scotch – a triple, Langham judged – and Charles had the foresight to change the subject. 'How many other guests are we expecting, young man?'

'Just one,' Royce said. 'Lady Cecelia Albrighton. Oh, and Connaught's brother, Monty, arrived in the village this morning. He phoned to say he'd be up for drinks.'

'*Lady* Cecelia? Gentry?' Colonel Haxby snorted. 'Don't like the sound of that. Bloody aristocrats can't be trusted. In bed with the ruddy Nazis, they were. All the dashed lot of 'em.'

'Isn't that going a bit far, old boy?' Pandora said, and Langham received the impression that she was enjoying herself.

Haxby ignored her. 'Anyway, why's Connaught hobnobbing with aristocracy?'

'Apparently, he knew Lady Cecelia during the war,' Royce said.

Pandora snorted. '"Knew" in what sense, Wilson?'

'I'm sure I've no idea,' the young man said. 'You'll have to ask Connaught himself.'

Langham looked at his watch. It was almost four fifty. 'Time we were pushing off if we're to make the appointment with Annabelle,' he said to Maria. 'Charles, would you care to accompany us?'

'I think, my boy, that I might retire to my room and rest for a spell before dinner, if you'll excuse me.'

Wilson Royce took the opportunity to suggest he show the rest of the guests to their respective rooms.

'Forty winks before grubs up,' Colonel Haxby said. 'But do the honours and fill me up before we go, laddie.'

Langham took Maria's hand and they escaped.

SEVEN

'Well,' Langham said as they drove through the gates of Connaught House and along the lane towards the village of Trennor Pendennis, 'what did you make of that?'

'I feel as if we've just escaped from a lunatic asylum.' Maria laughed.

'What I'd like to know is why Connaught is gathering all these misfits?'

'Misfits who have a grievance against him,' she said, 'and to whom he wishes to apologize.'

'Curiouser and curiouser. Perhaps Annabelle might be able to shed light on the situation.'

They drove into the cobbled harbour. An old fisherman sat outside the Fisherman's Arms, mending a fishing net. Langham drew up and asked him where he might find Threepenny Cottage on Bramble Lane. The old man gargled something incomprehensible and pointed to the opposite headland. Langham thanked him and set off.

'Was he speaking French, by any chance?' he asked as they left the village.

Maria said, 'Cornish, I think.' She pointed. 'That way.'

He turned down a lane that branched off the main road and veered towards the headland across the bay from Connaught House.

'And there's Bramble Lane,' she said.

Langham eased the Rover down the lane and, a mile further on, made out the roof of a honey-stoned cottage.

'How quaint,' Maria said as they pulled up outside Threepenny Cottage.

They climbed out, and the mystery of the cottage's appellation became obvious. The cottage's extension had the twelve sides of a threepenny piece.

Annabelle Connaught was sitting at a garden table when Langham unlatched the gate. She looked up, shielding her eyes from the sun, and waved in greeting.

They crossed the lawn and Langham made the introductions. Annabelle wore a vast floppy sun hat and a low-cut summer dress patterned with huge red poppies. She indicated a pair of binoculars on the table. 'I saw you set off, so I put the kettle on. Or would you prefer alcohol?'

'Tea will be perfect,' Langham said. 'Earl Grey, if you have it. Black.'

Maria asked for Earl Grey too, but with milk, and they sat at the table as Annabelle returned to the cottage.

'She seems nice,' Maria said.

'Sane, you mean, after that lot back there?'

'She reminds me rather of the Lady of Shallot.'

He picked up the binoculars and swung them across the bay in the direction of Connaught House. Pandora Jade and Wilson Royce were strolling across a side lawn, deep in conversation. He passed the binoculars to Maria.

She fixed them to her eyes, frowning as she adjusted the focus. 'My word, it brings it so close. It's strange, Donald . . . like watching a film with a different soundtrack.'

He smiled. 'Nice way of putting it.'

'Oh, and this must be Denbigh Connaught himself.'

Langham screwed up his eyes, but the house was so far away that he was unable to make out individual figures.

'He looks huge,' Maria reported. 'Like a bear dressed up in a sailor's uniform.'

'A uniform? Here, let me look.'

She passed him the binoculars. 'Behind the house, towards the sea. Near that odd-looking wooden building.'

He readjusted the focus and viewed the scene behind the house. He found the circular timber construction, hidden from the house by a high boxwood hedge, and before it the flaxen-haired figure of Denbigh Connaught. He was garbed in baggy pants and a navy blue roll-neck sweater, and Langham understood why Maria thought he resembled a sailor, though a local fisherman would be a more accurate description. He stood beside the stump of an old tree trunk, as if lost in thought, and appeared to be caressing the wood almost tenderly. As Langham watched, Connaught turned, walked across to the timber building Maria had mentioned and disappeared inside.

Annabelle returned bearing a tray piled with scones, clotted cream and a teapot. 'I thought you might like to try a local delicacy – just one won't spoil dinner, I'm sure.'

She poured the tea and they helped themselves.

'I saw you admiring the extension,' she said to Maria. 'My father was so taken with it that when he came to have his study built in 'forty-eight he copied its twelve-sided design.'

Langham indicated the binoculars. 'I noticed the odd timber building.'

'The shape is not the study's only peculiarity,' she said. 'It revolves, keeping pace with the sun. My father knew George Bernard Shaw in the thirties, and was rather taken with his revolving study. He practically lives in the thing these days. But enough of my father.' She smiled at Langham. 'Did you manage to . . .?'

'I'm sorry I didn't get through to you last night,' he said, licking cream from his fingers. 'I did call, but there was no reply. I wanted to report progress.'

'Don't apologize. I was out. So . . . there *has* been progress?'

'Well, not much, I admit.' He told her what he'd learned about Wilson Royce's trip to London. 'I caught up with him in a pub, where he was bragging about making a killing in the art market.'

Annabelle pulled a face. 'The art market? How odd. I suppose it's a sideline.'

'That's what he said. My colleague's looking into the matter while we're down here.'

'What impression, if any, did you get from his activities?' Annabelle asked.

'A little early to tell. My colleague has been speaking to Royce's contacts in London today. I did learn that he fancies himself with the ladies.'

Annabelle rolled her eyes. 'He's so pathetic, it's almost pitiable.'

'Do you know why your father employed Royce as his business manager?'

Annabelle shrugged. 'He said something about his no longer wanting to bother himself with business matters.'

Langham nodded and sipped his tea. 'Did your father tell you why he wanted to change agents?'

'He mentioned it last year, just before Christmas. He said that Pritchard and Pryce were getting a bit stale, whatever that meant. I was against the move. Old Pritchard knew my father and his work intimately, and I could see no benefit from his joining another agency.' She smiled at Maria. 'I hope you'll understand my candour, Mrs Langham? Well, my father took umbrage, arguing that I didn't know what I was talking about. Then he almost kicked me out of the house.'

'How rude!' Maria exclaimed.

Annabelle sighed. 'My father is like that. He's dominated my life, controlled me, for almost thirty years . . . So why should I have been in the least surprised?'

'Your mother . . .?' Langham asked tentatively.

'Died when I was a couple of months old,' she said. 'Of course, I don't remember her. And my father doesn't keep photographs or any other memorabilia.'

'Obviously, his loss—' Maria began.

Annabelle shook her head. 'He's not in the least sentimental. I think he soon got over my mother's death. He's so caught up in his work, so absorbed in the inner life of his imagination, that personal relations are not in the least important to him.'

'But as a novelist,' Langham said, 'I would have thought they would be of prime importance.'

'Have you read any of his books, Mr Langham?'

'I must admit that I haven't.'

'They deal with human beings solely as embodiments of ideas and theories. He deals in mythic archetypes and eschews – *detests* – the current trend of kitchen-sink realism. My theory is that he disdains writing about real human beings because he's so egotistical that he understands no one but himself – and he sees himself as one of his mythic heroes.'

'I see,' Langham said, intrigued. He was looking forward to meeting Denbigh Connaught.

'So when he flew into a rage and threw me out, a part of me was hurt, but another part of me understood . . . and I pitied him for his lack of empathy.'

Maria said, softly, 'You see your father as a damaged person, Annabelle?'

The woman smiled, as if grateful for Maria's insight. 'Very damaged,' she said.

'Do you have any idea what made him that way?'

Annabelle leaned back in her seat and stared across the bay at Connaught House. 'His father was a distant figure and his mother doted on him, spoilt him something rotten. I think this formed his world view – that is, that the entire universe revolved around his needs and desires. In essence, he never really grew up. He's in the grip of a terrible infantilism that has corrupted his relationship with everyone he's ever met.'

Langham smiled. 'You didn't by any chance study psychiatry, did you?'

She nodded. 'For a year, before I decided to switch to general medicine.'

'The odd thing,' he said, 'is your father's desire to apologize to the people he invited to Connaught House. This doesn't seem the behaviour of someone unable to empathize.'

Annabelle looked surprised. 'I'm not sure that I understand. Apologize?'

He glanced at Maria, then said, 'Several of his guests – my friend Charles Elder, Pandora Jade and Colonel Haxby – all mentioned the fact that your father had invited them down in order to apologize to them.'

'That's the first I've heard about this. Are you quite sure?'

'Charles had it in writing,' Langham said, 'and the others mentioned it earlier.'

Annabelle shook her head. 'I thought it odd that he should invite so many people down to the house at the same time. He's usually very reclusive. He cherishes his own company, especially when working on a book.'

'Is he working at the moment?'

'Apparently, he's finishing off his latest novel, but then he's always rewriting. He can take up to two years to knock a book into shape. He's a perfectionist, you see.'

'So his inviting so many people at one time is an anomaly?'

'Very much so,' she said. 'He told me he was inviting a few people, and suggested I stay out of the way.'

Langham stared at her. 'What an odd thing to say.'

She sipped her tea, then sighed. 'My father keeps people in compartments, and is averse to allowing his various acquaintances to mix. He shows a different side of his personality to each one. To me, he is authoritative and domineering; to others, he plays the role of the great man of letters, or the tragic, widowed recluse, or the suffering artist. Perhaps it's a reflection of his damaged personality that he hasn't been able to integrate his psyche and present a whole man to the world at large. Perhaps, on some level, he has the self-awareness to realize this, which is why he doesn't care for people to see his many, diverse selves.'

Langham finished his scone. 'Do you happen to know any of his guests?'

'No, but my father's mentioned them on and off over the years. I gather he had a fling with Pandora Jade in his younger days, but as far as I know he hasn't seen her for decades. As for the colonel . . . They were friends, or acquaintances, before the war, when my father lived in London. I think my father loaned him some money at one point, but I can't be certain about that.'

'And Lady Cecilia?'

'They had an affair, during the war, when my father was working on her estate. He was a conscientious objector, you see, and he worked on the land. Lady Cecelia was married. She suffered a nervous breakdown at the time, and I've often wondered if it might have had something to do with their clandestine affair.'

'Perhaps,' Langham ventured, 'this is what's preying on your father's conscience. How did the affair end? Did he leave her?'

'I don't know the details, but I do know that she was hospitalized for a number of years.'

'*Years?*'

'Apparently so.'

Maria replaced her tea cup on the saucer. 'Were you with your father during the war?'

She laughed, but there was a certain brittleness in the sound. 'Good Lord, no. He packed me off to a boarding school in Scotland. He said it was for my own good. I saw him about once a year . . .' She stopped suddenly, and Langham received the impression that Maria's question had touched upon a raw nerve.

He stared down the length of the garden, to where a white picket fence ran the length of the clifftop.

As if eager to change the subject, Annabelle said, 'Come, I'll show you the view.'

Langham took Maria's hand and they strolled with Annabelle to the end of the garden. He approached the fence with caution and peered over, his nausea rising. A sheer drop of a hundred feet was traversed by a flight of steps cut into the cliff face. Far below, he made out a concrete jetty, with a small, bobbing motorboat moored to a rusting capstan.

'At some point over the weekend,' Annabelle said, 'I'll take you out on my boat and show you the spectacular caves along the coast.'

Langham nodded queasily, taking in the narrowness of the precipitous steps and the chain hand-rail pegged into the cliff face. 'That would be . . . interesting.'

Maria, sensing his unease, squeezed his hand.

They strolled across the garden and paused to admire the inland view, the golden cottages of the village rising up the hillside and the hazy verdure of the surrounding forests.

Annabelle reminisced about how she had been drawn back to Cornwall after three years in London.

'A practice at St Austell, a few miles along the coast, advertised a position for a GP, and it was an opportunity too good to spurn.'

'With the advantage that it was close to your father,' Maria said.

Annabelle gave a grim smile. 'I cannot honestly say that that was part of the attraction. No, I missed the *place*. After all, I spent the first ten years of my life here.'

They returned to the table and finished their tea, while Annabelle chatted about the beauty of the area.

A little later, noting the time, Langham said, 'My word, it's almost six. We'd better be pushing off.'

'I'll be in touch about the scenic tour,' Annabelle promised. 'Perhaps Sunday afternoon?'

'That would be wonderful,' Maria said.

They returned to the Rover. As they drove off, Maria said, 'I like her, Donald. I'm intrigued by her relationship with her father.'

'In what way?'

'Oh, in her ambivalence; she obviously loves him, but also hates him at the same time.'

'You think so?'

She nodded. 'Well, I think I would, if *I* were his daughter.'

They drove through the village, up the hillside and through the forest towards Connaught House.

'And now for a quick drink before dinner – and the appearance of Denbigh Connaught,' Langham said. 'I think we're in for fireworks before the evening's out, my girl.'

EIGHT

They entered the drawing room to find Charles holding forth, his gargantuan, brandy-glass figure a central primary around which the other guests orbited.

The gathering had been augmented by the arrival of two more guests, Lady Cecelia Albrighton and Monty Connaught. Lady Cecelia was a tall, spindly woman in her early sixties, whose silver lamé evening dress might have suited a woman thirty years her junior but which, draped on her angular frame, merely pointed up the fact that the passage of time had not been kind to her. Everything about her was grey, from her distant eyes and distressed hair to the tone of her skin. Langham did discern, however, something of the vanished beauty of her younger days in her elegant face and long neck.

Monty Connaught was a tall, powerfully built man in his early fifties, dressed in casual flannels and a light blue cotton jacket. His sunburnt face and head of tight, gunmetal grey curls gave him the distinguished appearance, Langham thought, of a Roman senator. His most striking feature, however, was not his patrician face but his right hand, which had been horribly injured in an accident: the three middle fingers were missing, leaving only the thumb and little finger. The silvered scars scoring the ill-carpentered metacarpus suggested a burns injury.

He pincered his whisky glass, crab-like, between the thumb and remaining finger.

The butler hovered with a tray of sherry, and Langham and Maria helped themselves. Charles made introductions.

'I won't shake,' Monty Connaught said to Langham, lifting his injured hand. 'Some people are a bit put off by the claw. Pleased to meet you, Donald, Maria.' He had a rich, pleasant voice and an affirmative smile. Langham wondered why he didn't offer his left hand, which he kept in the pocket of his jacket.

'Just a tick,' Langham said. 'M. J. Connaught. *Iberian Sojourn.* I thought I recognized the face.'

Monty smiled. His light blue eyes were striking, even more so for their contrast with his suntan. 'You've read it? You must be one of a very select few. That was one of my early ones – it sold about fifty copies.'

'I enjoyed it. I was researching the coast of Spain for one of my thrillers. I thought you brought the country to life.'

'You're too kind.'

'Are you working on a book at the moment?' Langham asked.

'As a matter of fact, I've just been commissioned to write about a trip along the Moroccan coast. That's where I'm heading in a few days.' He paused, staring down at his whisky. 'I don't know about you, Donald, but I'm finding it harder and harder to make a living from the pen.'

'I went through a lean spell just after the war,' Langham said, 'but I'm not doing too badly now. Selling enough to keep the wolf from the door, at any rate.'

Monty smiled. 'Oddly enough, it was just after the war when I was doing well. Halcyon days. You see, everyone wanted to escape, lose themselves in exotic climes and far-flung adventures. I did a couple of slim books a year and the lending libraries couldn't get enough of 'em.'

'But these days?'

'I'm lucky if I get one commission a year. The market's still stable, but there are more and more scribblers cashing in on the racket. Everyone with half an education is writing an account of their summer holidays.'

'That must be more than a little galling.'

Monty laughed. 'I suppose I shouldn't complain. I don't live in Britain. I spend the summer sailing around the Med, doing the research for my books, then dock in Athens for the winter, batten the hatches and write the things. Few places cheaper to live than Athens, Donald. I get by.'

Langham wondered how Monty viewed the literary success of his brother, whose books were well reviewed and often appeared on bestseller lists.

To their left, Charles was finishing off an account of his friendship with Lord Alfred Douglas. 'And the sweet thing was his devotion to Wilde, and his acknowledgement of his part in the great man's downfall.'

Colonel Haxby harrumphed and smote the parquet with his stick. 'Great man?' he muttered. 'Chap deserved everything that came to him. Jumped-up Irish invert that he was.'

Pandora Jade, dressed for dinner in a pin-striped trouser suit, challenged the old soldier. 'I don't see how you can use his nationality, or his sexual persuasion, to tarnish the undoubted fact of his genius. Have you seen any of his plays, Haxby?'

'Plays? Haven't the time to go running around the West End!'

Wilson Royce, gripping a glass of whisky to his chest and looking, Langham thought, more than a little inebriated, whispered, 'The old sot hasn't lived.'

'Charles was telling me about your recent marriage,' Lady Cecelia said to Maria. 'How I do love a romantic story. Now tell me,' she said, 'was it love at first sight?'

Maria laughed. 'I first saw Donald in a photograph on the back of one of his books. And I have to admit that I did think him rather dashing.'

'My word, what a remarkable coincidence! Do you know,' Lady Cecelia went on, smiling around the group, 'my first encounter with Denbigh was, as it were, through one of his early novels. My husband was a critic for *The Times*, before the war, and the house was positively inundated with review copies. Of course, I browsed through them from time to time, and I well recall the occasion I happened upon *A Winter's Harvest*. And the picture of the young author! Why, my head was turned, if I'm not being *too* indiscreet. And I thought the novel a masterpiece.'

'How did you come to meet Connaught in person?' Pandora wanted to know.

Lady Cecelia laid her long, pewter fingers on the woman's arm. 'It was through a remarkable coincidence. My husband farmed the estate before the war, and when many of his workers were called into the services, their places were taken by Land Girls and conscientious objectors. One of the latter was a man whom I thought rather familiar, and then the penny dropped. It was none other than Denbigh Connaught.' Her gaze became distant as she thought back to the early years of the war.

'It's remarkable,' she went on in a quieter voice, 'how one's life can change because of random chance, isn't it? Had it not been for Denbigh's posting to Lincolnshire . . .'

'You would not be here today,' Pandora finished.

'Which begs the ruddy question,' Colonel Haxby said, 'why *are* we here? Why did Connaught drag you down here, Lady Cecelia?'

Lady Cecelia blinked, returning to the present. 'I received a letter inviting me for the weekend.'

'Did he, by any chance,' Pandora ventured, 'mention anything about an apology? You see, to the rest of us he mentioned the need to apologize.'

Lady Cecelia regarded her sherry. 'As a matter of fact, he did. But that's not the reason I came. I don't hold grudges, my dear. Life is too short to harbour ill-will towards others, don't you think? What passed between Denbigh and me all those years ago . . . It's all water under the bridge as far as I'm concerned. When I received the letter, I thought how nice it was that he still remembered me, and how wonderful it would be to renew our acquaintance.'

Langham glanced at Maria, who was smiling at the woman's words.

'Can't say the same in my case,' Colonel Haxby barked. 'Letter stirred up memories I thought I'd buried long ago.'

'So why,' Wilson Royce said, 'did you accept the invitation?'

The old soldier drained his Scotch and signalled to the butler for a refill. 'Despite what I said earlier, I didn't come to shoot the old reprobate. Considered it, mind you. Chap deserves a round of lead, for what he did.'

'And what might that have been?' Langham asked.

'That's between me and Connaught,' Haxby muttered.

'So if not to dispense summary justice,' Pandora said, winking at Maria, 'why did you accept his invitation?'

Haxby waited until the butler had topped up his glass, took a swallow, then said, 'Because not only did Connaught say he wanted to apologize, but he also said . . . said he wanted to make amends – to give me something.'

Wilson Royce blinked. 'Give you something? Did he say what?'

The colonel shook his head. 'Kept mum on that front, laddie. That was the bait, you see, to bring me here. I've no idea what he meant, but I'm intrigued.'

Langham looked around the little group. 'Would it be indelicate to ask what inducement he made to the rest of you?'

Charles said, 'You know what it was in my case, my boy – Connaught promised me his next novel.'

Pandora said, 'Merely said he wanted to apologize, and sent me a cheque for travelling expenses.'

'To me he mentioned merely the need to apologize,' Lady Cecelia said. 'I would need no *inducement*. It is enough to think that I will soon be renewing my acquaintance with Denbigh.'

Monty Connaught finished his whisky. 'I received a telegram from him at my club on Wednesday. Said he needed to see me urgently. I arrived this morning, but Denbigh's been holed up in his study all day. Haven't had sight or sound of him.'

Colonel Haxby pushed up the sleeve of his blazer and blinked at his wristwatch. 'It's past six. I thought you said he'd be with us by now, Royce? Where the blazes is he?'

Wilson Royce looked uncomfortable. 'Punctuality, I'm afraid, is not Mr Connaught's strong point. When he's working, he tends to forget things like the passage of time, and meals.'

'But for God's sake,' Pandora said, 'he invited us down expressly to see him, so he should damn well keep to schedule. He said drinks at six, and it's a quarter past now.'

'I've heard all about this study of his,' Colonel Haxby said. 'Read about it in some newspaper. Stole the idea off Bernard Shaw, if I'm not mistaken.'

Royce said, 'But Shaw's study rotated manually, Colonel. The beauty of Connaught's study is that it's automatic. It's mounted on a cross-frame, and the upper part of it turns to follow the sun, powered by an electric motor. Connaught designed it himself.'

Colonel Haxby raised his stick. 'Tell you what. We should mount a raid. A little sortie, beard the lion in his den. Lead the way to this revolving study, young Royce!'

'I . . . I don't think that would be a very good idea,' the young man said.

'I think it a damned good notion!' Pandora declared. 'And it's such a lovely evening; let's go and visit the great man.'

Maria smiled at Langham and raised her shoulders in a shrug of excited delight.

Lady Cecelia looked unsure. 'Well, if you don't think it would anger . . .'

Charles glanced at Langham. 'I've heard that his rage is legendary, my boy. I think caution might be the watchword here.'

The colonel bellowed a laugh. 'Balderdash! Let's surprise the fellow!'

Monty Connaught caught Langham's eye. 'I'll be pushing off, Donald. I'm not stopping for dinner – due to meet a few friends in the village at seven. Let's get together for a drink and a natter at some point over the weekend.'

'I'd like that,' Langham said.

Monty nodded around the group and strode from the room.

Colonel Haxby made for the French windows, lofting his walking stick. 'Tally-ho!' he called out, and led the guests out into the balmy evening.

Langham, Maria and Charles brought up the rear of the little group as it crossed the lawn.

'I'm not sure I want to be leading the charge,' Maria said.

'Wise of you, my girl,' Charles agreed.

To the south, the extensive lawn sloped towards the edge of the cliff. To the right of the greensward, concealed from the house behind the boxwood hedge, was Denbigh Connaught's singular study. Twelve-sided and constructed from pitch pine, it resembled a rather plain musical box with a conical roof. It might have been revolving, but at such a rate that, as it followed the sun, its movement was undetectable to the naked eye.

A circular, stepped plinth surrounded the foot of the study, and without preamble Colonel Haxby mounted this and rapped sharply on the glass of the door with his walking stick. He applied his nose to the window, but a rattan blind hid the study's interior from view.

Haxby tried the door handle, found it locked and raised his stick again. Wilson Royce winced and began, 'I don't think . . .' but to no avail, as the colonel tapped again fit to break the glass.

'Hell hath no fury,' Charles whispered, gripping Langham's elbow, 'like a writer rudely plucked from his muse.'

'Perhaps Connaught is already in the house,' Maria said, 'which would be just as well.'

Royce said, 'But he would have joined us for drinks, if . . .'

'Perhaps,' Pandora said, with a hint of mischief that Langham realized was becoming her stock in trade, 'one of us has decided to do away with the reprobate? You said you wanted to shoot him earlier, Colonel. And the rest of us, with a couple of exceptions, wouldn't be averse to pulling the trigger.'

'I don't think that kind of humour . . .' Royce began.

Pandora beamed around the dithering group. 'Can we all account for our whereabouts since arriving here?'

Charles said, 'Does anyone have a spare key? Perhaps it might be prudent to check?'

'My money's on finding him seated before the typewriter with a bullet in his brain,' Pandora said with ghoulish glee.

Lady Cecelia touched Maria's arm and murmured, 'Why does the awful woman go on so, my dear?'

Maria smiled in reassurance. 'I'm sure there's nothing to be worried about.'

Royce looked around the group, and his gaze alighted on Langham. 'Do you think I should fetch the spare key and check?'

Langham nodded. 'Might be wise,' he said.

At that second, a large, looming figure appeared from around the side of the study and stood regarding the group.

'What the hell,' boomed the man, 'd'you think you're all doing out here, milling around like a flock of sheep?'

'Mr Connaught!' Royce cried with relief. 'We wondered . . .'

'We thought you'd had a heart attack, old boy,' Colonel Haxby said.

'No, we didn't,' Pandora piped up. 'We thought someone had finally done the honourable thing and bumped you off.'

Denbigh Connaught stared at the artist. 'Typical of your gallows humour, Pandy. You haven't changed in the slightest, have you? I've neither succumbed to a heart attack nor been bumped off. I've just finished my constitutional, I'll have you know.'

His face was large and fleshy, in repose melancholy but now animated by disdain. He had a curious head of hair, spun gold and bunched above his ears, with thin strands cross-hatched sparsely over his scalp.

Langham glanced at Charles to see how he'd reacted to the appearance of his *bête noire*. His friend had taken a step backwards, a hand lifted to his mouth, and was staring at Connaught with evident distaste.

'So here you all are,' the novelist said in a low, baritone rumble, his eyes raking the quivering group. 'Here you all are . . . Pandy, still the jester, the *agent provocateur*. And Colonel Haxby . . . It's been a long time, Haxby. Charles, Charles . . . even longer. My word, how the sands of time change us all.' He smiled at Cecelia, it seemed with genuine warmth. 'It's good to see you, Lady Cee.'

He clapped his hands suddenly, making several people jump. 'Now in with you! Go on! I need a drink . . . Inside!'

And, running at the group, he chivvied them back into Connaught House as if they were a gaggle of errant geese.

NINE

'If you'd care to follow me through to the dining hall,' Connaught said as they entered the drawing room.

He led the way through a side door and along a gloomy, panelled corridor hung with Victorian landscapes. 'This part of the house is a hundred years old,' he expounded as they walked, 'but the dining hall and the rest of the west wing are Georgian. Much of the house was destroyed by fire in the eighteen-fifties. Only the west wing survived. Here we are.'

The oak-panelled walls of the dining hall were hung with dusty landscapes and several portraits of Victorian worthies, presumably Connaught's ancestors.

The novelist seated himself in a massive oaken chair at the head of the table. Wilson Royce murmured to the guests, 'You'll find that you have each been assigned a place.'

Langham found his name written on a folded card and wondered if Connaught had arranged the seating plan to achieve a desired effect. He was seated to the novelist's right, across from Lady Cecelia; to Langham's right was Maria, and Pandora Jade faced her. Charles, Wilson Royce and Colonel Haxby were seated furthest from Connaught.

They were served dinner by the old butler, Watkins.

Langham glanced at Charles, who was sipping his wine and casting the occasional wary glance towards Denbigh Connaught. He caught his agent's eye and smiled; Charles raised his glass in acknowledgement. A strained hush hung over the gathering, all the more pronounced for a guest occasionally attempting to strike up conversation which might engage the whole group: Pandora praised the consommé, and Colonel Haxby splashed a mouthful of claret around his gums and pronounced, 'A decent drop of Bordeaux, Connaught.'

Connaught looked up and said, almost under his breath, 'As if you would know, Haxby.'

He scanned the guests and, noting his brother's absence, muttered, 'I thought Monty was joining us?'

'He was here for drinks earlier,' Langham said, 'but he said he had to get off to meet friends at seven.'

'That was his excuse, was it?' the novelist grunted. 'Fact is, he doesn't like to be seen eating, on account of his hand.'

'That must be awkward,' Langham said, feeling the need to defend the man. 'It must be difficult, operating his boat . . .'

Connaught shook his head. 'Not difficult in the slightest. He has a couple of deckhands who do all the heavy work. All Monty does is sit, soak up the sun and type his terrible books.'

As they made their way through the first course, conversation broke out around the table; Maria asked Pandora about her paintings, and Charles quizzed the colonel about his time in Egypt.

Connaught said to Langham, 'Annabelle mentioned that you're a writer yourself.'

'Well, I turn out a thriller a year,' he said, and cursed himself for sounding so apologetic.

'Must admit I don't read modern writers,' Connaught went on. 'I don't want to be influenced. Also – and I don't mean this personally – I find that what concerns my contemporaries doesn't in the slightest interest me.'

'In terms of ideas?'

'Just so.' The novelist nodded. He ate slowly, reflectively; he wheezed between mouthfuls, smelled overpoweringly of cigarette tobacco and blinked at his guests short-sightedly.

'What do you read?' Langham asked.

'History, philosophy,' Connaught said, 'and, of course, the Greeks. I find that they really said it all in terms of the summation of the lot of humanity. What followed, with the advent of Christianity . . .' He waved, as if in disgust. 'Fah! Two thousand years of indoctrination designed with one end in mind: to inculcate the idea of guilt into the human race.' He stared around the table, as if seeking opposition. 'Though, I admit, it's a brilliant ruse: strike guilt into the heart of the populace and you have them by the balls.'

'At least the Christian ethos,' Pandora was brave enough to opine, 'did promote the idea of the sanctity of the individual.'

Connaught pointed his soup spoon at the artist. 'That's the girl! You're no more Christian than I am – or have you been converted, Pandy? No, you're just being contentious for the sheer bloody hell of it.' He waved. 'Anyway, look what the sanctity of the individual ended up with: a citizenry cowed by collective guilt and an appalling Sunday school morality. It makes me sick!'

Colonel Haxby leaned forward, spilling claret down his blazer as he did so. 'And what, sir, what . . . what do you intend to do about it? It's . . . it's all very well shouting one's mouth off about the perceived ills . . . ills of the world, but what the ruddy hell . . .?' He lost the thread of his argument and lapsed into silence.

Smiling tolerantly, Connaught said, 'I write, my friend. That's all I can bloody well do. I write to the best of my ability. My latest is all about . . . But I'll tell you all about it tomorrow, Charles.'

Surprised at the mention of his name, Charles raised his glass and smiled unsurely. 'I shall look forward to that,' he murmured dubiously.

The soup course finished, they were served game pie with roast potatoes, green beans and carrots – basic fare but expertly cooked.

'Woman in the village comes in every afternoon and does for me,' Connaught said when Maria praised the meal. 'Watkins does breakfast, by the way, between eight and nine, so make sure you're down in time or you'll be making your own toast.'

Having said his piece about the ills of Christianity, Connaught seemed happy to retreat into silence, knock back whisky after whisky and allow others to take up the conversation.

From time to time, Langham caught Wilson Royce looking at him across the table, as if the young man was attempting to recall just where he'd seen his face before. Pandora Jade bombarded Charles with questions about his literary agency, then said that she was thinking of writing her autobiography. Colonel Haxby drank to excess and by some miracle of long practice managed to finish the food on his plate. Lady Cecelia ate with decorum, her arthritic fingers kinked around the cutlery, and from time to time addressed a quiet aside to Wilson Royce or Charles.

Maria asked Royce what he did before becoming Denbigh Connaught's business manager, and he told her that on leaving Oxford he'd worked in the accounts department of a London publisher. Langham wondered when the young man had begun to take an interest in art.

The light beyond the French windows waned as the sun sank, and the twinkling points of a thousand stars appeared above the shipping lanes. The errant power supply made the electric lights in the room dim and surge, creating an effect like candles in a draught. Connaught ordered the butler to break out the port.

At one point a little later, during a lull in the conversation, Connaught slumped further down in his seat – resembling a bear that had failed to accommodate itself to the constraints of human furniture – and gazed around his guests.

The silence deepened and, as if by some unspoken consent, all eyes turned to the host.

Connaught, nursing a tumbler of whisky on his chest, purred, 'C'mon, then. Tell me a little about yourselves.'

Into the startled silence, Colonel Haxby hiccupped. 'What was that, old boy? Tell you about . . . about ourselves?'

'Just the four of you: my *old* friends. The people I knew so long ago. You, Haxby, and Pandora, and you, Charles, and Lady Cee. I'd like to know . . . It's been so long. Years and years. How . . . how has life treated you?'

Colonel Haxby opened his mouth, but remained silent. Pandora regarded the novelist with an amused expression on her round, owlish face. Charles looked uneasy, lost, for once, for words. Only Lady Cecelia smiled, as if taking the question in her stride.

'The years have, all things considered, treated me well,' she said. 'After the war . . . after what happened . . . Well, my husband left me, but, to his credit, settled an annuity to ensure I was not forced into the poorhouse.' She smiled at her little joke. 'For the last ten years I have lived in a small flat in Knightsbridge, and I busy myself with charity work. I have friends whom I see every week. And living in London' – she smiled around the table – 'well, there is always so much to see and do, isn't there? The theatre, and recently I've taken an interest in the cinema.'

'And you never remarried, Lady Cee?' Connaught asked.

Her smile was tremulous, and Langham's heart ached for her. 'No,' she said. 'No, I never remarried.' She brightened. 'But then, I never met the right man.' She beamed across at Maria. 'Which perhaps is why I do so like to hear about young love.'

Connaught swivelled his bleary eyes to focus on Pandora. 'And you, Pandy? How has the fickle finger of fate treated you?'

The artist sat back, twirling her wine glass and regarding Connaught evenly, her red lips twisted into an amused moue. 'I wonder why you want to know, after so many years?' She shrugged. 'I get by, doing what I always wanted to do. I sell my paintings,

always for amounts that make it necessary to do the next one faster
than I would like.'

'And lovers?'

'I . . . I don't stint myself in that department, Connaught.'

'I bet you don't,' he said. 'But are you happy, Pandy?'

'Happy?' she snorted. 'What a bloody stupid question! How can
anyone with half a brain claim to be happy? We're born into chaos,
heir to a plethora of ills, and die before we can fully realize ourselves.
Of course I'm not bloody happy. But in the face of a hostile universe,
as one must, I endure, Connaught. I endure.'

The novelist raised his glass, the gesture mocking. 'And I applaud
your spirit, my dear.' His large head swung to the left of the table.
'Colonel?'

'What she says,' he belched, pointing at Pandora Jade. 'What the
little round lady over there so wisely says. I endure, with a little
help from the cup that cheers. Who said that drink hath charms to
soothe the savage breast? Well, I agree with him!' He slipped down
in his seat, closed his eyes, and was lost to further rational debate.

Connaught said, 'And you, Charles?'

Charles sat back in his chair and stared into his port. At last he
looked up, into Connaught's gaze, and said, 'I think that one can
be happy, *pace* Pandora, and not be consigned to the realm of fools.
One must be a realist, and not wish for, or dream of, too much.
Enjoy the fine things of life – always the finest, in books, art, and'
– he smiled across at Maria and Langham – 'and friends. Give unto
others as one would wish to be given.' He fixed Connaught with a
steely stare, which surprised Langham, and went on, 'Remember
the past, but do not be beaten by it. Remember that grief abates in
time and, like memory, fades.'

'Do you consider yourself a success, Charles?'

'I run a successful agency, so yes, I think I do.'

'I meant,' said the novelist, 'do you consider yourself a success,
personally?'

Rather than wither under Connaught's onslaught, Charles rallied.
'I have had my burdens to bear, Denbigh. I have suffered loss and
pain, as you well know. And though I might not concur with Pandora
that happiness and foolishness are synonymous, I do agree with her
that one endures.'

Connaught nodded, as if satisfied with what he had heard. At last
he said, 'You're all probably wondering why I invited you down

here. Or, rather, why now I find it in my heart to apologize to you for sins committed many years ago.'

In the tense silence that followed, he looked around the group, one by one, and then went on, 'And tomorrow I will tell you. Usually, when writing a novel, I would work on Saturday. But as I have almost finished . . . tomorrow I will see you all. Lady Cee first, and then you, Charles, and then the colonel – if you would be good enough to remind him, Royce? – and Pandy. I'll see you each every half hour, beginning at ten, in my study.' He pointed over his shoulder. 'I'll see Monty later. He's staying at the Fisherman's, for some damned reason. Royce, give him a call and get him up here after lunch – understood?'

Langham looked around the group. Lady Cecelia was gazing at Connaught with tenderness. Charles, his lips pursed, was staring down at his port, as if perplexed. Colonel Haxby was by now snoring, oblivious to the novelist's words. Pandora Jade watched Connaught with calculation, as if she suspected him of planning some ruse but not knowing quite what it might be.

Connaught stood suddenly, muttered, 'Until then, goodnight,' and stumped drunkenly from the room.

'I think that,' Pandora Jade declared, 'calls for another drink.'

TEN

Maria awoke to sunlight and birdsong flooding the east-facing room. She turned on to her side, propped her head on her hand and stared at her husband. He was fast asleep, his head buried in the feather pillow, his dark hair mussed. She'd had a nightmare in the early hours – she was a child again, chased by a poodle – and had come awake with a startled cry to find that Donald was soothing her with quiet, reassuring words. She'd fallen asleep in his arms a little later.

She slid out of bed, bathed quickly and returned to find Donald awake and yawning.

'Sleep well?' she asked.

'Like a log. You?'

'Fine, apart from the nightmare.'

'Oh, yes. I remember. All right now?'

'I'm fine,' she said.

Donald climbed from bed and dressed. 'I wonder how Charles is this morning?'

'I had a quiet word with him last night, before we turned in. I insisted that I accompany him when he met Connaught this morning.'

He glanced at her as he knotted his tie. 'And what did he say?'

'You know Charles. He's fiercely independent. But in this case, I think he was secretly grateful for the offer.'

Donald strolled to the window and stared out. He turned and asked her, 'What did you make of last night?'

'Connaught's performance?' She bit her lip, considering. 'To be honest, I'm not sure that I trust the man. I mean, all that business about two thousand years of collective guilt, thanks to Christianity, and his calling his old friends – or acquaintances – here to apologize.'

Donald shrugged. 'Perhaps, in his old age, he's been stricken by the dread Christian guilt.'

'He's not that old. The same age as Charles – fifty-six.' She considered. 'But perhaps you're right. Perhaps he's had cause to look back and reassess his life . . . and is overcome by guilt and the need to make reparations.'

He looked at her, frowning. 'I'm intrigued. It's given me an idea for a book. *Sam Brooke Investigates the Case of the Guilt-Stricken Novelist.*'

'Interesting,' she said. 'But I think the title needs a little work.'

'I agree.' He offered his arm. 'Breakfast?'

They descended to the dining room to find Wilson Royce seated at the long table, tucking into bacon and scrambled eggs.

'All alone?' Donald asked.

'Lady Cee requested tea in her room,' Royce said, 'and Pandora was down earlier, looking like death after indulging last night. She had a couple of sips of coffee and fled back to her room.'

Maria helped herself to toast, eggs and coffee.

'After you retired last night,' Royce went on, 'we repaired to the drawing room, and the colonel and Pandora were still knocking it back when I turned in at one. I wouldn't like to have the colonel's head this morning.'

Donald smiled. 'I should think he's quite accustomed to the effect,' he said, pouring himself a cup of Earl Grey.

Maria attended to her eggs and toast. The coffee was excellent, surprising her. If there was one thing she'd learned from drinking coffee in England, it was that the experience was often disappointing.

They ate in silence for a time, before she asked Royce, 'I don't suppose Connaught said anything to you about his wish to apologize to some of his guests?'

Royce dabbed his lips with a napkin. 'No, and no one was as surprised as I was. Apologies are the last thing I'd expect from him.'

Maria glanced at Donald. He was staring at the young man as if calculating something.

'Tell me, did Connaught remarry after the death of his wife?' Donald asked.

Royce lowered his tea cup. 'Remarry? But he was never married. What made you think . . .?'

Donald frowned. 'It was something Annabelle said yesterday. I must have picked up the wrong end of the stick. She said that her mother died when she, Annabelle, was very young.'

Royce shrugged. 'Connaught had a legion of women in the past, but he never married.'

Maria refilled her cup and asked, 'Do you think he'll be down for breakfast?'

'He doesn't have breakfast. Watkins takes tea to his room at six.' Royce finished his own tea. 'If you'll excuse me, I'd better get to it.'

'Day off?'

'Half a day. A round of golf this morning, and this afternoon Connaught wants me to go through his papers, sorting out what can be burnt. He's finally decided that the accumulated paraphernalia of a lifetime can be discarded.' He pointed towards the ceiling. 'I'll be locked in his old study all afternoon, amid dust and mouse droppings. No rest for the wicked.'

He smiled at Maria, sunlight glinting off his eye-tooth, nodded at Donald and hurried from the room.

She pointed to the bacon, sausage and eggs on Donald's plate. 'You certainly have an appetite. Not hungover?'

'Didn't you notice?' he said. 'I paced myself last night, too interested in what was going on. I'm intrigued by Lady Cee, as Connaught calls her.'

'In what way?'

'She appears, of the four old "friends" he invited down here, to be the only one who doesn't bear him a grudge. In fact, I'd say that she's still fond of the old goat.'

Maria sat back and nursed her coffee. 'Mmm. I wonder what happened between them, during the war? I mean, for Connaught to apologize about?'

'I think, my darling, that that will remain their secret until the grave.'

The door opened and Charles eased his bulk through the opening, with not much room to spare.

'How delightful!' he sang. 'Newlyweds at breakfast. And what a spread!' He cast an epicurean eye along the sideboard laden with silver salvers and hot plates. 'Oddly enough, I have an appetite this morning.'

'I'm pleased to hear that,' she said. 'I'd recommend the scrambled eggs. And the coffee is rather good.'

'My word! Kidneys!' Charles declared. 'I could write an ode to the delight of the humble kidney!'

While Charles was filling his plate, Donald caught Maria's eye and murmured, 'He's on form.'

She nodded, frowning. 'Suspiciously so,' she whispered.

'Making the best of a bad job?'

'I think so.'

Charles came to the table with a laden plate, sat beside Maria and poured himself a cup of coffee.

'What a wonderful morning,' he said. 'Later, perhaps – when we have satisfied Connaught's desire for amateur theatricals – we might venture abroad.'

'Good idea,' Donald said. 'How about a drive? Tell you what, how about we motor along to St Austell and have lunch?'

'Capital idea,' Charles agreed, munching on a kidney.

'Yesterday,' he went on, 'Lady Cecelia was telling me about her friends in London, and it so happens that we have someone in common. Cecelia knows Caroline Dequincy.'

'What a small world,' Maria said, and for the next five minutes they chatted about the American actress.

Through the window, Maria saw Monty Connaught striding up the drive towards the house, and a minute later the double doors at the far end of the room opened. Monty greeted Maria, Donald and Charles, poured himself a coffee, and leaned back against the sideboard, clutching the cup in his mangled hand.

'I won't join you,' he said. 'I find that all I can stomach in the morning is strong coffee.'

Maria recalled overhearing what Denbigh Connaught had told Donald yesterday, about Monty being self-conscious about eating in public. She felt sorry for him.

'I had a call last night from young Royce,' Monty said, 'summoning me to see Denbigh this afternoon. I thought I'd come up early and make a day of it. I left most of my books here twenty-five years ago when I fled the nest, you see, and I need to do a little research.'

'For your next one?' Charles asked.

'My publisher just commissioned a book about the coast of Morocco. I'm heading off in a day or two.'

'Did Denbigh say why he wanted to see you?' Donald asked. 'He's gathered most of the other guests here so that he can apologize.'

Monty's tanned face cracked into a smile. 'Well, he'll have plenty to apologize about, if even only half the tales are true.' He shook his head. 'That said, it's not like the old rogue to say sorry to anyone.'

'Not even to you?' Maria asked.

Monty shook his head, staring down at his coffee. 'He's never apologized to me in his life, and God knows he has plenty to be sorry about. Denbigh's five years my senior, and in our youth he lorded it over me. Between you and me, I think he resented my appearance on the scene. Stole his limelight somewhat.'

'How do you get on now?' Donald asked.

Monty smiled, showing white teeth. 'I haven't seen him for almost ten years, and back then there was no love lost. I must admit, though, that I'm intrigued. His telegram said he needed to see me urgently.'

'I think most people are wondering what he's up to,' Donald said.

Monty shrugged and poured more coffee. 'Right, mustn't dally,' he said. 'Work to do.'

Carrying his replenished coffee cup, he left the room.

'I wonder if we should take a stroll around the grounds,' Donald suggested, 'before . . .'

'The view from the clifftop,' Charles said, 'will be divine.'

They left the dining room and crossed the sloping lawn to the precipitous drop some two hundred yards from the house. Maria, knowing Donald's fear of heights, gripped his hand as they came to the tussocky edge of the cliff.

The sea was a flat expanse of blue and silver sequins; to their right, the coastline receded into the hazy distance in a series of scalloped coves and bays. Maria released Donald's hand, approached the edge and peered over.

'Careful,' he said.

Ten yards to their right, a steep flight of concrete steps led down to a small timber jetty. 'Perhaps, later,' she said mischievously, squinting at Donald, 'we should climb down and walk along the jetty?'

'Not on your nelly!' he said.

'I'd hold your hand all the way, Donald.'

He joined her and peered down, wincing. 'Doesn't look wide enough to walk two abreast,' he said.

She sighed. 'Oh, then we will have to think of some other form of entertainment.'

Charles laughed. 'Stop being so cruel to the poor man, Maria!'

Donald dragged her away from the edge and they strolled across the lawn.

He lit his pipe and puffed it into life. She was becoming accustomed to the rich smell of his tobacco which, together with the Brylcreem he used on his hair, she thought of as Donald's distinctive odour. She kissed his cheek.

'What was that for?' he laughed.

'Because you look so oddly serious when you puff away at that funny pipe of yours.'

'Is it funny?'

'A little, the way it sticks out from your manly jaw, with its little smoking chimney.'

In the distance, its windows glinting in the sunlight, was Denbigh Connaught's study. The door opened and Lady Cecelia appeared; she stepped from the building and hurried towards the house, her head down and a hand pressed to her chest.

'There goes Lady Cee,' Donald said. 'I wonder what transpired.'

Charles glanced at his watch. 'Ten fifteen,' he said. 'We might have been summoned into the great man's presence at ten thirty, but I refuse to kick my heels out here until then. What do you think, Maria?'

She was about to suggest they explore the walled garden on the far side of the house for fifteen minutes, but Charles lofted his silver-topped malacca and set off without awaiting her reply. 'Onward!' he declared.

Maria gave Donald a quick kiss. 'See you later, *mon cheri*.'

'Look after the old boy, Maria.'

'I'll do that,' she said. She caught up with Charles and took his hand as they walked around the study to reach the door, which at this time of the morning was facing the sea.

Charles rapped sharply on the glass with his cane. Maria hung back, anticipating Connaught's adverse reaction to her presence.

The door was snatched open precipitously and Connaught glared out. 'What time do you call this?' he barked, glancing at his wristwatch. 'You're early. I expressly said ten thirty.'

'You've dallied over this for forty years,' Charles replied sweetly. 'A few minutes are neither here nor there.'

Connaught grumbled something, then glared at Maria. 'And I didn't say anything about bringing a guest.'

'Maria is my business partner, Connaught. We come, as it were, as a package. Of course, if you'd rather not . . .' He turned as if making to leave.

Connaught snapped, 'Come in, then.'

Charles gestured for her to precede him, then squeezed through the narrow opening after her.

A battered settee and two wicker chairs were positioned to the left. Before the settee was a coffee table bearing a portable typewriter. The floor was of herringbone parquet, covered by a faded Persian rug. To the right, opposite the settee, stood an upright piano.

'Drink?' Connaught asked with ill grace.

'I'd rather conduct this meeting sober, if it is all the same to you,' Charles said primly.

'You?' the novelist asked, glaring at Maria.

'No, thank you.'

'Take a pew.' Connaught indicated the wicker chairs, pulling one of them closer for Maria. Having poured himself a Scotch, he dropped into the settee and stared at the pair.

Charles squeezed himself into a chair; it was a tight fit, and the wicker squeaked its protest. Connaught, Maria noted as she took her seat, appeared a little drunk; his face was flushed, the hair on either side of his thinning pate even more dishevelled than usual.

He glared from Maria to Charles. 'You're probably wondering what the hell all this is about.'

'That, Connaught, is something of an understatement. You remain incommunicado for forty years, and then—'

'And then summon you out of the blue to apologize. Must seem a bit rum, what?'

Charles smiled. 'You employ the phrase somewhat glibly.'

Connaught leaned back. He regarded Charles with a calculating gaze. 'It happened a long time ago, Charles.'

'Time does not diminish the pain, nor—'

'Don't go all poesy on me. I had enough of that at Winchester. Do you realize how much your constant soliloquizing grated on my nerves?'

'I might counter, Connaught, by asking if you realize how your ego tested the patience of our little group of pals.'

'We're even, then. But as I said, all this happened a long time ago. If you think I don't regret what I did then, you're sorely mistaken. Not a day goes by without—'

'If you're trying to elicit my sympathy, I suggest that you consider what it might have been like for me. After all, it was I who suffered.'

'And I, too, Charles. I was young – a mere boy. A fool, and damned fool, I'll grant you that. I suffered, and still suffer, the crushing guilt. And I might say that, as a burden, guilt is far harder to bear than grief after so long . . .'

Maria looked at Charles. His mouth was open, frozen in speechlessness. He gathered his wits and said, 'If you are trying to claim that your guilt is in any way comparable to the torture I suffered, at the time and in the years that followed, then you have an insufferable cheek, sir! "Guilt is far harder to bear than grief . . ." You astound me with your ignorance.'

Connaught took a mouthful of whisky. He remained quiet for a while, as if to allow Charles to calm himself, and then said very quietly, 'The nightmares began a few months ago.'

Charles blinked. 'The nightmares?'

'I am being haunted, Charles, for what I did that summer in 1917.'

Maria glanced at Charles. He was staring at the novelist, his eyes narrowed.

'Every night,' Connaught went on, 'every night he comes to me . . .'

'"He"?' Charles whispered.

'Who else?' Connaught said. 'Daniel . . .'

Beside her, Charles gave an almost imperceptible moan.

Connaught said, 'Do you have any idea, Charles, what it is like to know that you are responsible, directly responsible, for the death of another human being? To know that, through one's actions when one was a stupid, callow youth, a young boy died . . . Do you know what it's like to wake up in the early hours of the morning, wake up screaming from dreams in which Daniel is pointing at me, *accusing*?' The novelist hung his head, took a deep breath as if fighting against the desire to sob, then went on, 'He comes to me every night, Charles, *every night*; Daniel – as innocent and youthful . . . and as beautiful . . . as he was then, and he says to me, "Why?"'

Charles opened his mouth to speak. His hands were trembling on his lap. He said at last, 'What you did – your actions – you killed him just as if you'd taken a pistol and shot him through the heart!'

Connaught stared at Charles, his gaze stricken. 'Don't you think I know that, for Christ's sake! Don't you see that I've had to live with the guilt for every single day of my life? Trying to remain sane with the knowledge of my guilt, the knowledge that gnaws at the very core of my being. Over the years I've . . . by Christ, I've come to hate myself, been driven to the very brink of insanity!'

Charles stood up suddenly, skittling the wicker chair. At first Maria thought that her friend was about to launch himself at the novelist, but instead he hurried around the upturned chair, reached the door and turned.

'And you wish to placate me by offering your next novel?' His voice sounded strangled; his face was red, and tears rolled down his cheeks.

Connaught stretched out a hand, as if pleading. 'It is all I can give you, Charles, other than my heartfelt apology.'

Charles, standing with one hand on the door handle, shook his head and said, 'I cannot bring myself to forgive you, Connaught.'

'I don't want your forgiveness, for Christ's sake! I want your understanding!'

The two men stared at each other. Maria heard her heart thudding.

'My understanding?' Charles shook his head, uncomprehending.

Maria stared at Connaught as he searched for the words; he tore his gaze from Charles, his face contorting in pain. At last he managed, on the verge of tears, his mouth twisting, 'When I saw you two, that day, beside the river . . . When I saw how . . . how much Daniel obviously cared for you . . . Do you have any idea, any idea at all, Charles, how that made me feel?'

Charles shook his head. 'Feel?' he echoed.

'I . . . I was consumed with jealousy,' Connaught whispered, and hung his head in silence.

'Jealousy?'

'I loved Daniel, for Christ's sake! I *loved* him!'

Charles collapsed against the door, staring at the stricken novelist. He shook his head, then gathered himself and said, his words strangled, 'So . . . so you decided to destroy what I had? If you could not claim Daniel's affection, you ensured that neither I nor anyone else would enjoy his love.'

Connaught rose unsteadily to his feet. 'How could I foresee what my actions would lead to?' he wept. 'I swear to you, Charles, I did what I did not to punish Daniel, but because I was jealous of his love for you . . . I did what I did, I admit, so that *you* might suffer.'

Charles stared at the novelist, aghast. Tears spilled down his cheeks as he struggled to find an adequate response, and Maria wanted to stand and take him in her arms.

Charles said, in little more than a horrified murmur, 'And in God's name you have made me suffer, you *monster!*'

'Charles, I beg you.' Connaught moved. He took three paces across the study to a bookcase and snatched up a great sheaf of typescript.

He held it out to Charles, 'Please, take it.'

'Damn your accursed novel!' Charles cried, snatching open the door. 'And damn you, Connaught!'

He turned and fled from the study.

As if released from paralysis, Maria stood quickly and crossed to the door. Connaught moved to her, thrusting the manuscript into her hands.

Without meeting his eyes, she took the bundle, stepped through the door and hurried across the lawn.

ELEVEN

Langham sat on a bench outside the drawing room, smoking his pipe and leafing through *The Times*. He was contemplating the crossword when he heard a door slam beyond the high wall of the boxwood hedge, and seconds later Charles appeared at the

far end of the hedge. His friend seemed agitated and hurried through
the timber door of the walled garden.

Langham was debating whether or not to follow him when Maria
rounded the hedge before him and stopped in her tracks.

'Maria? What is—'

'Have you seen Charles?' she asked urgently.

'Yes.' He pointed with the stem of his pipe, indicating the narrow
length of lawn that ran between the hedge and the house. 'He entered
the walled garden just seconds ago.'

'We need to talk to him . . .'

He stood and took her arm. 'What happened?'

'Oh, it was awful, Donald. Awful!' She set off towards the garden,
Langham at her side. 'It seems that Connaught was responsible for
the death of a boy while they were at school, someone very close
to Charles.'

'My word . . .'

They came to the walled garden and pushed through a green-
painted door. Langham scanned the geometrical pathways. Charles
was seated on a bench, one of four arranged in a square at the centre
of the garden.

Maria set off at a run and Langham followed.

Charles looked up, saw them and quickly dried his tears with a
handkerchief.

They hurried along the gravelled pathway and arrived at the centre
of the garden.

'Please,' Charles said, indicating the bench placed at right angles
to his own. 'I think I owe you an explanation, Maria, and an apology.'

'You've really no need.'

'I insist!' Charles smiled through his tears as they sat down. 'My
behaviour in the study . . . I should not have lost my temper.'

'You were provoked,' she said.

'Nevertheless . . .' he began. 'My apologies, Maria, for running
off like that.'

She reached out and took his hand. 'Charles, I understand.'

'I really must tell you all about what happened. Who better to
tell than good friends?'

Maria glanced at Langham; he nodded minimally.

She murmured, 'Very well.'

They sat in silence for a while, and then Charles said quietly, 'In
retrospect, my later schooldays seem a halcyon time.' He paused.

'I was truly happy; the world was young, and all my life stretched ahead.' He smiled to himself and quoted, '"That is the land of lost content, I see it shining plain, the happy highways where I went, and cannot come again . . ."'

He stared into space, lost in thought, then went on, 'Perhaps my being so happy at the time made what happened that summer seem all the more . . . tragic. But no – in any circumstances it would have been terrible.'

Maria said, 'Charles, honestly, you don't have to . . .'

His eyes appealed to her, and then to Langham. 'But I *need* to, my children. I need to unburden myself. I *want* to.'

Maria sighed. 'But only if you're absolutely sure.'

'I have never been surer,' Charles said. 'I want you to understand what Denbigh Connaught did, all those years ago.'

He tucked his handkerchief into his breast pocket and smiled at them.

'There was a boy,' he began, 'Daniel. Daniel Lattimer; he was the same age as me. He combined athleticism with a rare, golden beauty, and a winning gentleness that put everyone under his spell. He came to Winchester at the age of fourteen, and we became fast friends. We were inseparable. Of course, that sort of thing was not uncommon. Throw a group of boys together at that age and it is inevitable that crushes and . . . *pashes*, as they were known . . . should propagate. But what Daniel and I shared, I tell myself, was something special.'

He fell silent, his eyes pooled with unshed tears. He stirred himself and continued. 'Connaught – Denbigh Connaught – was part of our little coterie, but always somewhat on the fringe. Daniel and I and two or three others were smitten with Christianity – we had a school chaplain who made it all seem so real, so modern and relevant. Connaught, however, wanted nothing to do with all that. I could not decide, at the time, if he acted as he did to shock us, or if he was genuine in his . . . in his avowal to live life to the full, to please himself and beggar the consequences. He bragged about going up to London and sleeping with prostitutes, and there was a rumour that he'd seduced a shop-girl. I wonder, now, considering what he said in the study, if it had merely been an attempt to show Daniel that he didn't care.

'In the summer of 1917, my friendship with Daniel became more . . . intense. We hovered on the brink of intimacy for weeks; oh, how I tortured myself with longing, spent sleepless nights dwelling on my love for the boy! I could not be sure if Daniel reciprocated my feelings. I know he regarded me as a true friend, but as anything more?' He paused, took a deep breath and plunged on. 'It happened one afternoon after the annual cricket match against Harrow. We were strolling through woodland, behind the school . . . We came to a stream, and I suggested that we swim. We had not brought our costumes, of course.' He swallowed, his voice catching. 'We swam naked, and then lay on the bank, in the sunlight, and talked, and . . . and . . . You can imagine the rest. I . . . I will say nothing other than it was quite the most wonderful experience of my young life.'

Maria glanced at Langham and smiled.

'The future stretched ahead,' Charles said, 'so full of promise. We were both due to go up to Oxford that autumn, and the thought of the shining spires in the company of Daniel . . .' He shook his head, his expression clouding. 'And then one day Daniel was called out of Latin and told to report to the headmaster. Later, in tears, he told me that we'd been seen on the riverbank and had been reported. The headmaster had told him that our respective parents were to be informed, and if it happened again, he'd said, we would be expelled. I, for my part, was not so much concerned as to the reaction of my mother – we were not close – and my father had passed away when I was ten, but I was beside myself at the thought of what Daniel's parents might say and do. His father was an Anglican clergyman with a parish in Norfolk, a hellfire tyrant who ruled with a rod of iron. Daniel, understandably, was terrified.'

Charles closed his eyes suddenly; he took a deep breath, opened his eyes and continued. 'Daniel was discovered by the chaplain, early one morning, at the foot of the bell tower. He had left the dorm in the early hours and, unable to bear the thought of his father's ire and his mother's shame, thrown himself from the tower. I . . . I found a note under my pillow, in his beautiful handwriting. He simply stated that he was sorry, and that he hoped that I, and God, might forgive him . . .'

Charles wept in silence; Maria reached out and squeezed his hand. He rallied, smiled at them and went on, 'I was riven by grief and guilt. The thought of life without Daniel, of a future in which he did not feature . . . You see, I had built so many dreams, constructed a future for us together at Oxford, and to have that so cruelly ripped away . . .

'I was summoned to the headmaster's study. He . . . he said it was a tragic accident, that Daniel had been sleepwalking . . . He also told me that he had not yet approached our parents with the details of our . . . our "indiscretion", and, in light of what had happened, would not do so. I did not tell him about Daniel's note.' Charles fell silent, and it was a minute before he continued. 'And then a few days later, on the very last day of term, Denbigh Connaught sought me out in the library where I'd gone to brood. I assumed he'd come to offer his condolences. He . . . he seemed frozen, almost terrified, as he admitted that it was he who had informed on Daniel and me; he had followed us that day from the cricket field, and had watched us on the riverbank. Then he had gone to the headmaster and told him, because, he said, "it had been the right thing to do".' Charles shook his head and repeated, slowly, '"The right thing to do"? I never really understood what he meant, then or in the years that followed, as I tried to parse his motivation. It seemed so . . . so *cruel*, and counter to everything that Connaught, as a disciple of Greek hedonism, believed.' He looked up and smiled. 'Of course, now I understand.'

He looked from Langham to Maria. 'You heard him say so himself, Maria. He was jealous. He adored Daniel – I see that now – and resented my relationship with the boy . . . And in his jealousy, in order to hurt me, he did something so selfish, so thoughtless . . .'

Maria reached out and took his hand. 'I'm sorry.'

'And now, after all these years, he has found it in himself to acknowledge his sin, and ask for my understanding and forgiveness.'

'And,' Langham began tentatively, 'will you?'

'Will I accept his apology?' Charles fell silent, contemplating. 'Do you know something, my children, until just minutes ago I was consumed by such anger that I would have damned Denbigh Connaught to hell.'

'But now?' Maria asked.

Charles sighed. 'I need time, my friends. I know I *should* find it in myself to accept his repentance . . . But it will take a little while.'

Maria murmured, 'I'm glad, Charles, and proud of you.'

They fell silent and contemplated the beauty of the garden. Langham refilled his pipe and puffed it into life, and steered the conversation on to other subjects. For the next twenty minutes he told Charles of their plans to find a little cottage in the country close to their friend's stately pile in Suffolk, and Charles positively beamed at the prospect.

A little later Langham said, 'And now, how about a drink before lunch?'

Maria looked at Charles, who smiled. 'Do you know, a little drink is *just* what I need at this moment.'

They left the benches and strolled towards the exit, Maria taking Charles's hand and squeezing.

As they stepped from the garden, Langham looked up and saw, at the far end of the narrow lawn, Colonel Haxby emerge at speed from the French windows of the drawing room, followed by Pandora Jade. The colonel disappeared around the far end of the hedge.

Pandora stopped when she saw the trio, then dashed towards them in evident distress.

She stared at Langham, her lips trembling in shock. 'Thank Christ,' she panted. 'You've got to come. It's Colonel Haxby . . .'

'What is?' he said.

'He has his gun,' she said, 'and he's threatening to kill Connaught!'

And, with that, she turned on her heel and raced around the boxwood hedge and out of sight.

TWELVE

R yland left Lewisham at eleven o'clock on Saturday morning, crossed the river and drove north to Belsize Park. On the way he passed within half a mile of St Mary's, where Don and Maria had tied the knot.

For months beforehand he'd dreaded the reception and his duties as best man. In the event, after a few pints of Fuller's, his nerves had evaporated and he'd hobnobbed with all sorts, from the staff of the French embassy where Maria's father was the cultural attaché, to drink-sodden old hacks who kept the wolf from the door by penning a dozen westerns a year.

Came the time for him to make the best man's speech, and he was raring to go. He forgot his nerves – and the few lines he'd prepared – and launched into a full-blown account of what an all-round good fellow Donald Langham was, finishing with the story of how Captain Langham had saved his life at Diego Suarez. At the end of the ten minutes, the room was silent, with hardly a dry eye to be seen. But best of all was the expression of appreciation on Don's face as Ryland proposed a toast to the groom.

And then, his duties dispensed with, he'd proceeded to get royally blathered.

He turned into a leafy road off Belsize Park High Street and inched along in search of the premises of Harker Fine Arts.

He found the imposing, double-fronted gallery fifty yards along the road and whistled. 'Would you look at that . . .' Talk about going from the ridiculous to the sublime, he thought: yesterday he'd slummed it in a Rotherhithe junk yard, and now he was about to enter the portals of a place which, by the looks of it, catered for aristocrats and royalty. The door was painted a rich navy blue, and the window frames on either side glinted with a border of gold leaf. In the windows, exquisite miniatures nestled on beds of black velvet.

Ryland smiled to himself. So William Harker might deal with the rich and famous, but it was heartening to know that he also maintained contact with the likes of Bernie Radley, rag-and-bone man and notorious fence.

He crossed the pavement and entered the gallery.

A discreet bell above the door tinkled his arrival, and a thick carpet underfoot deadened his tread. He looked down, feeling a twinge of guilt at not having wiped his feet. Oil paintings hung on the walls, and more were arranged on easels down the centre of the long, narrow room. A young woman, as pretty as a film star with piled-up hair and pearls, sat behind a desk and regarded him curiously, a finger pressed to her carmine lips.

Ryland nodded to her, pulled a cigarette from behind his right ear and lit up. He strolled down the gallery, moving from picture to picture. They depicted geezers from centuries ago with ridiculous wigs and tiny, prim mouths. All very well, he thought, but give me a snap of Brighton seafront any day.

'Can I help you, sir?' the young woman asked in cut-glass tones.

Ryland turned. 'I'd like to speak with William Harker.'

'Mr Harker will not be in until twelve, sir.'

'Sleeps in on Saturday mornings, does he?'

She smiled, almost conspiratorially. 'He arrives at twelve every day.'

'It's all right for some.' He looked at his watch. It was ten to twelve. 'I'll wait.'

'Are you interested in making a purchase?'

'I wish!' he laughed. 'What are they going for? This one, for example?' He pointed at a painting of a knickerbockered youth who looked as if he was chewing a lemon.

'That would be one thousand pounds.'

Ryland whistled.

The girl laughed. 'I know,' she said, dropping what she'd learned in her elocution lessons. 'Crazy, ain't it?'

'Strewth, and I had you down as one of the Mayfair set.'

'Stepney, but I can talk posh when I want to.'

'Stepney? Lordy, I was born next door in Bow. Ralph Ryland.'

'Pamela Baker.'

'So how'd you find yourself a cushy number like this, Pamela?'

'Me dad knows someone who knows Mr Harker,' she said. 'He was looking for a receptionist last year, and I'd just finished this course at night school, hadn't I?'

'Good for you,' Ryland said. 'What's this Mr Harker like as a boss?'

'He's all right, I suppose. But he thinks he's better than everyone else. Earn a bit of money and they think they own the world.'

'Maybe you can help me.' He pulled out his accreditation and showed it to the girl.

Her eyes went wide. '"Coo", as they say in the films. A private eye. Mr Harker in trouble again?'

'Again? Makes a habit of it, does he?'

'Mixes with the wrong type, in my opinion. See, years back he did a bit of bird in the Scrubs. Receiving stolen. Not that he likes being reminded of it.'

'I can imagine,' he said. 'I wonder . . .' He pulled the photograph of Wilson Royce from his pocket and showed it to the girl. 'You don't happen to have seen—'

'Seen him?' Pamela said, snatching the photo and staring at it with venom in her eyes. 'I'll say.'

Ryland sat on the corner of the desk and said, sympathetically, 'What happened?'

'He swans in here one day last summer, he does. "Hello," I says. "This chap thinks he's God's gift." All smiles and gab. Charming, I'll give him that. And good-looking in a wet kind of way. He does some business with Mr Harker in the back office, then comes out here and works his charms on me.'

'And I hope you told him to go sling his hook,' Ryland said, thinking that he must sound like her father.

Pamela blushed. 'That's what I should have done. Only . . .' She faltered. 'He had this way with him, see. Said I was beautiful, that I should be in the films. Then he said that he had contacts, people in the business. So we went out for a drink, and then dinner, and a few nights later he took me to this big hotel in the West End and he introduced me to these men in black suits smoking fat cigars, and they looked me over like I was meat on a slab. Wilson said they were money men, producers, and if I stuck by him, he'd see me right.'

'What happened?'

'Nothing. Well, I saw Mr Wilson Royce for a month, if you know what I mean. I asked him about these money men, but he just shrugged and said that these things take time. And then he goes and drops me, just like that. Didn't answer my calls, and didn't show his evil face in here ever again.'

'I'm sorry.'

'Yes, well . . . It taught me a lesson, didn't it? Trust no one, especially smooth-talking Johnnies like Mr Royce.' She smiled at him. 'So, what's he up to now? I hope it's something illegal and you nab him.'

'I'm not exactly sure what his racket is. But I think he's up to no good. Do you know how often he met Mr Harker?'

'Maybe two or three times, I'd say, before he vanished.'

'And do you know what business he conducted with your boss? Did he want to sell Harker a painting?'

'I'm not sure, but Mr Harker did introduce him to . . . Oh!' Pamela sat up ramrod straight and nodded towards the window. 'His nibs!' she hissed. 'Don't tell him about what I said. I think he took a bit of a shine to Mr bloody Royce.'

'Mum's the word,' Ryland promised, looking through the window as a large man emerged from the back of a chauffeur-driven Daimler and waddled towards the gallery.

Ryland turned from the desk and affected an interest in the paintings.

Mr Harker eased himself through the door. 'Any phone calls?' he asked Pamela.

'No, Mr Harker, but a Mr Ryland is here to see you.'

Harker turned and regarded Ryland, and was clearly not impressed by his visitor's frayed suit and general down-at-heel appearance. A gold filling flashed as he smiled without the slightest degree of warmth. 'Yes?'

'I wonder if I might have a word?'

'Concerning?'

Ryland presented his accreditation. 'I'd like to talk to you about a mutual acquaintance.'

'And who might that be?'

'A certain Wilson Royce.'

Ryland thought he saw the man's lips purse as if in distaste. 'Come into my office.'

Harker led the way to a small, sumptuous room and seated himself behind an oak desk. Ryland leaned back against the door.

'Well?' Harker demanded.

'I'm investigating the activities of Mr Wilson Royce,' Ryland said, 'and I understand that you've had certain business dealings with the young man.'

'Who told you this?'

'Now, that'd be compromising my sources, wouldn't it, Mr Harker? I'm sure you understand that.'

'It was a long time ago,' Harker said. 'I hardly recall Mr Royce.'

'A long time ago? I'm given to understand it was just last year.'

'I'm a very busy man, Mr Ryland. I deal with hundreds of people in the course of the year. You can't expect me to remember everyone.'

'Then tell me the little you do recall about Mr Royce.'

Harker pursed his fat lips, then shook his head. 'He came in here once, I think, and expressed interest in buying a painting.'

Ryland regarded the end of his cigarette. 'Now that's very interesting, Mr Harker, because that isn't quite the story I had from my source, is it?'

'I can assure you—'

Ryland interrupted. 'You see, what I heard was this: our young Mr Royce came in here trying to *sell* you a painting.'

'I would have a record of the transaction if that occurred.'

Ryland smiled. 'Would you? I would've thought you'd keep that kind of deal under wraps, so to speak.'

'Just what are you insinuating?'

Ryland laughed. 'Come on, Harker. We're men of the world. You know very well what I'm "insinuating".'

Harker spread his fat hands on the desk and leaned forward, droplets of sweat beading his bald head. 'I run a respectable establishment here, Mr Ryland.'

'Oh, I'm sure you do – with a bit of shady business on the side, I dare say. Now,' he went on, relighting his cigarette and blowing out a plume of smoke, 'just what was Mr Royce trying to sell you?'

'As I said—'

'We can do this two ways, Harker,' Ryland cut in brutally. 'Either you spill the beans or I get the rozzers in to investigate. And I'm sure you wouldn't want to serve another spell in the clink, would you?'

'But that was years ago!'

'Do you think the judge would take that into consideration – as an "extenuating circumstance", perhaps?' Ryland sneered. 'Now, what did Royce want to sell?'

'I . . . I don't recall the exact details. A painting. A miniature, I think.'

'And don't tell me that you passed up the opportunity to buy it?'

'I . . . I was suspicious. Something didn't ring true. I suspected that he'd obtained the painting through less than legal means.'

'Which is a long-winded way of saying you think he nicked it?'

'I . . . As I said, I had my suspicions.'

'Which were? Just *why* did you think Royce wasn't on the straight and narrow?'

'He said something about a deceased aunt leaving him the painting, and that he was looking to make a quick sale.'

'And you didn't believe him?'

'Something didn't ring true. The deceased aunt is something of a cliché, after all.'

'So you didn't buy the painting?'

'I declined.'

Ryland nodded, regarding the smouldering tip of his cigarette and biding his time. 'So instead of buying the painting yourself, Mr Harker, you introduced him to someone who might?'

Harker's eyes widened as he stared at Ryland. 'What makes you think . . .?' he stammered.

'I have a very informative source,' Ryland said. 'Now, who did you introduce him to?'

'I did nothing of the kind,' Harker blustered. 'I told him I wasn't interested, and he left without a word.'

'I was given to understand that he visited you, here, on more than one occasion.'

'You were informed incorrectly.'

'And you're sure you can't recall who you introduced Mr Royce to?'

Losing his patience at last, Harker rose from his seat, rounded the desk on his tiny, surprisingly nimble feet and whisked open the door. 'Good day, Mr Ryland.'

'And not even the offer of a cup of tea?'

'Good day to you.'

Ryland gave the man an ironic salute, then turned and strolled from the office. The door slammed behind him.

At the reception desk, Pamela winced. 'No luck?'

'Well, I've certainly put the wind up your Mr Harker. He says he hardly recalls Mr Royce.'

Pamela pulled a face. 'Likely story! He was all over Royce when they met. "Yes, Mr Royce. No, Mr Royce . . ." I reckon he was on to a good thing with Roycey, I do.'

'You were about to tell me that Harker introduced Royce to someone.'

'That's right. I heard Mr Harker say he'd put Royce in touch with an acquaintance. The chap had a strange name . . . Ventnor, Vent . . . *Venture*? He was foreign, anyway. He came in here once and asked to see Mr Harker – a small, dark little man. An Eyetie, maybe.'

'Venture . . .' Ryland repeated. 'And that's all you know about him? No phone number?'

Pamela squinted towards the office, leaned forward and whispered, 'I think Mr Venture was one of Mr Harker's dodgy contacts, so he didn't keep anything like his phone number or address on the record.'

'You've been a star, Pamela,' Ryland said. He fished a ten-shilling note from his wallet and passed it to the startled girl. 'Buy yourself a little something, on me.'

'Why . . . That's very kind of you, Mr Ryland.'

He made to go, then paused. 'And how would you like to come and work as my secretary, one day? I plan to expand my little operation and move into the West End pretty soon, and we'll need someone with their head screwed on the right way to man the front desk.'

'Straight up?' Pamela beamed at him. 'Be more exciting than this place, I can tell you.'

'Then I'll be in touch,' Ryland said. He gave her a wink and tripped from the gallery.

The sooner Pamela was out of there, the better, he thought. She'd go far, that girl.

He sat in the car for a few minutes, considering what to do next, then drove south. He'd check the address Don had seen Wilson Royce entering on Thursday, and with luck talk to the blonde piece whom Don had glimpsed drawing the curtains soon after Royce's arrival.

He considered Harker and what he'd learned. Of all the people he met in this line of business, straight and bent, good and bad – and not all the bent were bad, in his opinion, nor the straight good – the likes of Mr Harker struck him as the lowest of the low. He hid his true self behind a veneer of respectability, and expected the world to take him at face value. Well, he'd seen through Harker's guise to the greedy, scheming con man that lurked beneath.

He turned on to the King's Road, drove for half a mile, then indicated right and pulled up outside number twenty-two.

He peered up at the three-story Regency town house. Nice, he thought. Mr Royce certainly liked to consort with those in the swim.

He climbed the steps to the front door. He'd expected to find multiple doorbells signifying that the house had been subdivided into separate flats by greedy property developers cashing in on the housing shortage after the war. To his surprise, there was only one bell – a big brass thing in the centre of the red-painted door. He pushed it and waited.

The door opened almost immediately, and a classy blonde in her later twenties, wearing a flaring summer dress and high heels, peered out at him.

'Not today, thank you,' she said. She carried a handbag and was clearly on her way out.

'Beatrice Reynolds?' he asked.

The woman looked surprised. 'And you are?'

Ryland showed her his accreditation. 'I'd like a few words, if I may.'

'I *am* in rather a hurry.'

'This won't take a minute,' he said. He'd give Wilson Royce this: he had taste when it came to women. This one was a looker, and no mistake. A slim version of Diana Dors, without the puppy fat, and posh with it.

Beatrice looked at her tiny gold wristwatch. 'I have a taxi due in two minutes . . .'

'Won't keep you that long,' Ryland assured her. 'Don't even need to go inside.'

'Very well, what is it? Don't tell me – Wilson Royce, right?'

'How did you guess?' Ryland smiled.

'What's the young fool done now?'

'That's what I'd like to find out,' he said. 'Always getting himself into trouble, is he?'

'What's the phrase?' she said, squinting against the sunlight. '"Sailing too close to the wind"? That's what Wilson does.'

'Buying and selling, wheeling and dealing?'

'Something like that.'

'Paintings and the like?'

'He's mentioned selling the occasional piece, yes.'

'Did he ever tell you about a contact of his, a Mr Venture?'

'Mr Venture?' She looked puzzled. 'Oh, you mean Mr Venturi? His business partner, he calls him. He's mentioned him in passing.'

'Mr Venturi . . .' Ryland repeated. 'Do you happen to know his first name? Or anything about him?'

Beatrice frowned. 'Paolo, Primo? I'm sure it began with a P. And all I know is that Wilson mentioned he was a displaced person, and came to England after the war.'

'I don't suppose you have his address?'

'I'm sorry. I never met the man. Wilson's just mentioned him once or twice. Oh,' she said. 'Do excuse me. Here's my taxi. Must dash.'

Ryland touched his forelock as she hurried down the steps. 'Have a pleasant day,' he called out. 'And thank you.'

Mr P. Venturi, he thought as he climbed back into his car and drove south to Lewisham. There would be dozens of Venturis in the phone book, no doubt, but at least it was a lead.

Well, he could forget Wilson bloody Royce for the rest of the day and enjoy the match this afternoon. He was cheered by the thought of the new football season, and the hope of a better showing for Millwall than last year's poor finish. And his boys were fired up for the match, too.

Annie was up to her elbows in soap suds, washing up, when he arrived home.

He crept up behind her, slapped her bottom and kissed the back of her neck.

She jumped. 'You devil, Ralph!' she cried, flicking soap at him. 'Who'd you think it was?'

'Cary Grant,' she said. She pointed to the kitchen table 'Sit down. I've made you a sandwich. Corned beef and pickle.'

His eight year-old, Terry, charged into the kitchen, making a hell of a racket with his football rattle. 'Come on the Lions!' he cried.

'Save it for the match, Terry,' Ryland said, aiming a punt at the boy's backside. 'Go on, scarper.'

'Oh,' Annie said, drying her hands. 'Harry from Brixton rang. He says he's done that key you wanted. He'll meet you after the match at the Nag's Head.'

'Diamond geezer.' He'd pick up the key later, and first thing Monday morning he'd drive up to Chelsea and have a poke round Wilson Royce's place.

'And I don't want you taking the boys into no pub after the match, Ralph,' Annie said, pouring two cups of strong tea.

'I'll only have a half, and we'll stand outside, I promise.'

'Don't want them turned into boozers,' she said. 'Anyway, what've you been up to all morning?'

She sat across the table from him and gave him a lovely smile, which lit up her face and made her look ten years younger.

He munched his sandwich and told her all about Mr Harker and his posh gallery.

THIRTEEN

L angham caught up with Pandora and they hurried towards Connaught's study.

'I saw Haxby race into the house,' she said, 'just after he'd had his audience with Connaught. He was spitting blood. And just now I passed him on the stairs, waving his revolver.'

Ahead, Langham made out the shambling figure of the colonel as he approached the study.

'Stay here,' he advised the artist. By now Maria and Charles had caught up with him, and he told them to remain where they were.

'Was the colonel drunk?' he asked Pandora.

'Have you ever seen him sober?'

'Wonderful.'

He took off, running after the drunken old soldier. He heard Maria calling out to be careful and raised a hand in acknowledgement. Haxby hobbled past Connaught's study and continued on towards the cliff's edge. Langham, at once relieved that Haxby was not bent on homicide, now feared what he might be contemplating.

He passed the study and ran down the sloping lawn.

'Colonel!' he called out.

The old soldier appeared to jump at the summons, though it was hard to tell as his artificial leg gave his gait a perpetual jerkiness. He came to the edge of the cliff and paused, looking frantically right and left.

'Colonel,' Langham said. 'I don't know what you're thinking of doing, but why not put the pistol down and talk to me?'

The colonel moved a step closer towards the edge and peered down. He stepped forward, and for a terrible second Langham thought he'd pitched himself over the edge.

Only then did he see that Haxby had found the precipitous stairway that dropped down the face of the cliff, and for whatever reason was stumping down towards the jetty.

Langham came to the top step and, nausea rising from his stomach, peered down.

'Colonel!'

Haxby ignored the call and continued his awkward descent.

Twenty-five feet down the cliff face, the old soldier turned and looked up. He swayed, blinking in the sunlight, then called out, 'You can't stop me, Langham. I advise you to . . .' He trailed off and continued his descent.

Langham turned to see Maria, Charles and Pandora approach him across the lawn. 'I thought I told you to—'

'And have you been shot by the drunkard?' Maria retorted.

Far below, the colonel had stopped at a point in the stairway that appeared to have crumbled. He was staring at the concrete step as if contemplating the wisdom of going on.

He sat down suddenly, his artificial leg sticking out over the edge, and slumped back against the rock. He looked back up the stairway, and Langham thought he saw desperation on the man's face.

He lifted the revolver to his temple and held it there.

Langham's stomach turned.

Against all his instincts, he found himself moving. He took a hesitant step forward, then another, fighting the rising nausea and pushing himself to descend. His every instinct cried at him to lie down.

'Donald!' Maria shouted.

He heard Charles reassuring her and called over his shoulder, 'Don't worry. I'll be fine.'

Down below, the old soldier pressed the barrel of the revolver to his greying temple and screwed his eyes shut.

'Colonel, please . . . I can help you.'

He reached out to the uneven cliff face, his legs trembling with every downward step. Far below, waves broke against the base of the cliff. It was a long way down – a hundred feet or more – and his gaze was drawn, against his better judgement, to the pounding surf.

He stopped, dragged in a lungful of sea air, and fought to control the shaking that had seized his entire body. He paused, closed his eyes and felt a little better.

The shriek of a seagull startled him, and he opened his eyes. All he needed now, he thought, was the attention of an angry gull.

On a grassy ledge three feet above him, the bird regarded him with its beady eyes.

The colonel called out, 'Stay where you are, Langham. I know you're on his side!'

The fact that the colonel was willing to enter into dialogue gave him hope. 'I'm on no one's side, Colonel – least of all Connaught's.'

He moved again, ignoring the pathetic trembling of his leg muscles, and descended step by painful step.

The old soldier was staring out to sea, the gun barrel still pressed to his temple.

Langham ventured, 'It's no way out, you know? Think of what you went through in the war. Did you face the threat of the Nazis just for it to end like this?'

'You've no idea!' Haxby shouted bitterly.

'Then tell me,' Langham said, moving ever closer. 'Listen to me, Colonel. Whatever you might think, there's no love lost between Connaught and me. If you want to know the truth, I don't particularly like the man.'

'He's a monster!' Haxby cried.

He was a dozen steps above the drunken old soldier now, and he was convinced that, had Haxby truly intended to put a bullet through his head, he would have done so already.

If he could only reach Haxby, talk to him and gain his trust . . .

'Tell me what happened,' Langham said.

'I . . . like a bloody fool, I obeyed his . . . his damned summons and went along.'

'And what did he want?'

The colonel didn't reply. He tightened his grip on the butt of the revolver and pressed the barrel to his skull with greater determination.

'Colonel,' Langham called. 'We can talk this over. I can help you, but I need to know what Connaught said.'

Haxby turned his head. For a terrible second, Langham thought that he was doing so in order to look into the eyes of another human being as he ended his life: there was a strange, almost fatalistic expression on the man's face.

Langham pleaded, 'Colonel, put the gun down, and then we can talk.'

He was just ten feet from Haxby now and getting closer with every step. When he reached him, he'd sit down a little way off, gain his confidence and talk.

He looked up. High above, a line of bobbing heads showed above the ragged line of the cliff edge: Maria, Charles and Pandora had been joined by two others, whose identity Langham could not make out. The sight of the peering heads, dark and rendered featureless against the bright blue sky, struck him as comical.

He turned his attention to Haxby and took another step. Amazingly, his nausea was abating; his heartbeat had slowed and he no longer felt dizzy. He still had the urge to press himself flat against solid earth, well away from the vertiginous drop, but that was an impossibility at the moment . . .

He was six feet above Haxby and stretched out his right hand so that he might receive the revolver. 'Give it to me,' he murmured as he took another couple of steps.

The colonel regarded him with his rheumy eyes. The hand gripping the revolver was shaking. Langham hoped he wouldn't pull the trigger by mistake.

Slowly, he lowered himself on to a crumbling stone step and sat down.

Surprising him, the colonel said, 'Would . . . would you like a drink?'

He was tempted to say that perhaps the last thing they should do now, given the circumstances, was to consume alcohol – but he feared the old man's reaction to a rebuttal and elected to accept the offer in the spirit of camaraderie.

He nodded. Haxby lowered the gun, placed it in his lap and pulled a small flask from his blazer pocket. Langham exhaled with relief.

The colonel took a swig from the flask and passed it to Langham.

He took the flask and pretended to drink, not allowing any of the brandy to pass his lips, and handed it back to Haxby.

The old soldier took another mouthful, smacked his lips, then said, 'Known him more than twenty years . . .'

Langham nodded. 'How did you meet?'

'At the Savile Club. Both liked a drop, y'see. Late at night, before the open fire, righting the wrongs of the world. Thought him a decent chap. Sound head on his shoulders. Didn't know he'd turn out to be a conchie – this was before the war, y'see.' He took another swig of brandy and passed it to Langham, who again faked taking a mouthful and returned the flask.

'What happened?'

The colonel blinked; he appeared confused. He took another long drink, belched, and this time did not pass the flask.

Langham considered the revolver sitting precariously in the colonel's flannel lap. He could easily make a grab for it, but that would merely risk a scuffle and endanger them both. Best to sit tight and talk.

'What do you mean, "What happened?"' Haxby asked.

'Back then,' Langham said, 'to make Connaught want to apologize now?'

Haxby shook his head, as if the memory was too painful to relate. His lips were puce, the same colour as the lattice of broken veins threading his cheeks.

At last he said, 'Killed a man.'

Langham blinked. 'Killed a man? You killed a man?'

'Me?' The colonel hiccupped. 'Killed plenty in me time. Jerries, that is. No, no . . . Connaught. He killed a man.'

'Connaught?' Langham said incredulously.

The colonel waved. 'Killed a man,' he said, 'and wanted to apologize to me.'

'But why?'

Haxby sat back against the rock, nursed the brandy flask and wept. 'Killed a man dead, he did, and didn't have the guts to admit as much!'

'When was this, Colonel?'

'When? 'Thirty-four, it'd be . . .'

'And who did he kill?'

Haxby shook his head. 'I . . . I can't rightly recall who.'

'How do you know this?'

'How? How do I know? B'cause I was ruddy well there, on the scene! I was bloody well . . .'

Then, without warning, the old soldier's head fell forward and his eyes flickered shut, out for the count. The flask slipped from his grip and hit the ground, and instinctively Langham made a grab for it. He caught the flask before it tumbled over the edge, and felt a sudden – if ridiculous – sense of achievement.

He took the revolver from Haxby's lap and ensured that the safety catch was fastened. He slipped it into his jacket pocket, alongside the flask, and regarded the unconscious old soldier.

Now here's a pretty problem, he thought; here I am, perched halfway up the side of a cliff with an unconscious old drunk and a personal fear of heights . . .

He stood shakily and climbed a dozen steps, then looked up and hissed, 'Maria!'

She peered down at him. 'What is happening, Donald?'

'The colonel's unconscious. Now listen to me – I need a rope, a long rope. Rouse the butler and rustle one up, would you?'

'A rope? *Oui.* I am going now.'

She disappeared, along with the other heads.

Five minutes later – though it seemed much longer to Langham – she appeared bearing a coiled rope and held it up. 'And now what, Donald?'

He pointed. 'Tie one end securely to that tree over there and throw the other end down to me.'

The heads vanished again, then reappeared a minute later. Maria tossed the coiled rope down to him; it landed on the steps above him and began to uncoil slowly of its own volition. He grabbed it, found the end and moved back down to the colonel.

Careful not to wake the old soldier, he eased the rope under the colonel's arms and around his chest. Knotting the thick rope was far from easy, but after struggling for minutes he secured the old man with a passable rendition of a bowline knot.

'Where . . . where the hell am I?' The colonel blinked at him, slowly coming to his senses.

'On the side of a cliff, tied to a rope, which is secured to a tree up there – so you can't fall, okey-dokey? Now, step by step we'll make our way back to the top. And for pity's sake, don't try to grab hold of me, because I don't have the luxury of being tied to a safety rope. Understood?'

'I'm in your capable hands, sir!' Haxby replied.

'Excellent. Now, easy does it, Colonel, one step at a time . . . Take my hand and follow me.'

Langham turned and, gripping Haxby's hand and avoiding looking down at the drop to his left, he made his slow way back up the narrow flight of steps.

'Just one thing,' Haxby said, 'how the bally hell did I come to find meself down here?'

'You don't remember anything?'

'Last I recall, I . . . I was closeted with . . . with Connaught,' he hiccuped, 'listening to his infernal blather.'

'You took whatever he said rather badly, Colonel.'

'Is it any wonder!'

Langham looked up and waved at Maria who was staring at him with concern etched on her face.

'Nearly there, Colonel. Easy does it.'

The colonel stumped up the steps, his artificial leg swinging wildly. He grimaced with the effort and clung on to Langham's hand for dear life.

Langham looked up again. To his relief, he saw that his head was almost level with the lawn. He smiled at Maria, who was biting her lip anxiously.

'Almost there,' he said. 'Just a few more steps . . .'

'You're a gent,' Haxby declared.

'My pleasure,' Langham said, 'and here we are. All's well that

ends well.' He took the last few steps and reached the sloping lawn
with an exultant sense of relief.

'Excellent work, my boy!' Charles carolled.

'Well done, Langham,' Pandora Jade said.

The butler and Wilson Royce grabbed the colonel, unfastened the
rope from around his chest and led him back to the house.

Maria embraced Langham tearfully and plastered his face with
kisses, then pulled away and regarded him with mock fury. 'And
don't you ever, Mr Langham, do anything like that again!'

'What, rescue an armed, suicidal, drunken, one-legged man from
halfway down the side of a cliff? You have my solemn word, my
darling, that I won't ever do anything half so stupid.'

'Thank you,' Maria said.

'I do think this calls for a little drink!' Charles declared.

Taking Maria's hand, Langham followed his friend back to the
house.

Denbigh Connaught said, 'Pass the wine, would you, Langham?
There's a good man.'

Langham did so, then topped up his own glass.

Colonel Haxby was absent from the dining table that evening,
laid up in bed. Wilson Royce had volunteered to take it in turns
with Watkins to sit with the colonel; earlier, Langham had asked
Royce if there was somewhere he might secrete Haxby's revolver,
and Royce had suggested the safe in Connaught's old study.

Monty Connaught had returned to the village immediately after
his meeting with his brother. According to Pandora, he'd stormed
from the study at two thirty, his face like thunder, and had said
farewell to no one.

Langham wondered what had passed between the travel writer
and his brother.

Denbigh Connaught, Lady Cecelia and Pandora Jade sat at one
end of the table, while Langham, Maria and Charles sat together in
the middle, chatting among themselves. Cook had prepared a side
of roast beef, new potatoes and vegetables.

Langham had little appetite. After the excitement on the cliff path
that morning, he, Maria and Charles had motored along the coast
to St Austell and enjoyed a lavish lunch at a public house overlooking
the bay.

He wondered how Denbigh Connaught was feeling now, having

offered his apologies to those he'd slighted down the years. The novelist appeared a little morose, enthroned in his high-backed oaken seat at the head of the table. Langham thought he resembled a dyspeptic monarch: Henry the Eighth, perhaps; he certainly had that king's bulk, with his jowly face and small, querulously pinched mouth and tiny, porcine eyes. Connaught hardly attended to what Lady Cecelia was saying to him, but concentrated on his food and wine.

Lady Cecelia, for her part, appeared to be in high spirits, addressing Pandora gaily when her overtures to Connaught fell on deaf ears. She asked the artist about her work and listened with polite, smiling attention while Pandora complained about the stranglehold that the major London galleries had on the art market.

After dessert of fruit salad and cream, Pandora made her excuses and said goodnight, soon followed by Lady Cecelia. Langham was about to suggest a turn around the garden to Maria and Charles when, from the end of the table, Connaught said, 'Heard all about your heroics this afternoon, Langham.' His tone suggested that Langham had committed some heinous deed.

'Hardly heroics,' he murmured.

'You should have let the old sot shoot himself.'

Charles, pointedly, turned his back on Connaught and addressed Maria.

Langham said, 'He was in a rather . . . agitated state.'

'Makes a change from his usual condition of inebriation, then,' Connaught grunted, finishing off his brandy and pouring another.

Langham sat back in his chair, considering his words. 'I thought your intentions, today, were to apologize? What happened in the colonel's case?'

Connaught scrutinized Langham with his piggy eyes. 'What did he say to you?'

Langham hesitated. 'Very little. He was a bit too far gone to say very much . . . other than to tell me how you first met.'

'Should never have bothered with the man,' Connaught said. 'But back then . . . there was something about him. Possessed a bit of vim and dash. Could've made something of his life . . .' He trailed off, his gaze distant.

'I suppose it does something to a man, losing a limb like that.'

Connaught grunted a grudging agreement.

Langham considered the colonel's claim that Connaught had

killed a man. 'What did you need to apologize to him for, if you don't mind my asking?'

'As it happens, I do mind your asking, young man. That's between me, Haxby and the devil.'

Langham smiled to himself and finished his wine.

Watkins approached the table, bent towards Langham and murmured, 'A telephone call for you, sir.'

Langham dabbed his lips and rose from the table. 'Excuse me.'

He followed Watkins from the room. 'It's Doctor Connaught, sir, about a boat trip.' He indicated the drawing room, and Langham closed the door behind him and crossed to the ivory-handled telephone.

'Donald, I hope I'm not interrupting dinner,' Annabelle Connaught said.

'Just finished.'

'It's about tomorrow. If you're still interested in a little trip out on the boat . . .'

'By all means.'

'Excellent. Aim to arrive around twelve, would you? The forecast is for continued fine weather, so the sea should be calm. I'll prepare a packed lunch.'

'That sounds wonderful. We'll see you tomorrow.'

Annabelle thanked him and rang off.

He was returning to the dining room when the door opened and Maria and Charles emerged.

'We made our excuses,' Charles said, 'and escaped. I really couldn't take much more of the man. He's the worse for drink, and insisted on disparaging a few of his contemporaries, and then moved on to the Angry Young Men.'

'I suggested we have a wander around the grounds,' Maria said. 'It's a lovely evening. Who was on the phone, Donald?'

As they left the house and strolled across the lawn towards the walled garden, he told her about the following day's boat trip. 'Would you care to accompany us, Charles?'

'Thank you for the invitation, my boy, but I shall decline. Small boats and the open sea hold terrors for me equivalent to your vertigo. So perhaps I should face them, as you so valorously did this afternoon. But no, I think I'll spend a quiet Sunday browsing Connaught's magnum opus.'

They stopped before the entrance to the walled garden and stared out to sea. A yacht sliced a white wake through the azure waters; the sun was westering and turning molten.

'Have you decided whether or not to represent Connaught?' Langham asked.

Charles struck an unconscious pose, his lips pursed in contemplation, his malacca cane lodged at an angle in the lawn. The warm breeze caught the drifts of his snow-white hair.

'I am still unsure,' he said at last. 'I think it might be churlish of me to refuse, after his apology, but . . .' He smiled at Maria. 'But we are in partnership, my dear, so perhaps we should discuss this when we return to London.'

Langham opened the timber gate and they walked widdershins around the walled garden. The scent of rose and honeysuckle filled the warm evening air.

He considered the prospect of the boat trip tomorrow, and the leisurely drive back to London on Monday. He had a new novel to think about; he'd work on the notes on Tuesday, and then put in his two-day shift at the agency. He wondered whether Ralph had turned up anything interesting on Wilson Royce.

They turned right along the path and came upon Lady Cecelia seated on a bench. She had been weeping and quickly dried her eyes on a tiny lace kerchief as they approached.

Another casualty of Denbigh Connaught's attempts at apologizing, Langham wondered.

She smiled up at them as Charles, as if to deflect attention from her distress, waxed lyrical about the beauty of the roses.

'I was just contemplating my good fortune,' Lady Cecelia said.

Charles appeared surprised, but rallied. 'Always a fine way to spend a late-summer evening, Lady Cecelia,' he said.

'Your good fortune?' Maria enquired.

'During the war,' Lady Cecelia said, 'when my husband and I separated . . .' She shook her head. 'I look back and wonder how I survived, and recently it has been something of a struggle to make ends meet. And then . . . and then something like this happens.' She looked up at them, tears pooling in her eyes again. 'Denbigh is such a wonderful, generous man, isn't he?'

Langham opened his mouth, but was too surprised to speak. Charles, ever the diplomat, murmured, 'Quite . . .'

'But don't let me interrupt your evening stroll,' Lady Cecelia said. 'I was just about to turn in. Goodnight.'

They returned her valediction and watched the dowager leave the garden.

'And what,' Maria said, 'was all that about?'

'It sounds as though Connaught has settled a sum on the old girl,' Langham said, 'by way of an apology.'

'But an apology for what, I wonder?' Charles said.

As they left the garden, Langham considered what Colonel Haxby had said that afternoon. He gazed across the lawn towards the cliff edge, lost in thought.

'What is it, old boy?' Charles asked.

'The colonel told me something while we were down there,' Langham said. 'He claimed that Connaught had killed someone, back before the war, and now wanted to apologize for it to Haxby.'

'Killed someone?' Maria exclaimed.

'That's what he said. But why,' he went on, looking from Charles to Maria, 'would Connaught want to apologize to the colonel?'

'You must remember that Haxby was in his cups,' Charles said. 'Talking tommyrot, in all likelihood.'

'I don't know,' Langham said. 'Something very odd is going on here, and I'd like to get to the bottom of it.'

FOURTEEN

Langham and Maria were leaving Connaught House late on Sunday morning when Langham heard a call from the hallway. Monty Connaught strode out into the sunlight, hitching his rucksack on to his shoulder. 'Donald! Pandora mentioned you were off to meet Annabelle. I don't suppose I could beg a lift into the village?'

'Of course. Hop in.'

'That's awfully good of you. It's a two-mile walk, and hell on my old pins.'

They climbed into the Rover and Langham drove from the grounds.

'How is the research coming along?' Maria asked, looking over her shoulder.

'I've been working up at the house since seven this morning,'

Monty said, 'scouring the maps I bought by the crate-load years ago. That's the disadvantage of living a life on the open sea, free of all worldly possessions. I must admit that I do miss my books and maps. At the same time, I couldn't bring myself to live on dry land again.'

They passed through the forest, sunlight flickering through the fir trees. 'How did your audience with Denbigh go yesterday?' Langham asked.

'Fine, fine . . . He just wanted to sort out one or two outstanding financial matters. Nothing "urgent" at all. In fact, it could have waited.'

Langham recalled Pandora's description of Monty's having a face like thunder on leaving his brother's study. 'He didn't want to apologize?' he asked.

'As I told you yesterday,' Monty said, 'if he started, he'd never stop. No, he owed me a couple of hundred pounds from some annuity he uncovered a few months ago, taken out for us by our father.'

'That will fund the Morocco trip,' Langham laughed.

'The more the merrier,' Monty said. 'Do you know, I live in perpetual fear of the bottom dropping out of the travel book market.'

Langham smiled. 'The nightmare of the professional scribbler,' he said.

'Only in this case, I think I have a legitimate reason to worry.'

'And why's that?' Langham asked.

'Reading between the lines after meeting my editor, Gilby and Watson are going through a bad time. I keep wondering when they'll pull the plug.'

Maria glanced over her shoulder. 'What would you do then?'

Monty gave a laugh that was far from humorous. 'I dread to think.'

Maria hesitated, then asked, 'Who is your agent, Mr Connaught?'

'Strange as it may seem, I don't have one. I sold my first book to Gilby just after the war, without an agent, and it's gone on from there. The thought of paying someone ten per cent of my scant earnings . . .'

Maria smiled. 'Well, if Gilby and Watson do fall on hard times, and you find yourself without a publisher, you could do worse than drop me a line, and I'll put some feelers out.'

'That's tremendously kind of you,' Monty said. 'I'll bear that in mind.' He pointed through the windscreen as they drove into the cobbled harbour. 'Anywhere around here will be fine. Thank you.'

Langham braked in front of the Fisherman's Arms and Monty climbed out. He leaned back towards the open window. 'It'd be nice to meet up for a drink and a chat at some point.'

'That sounds excellent,' Langham said.

Monty tapped the roof of the car and strode into the public house.

It was almost twelve o'clock when they drew up outside Threepenny Cottage. The sun shone from a blue sky innocent of a single cloud, and the sea, to Langham's inexpert eye, appeared perfect for boating: still and glassily calm.

'Will you be all right on the steps?' Maria asked as they climbed from the car.

'After yesterday, girl, I could scale Mount Everest in my sleep.'

Maria had dressed for the occasion. If her get-up wasn't quite nautical, it was certainly fetchingly casual: a white blouse with rolled up sleeves and green canvas slacks cut off just below the knee.

Annabelle Connaught was standing in the garden beside the timber picnic table, on which sat a wicker basket covered by a red-and-white checked cloth. She was staring across the bay at Connaught House and turned when they pushed through the gate. A pair of sunglasses sat like a tiara in her auburn hair. She looked like a film star got up for a publicity shoot.

'Excellent timing,' she said. 'If you're ready, we'll set off straight away.'

She picked up the basket and led the way to the steps. 'Ham and horseradish sandwiches, and an apple pie. I hope that's OK? Oh, and home-made lemonade to wash it down.'

'That sounds lovely,' Maria said.

Langham gestured for Maria to follow Annabelle down the steps, and hesitated before approaching the edge of the cliff. Despite his exploits the previous day, he felt queasy as he contemplated the long drop to the small boat rising and falling beside the concrete jetty.

Maria turned and looked up at him. 'Are you sure you're all right, Donald?'

'I'm fine,' he said, taking a breath and following her down.

At least on this descent, he thought, there was the chain pegged into the cliff face to assist him. He clutched the rusting links with a white-knuckled grip and stared at Maria's back all the way down. At the bottom she took his hand. 'You look as pale as a ghost.'

'Honestly, I'm fine.'

Annabelle stepped into the boat and reached out to help Maria. Langham followed and seated himself on a wooden bench that ran around the inside of the stern.

'Are you OK, Donald?' Annabelle sat at the tiller, staring at him with concern. 'You don't get seasick, do you?'

'I'm fine with the sea,' he said, and pointed back to the steps, 'but not so good with heights. You'd have thought that after yesterday . . .'

'What happened yesterday?'

Maria settled herself beside him. 'Donald saved the colonel's life,' she said.

'Well, hardly.' He put up a token protest. 'The colonel got himself into a drunken tizz and took himself off down the cliff path behind Connaught House.'

'With a gun,' Maria added.

Annabelle stared at them. 'A gun? What on earth . . .?'

'I followed him and talked him round. He was threatening to shoot himself.'

Annabelle stopped tinkering with the engine. 'But why would he do that?'

'I don't think his audience with your father went very well,' Langham explained. 'Brought back old memories. The upshot was that he got loaded and threatened to blow his brains out.'

'How is he now?'

'Royce and Watkins kept an eye on him overnight. I haven't seen him this morning.'

'I wonder what my father could have said to cause . . .' She trailed off. 'I told you that he had a propensity for annoying people. That's something of an understatement.'

She pulled the starting cord, turned the throttle and told them to hang on.

The engine caught and the boat puttered away from the jetty, riding the slight swell; as she increased speed, the boat smacked against the sea and water flew up from either side of the bow in a shower of jewelled spray.

Langham looked back at the way they had come. In the fold of the horseshoe bay, the village climbed the hillside, surrounded by meadows and forest. To the left, prominent on the headland, stood the turreted Gothic structure of Connaught House.

As they bounced from the bay and headed towards the open sea, Annabelle turned to them. 'What did my father say about his meeting with the colonel? I take it you asked him?'

'It did come up at dinner,' Langham said, glancing at Maria. 'He was far from sympathetic. Said I should have left him to blow his brains out.'

Annabelle winced. 'He can be so callous at times. All this speaking his mind malarkey . . . Drink talking, more like. Have you seen my father today?'

'He wasn't around at breakfast,' Maria said.

'No,' Annabelle said, 'he takes breakfast in his room, then locks himself away all day in his study, and woe betide anyone who tries to interrupt him.' She looked at Maria. 'Is that like all writers? Does Donald fly into a rage at the slightest interruption?'

Maria smiled. 'I haven't seen Donald fly into a rage about anything!'

'I've taught myself to scribble whatever the distraction,' he said. 'Before the war I rented a bedsit in Hackney next door to a family of ten.'

Annabelle eased the tiller to her right, and the boat described a great arc away from the bay and along the coast.

'I'm sorry to harp on about this,' Langham said a while later, 'but I'm intrigued by your father's dealings with the colonel. From the little that's been said, I get the impression that something happened to scupper their friendship, way back.' He hesitated. 'You said yesterday that he might have loaned the colonel some money?'

With the headwind tugging at her auburn tresses, Annabelle stared at the horizon. 'I was surmising, Donald. You see, I last saw the colonel when I was ten. This would have been back in 'thirty-five. You know what childhood memories are like . . . they can be almost dreamlike. I recall seeing Haxby in my father's flat in Islington; both men were drunk. I heard them talking . . . arguing . . . late one evening, and I must have got up to see what was happening. I don't know, but I have the impression that my father was giving something to the colonel . . . an envelope.' She shook her head, smiling at the errant memory of the girl she had been. 'I must have leapt to the conclusion that the envelope contained money, but it might have been anything.'

'And your father hasn't had anything to do with Haxby since then?'

'Not as far as I know. Of course, they might have met on one of my father's trips up to London. But no, he's never said anything about meeting him.'

Langham wondered at the wisdom of telling Annabelle what Colonel Haxby had said about her father having killed a man. He decided that he'd better keep it to himself.

'I'll take you to a famous smugglers' cave a mile or two along the coast,' Annabelle said a little later, 'and then we'll pull into an idyllic little cove, moor up and have lunch.'

Langham looked back at the coast. They were perhaps a mile from shore now and the changes that humankind had wrought on the landscape, in terms of roads and villages, appeared negligible against the greater evidence of the natural landscape, the vast swathes of woodland and wild meadow that stretched east and west as far as the eye could see. After London, this corner of Cornwall seemed an unpopulated paradise.

Annabelle steered them towards the coast, approaching an undulating line of cliffs. She throttled back and the boat slowed as they came to the high, arched opening of a gaping cave. She eased the boat out of the direct sunlight and into the cave's cool interior.

'It's known locally as Mad Eddy's Hole,' she said above the plashing of the waves. 'There's a ledge at the very back, and the story goes that Mad Eddy and his chums tunnelled up through the limestone to create a passage to the hamlet on the headland and used it to smuggle contraband. This was back in the seventeen hundreds. Rumour has it that a bit of smuggling still goes on.'

She turned the boat and they headed back out to the open sea.

She pointed ahead. 'And that inlet, there, is Kittiwake Cove. It's approachable only by boat and a perilously steep track, so with luck we'll dine alone. Hungry?'

'Famished,' Maria said.

They put into the cove and Annabelle moored the boat to the warped and salted timbers of a dilapidated jetty. Langham climbed out first, assisted the women on to the jetty and led the way along the treacherous boards to a shingle beach.

They ate their lunch in the shade of a wind-stunted hawthorn,

Maria and Annabelle chatting about their respective jobs and the merits of life in London compared with the delights of the countryside.

'But do you know,' Annabelle said at one point, 'a part of me would really like to get away from it all and live abroad. I really envy Uncle Monty and his lifestyle. It must be wonderful to explore exotic climes and write about one's exploits.'

'I'm not so sure that it's all plain sailing,' Langham said, biting into a sandwich. 'He was just telling me that he's going through a bit of a lean time.'

Annabelle laughed. 'Oh, don't be taken in by Uncle Monty's tales of penury. He doesn't do too badly, what with his commissions and the annual allowance my father makes him.'

Langham looked at the woman. 'An allowance?'

'Five hundred a year, I think it is,' she said. 'They never got on as children – hated each other, in fact. They were so very different, you see. Monty was always out adventuring, exploring the coast, building dens and playing with the local children. My father was somewhat solitary and bookish; he didn't mix with Monty's friends.'

'So the allowance . . .' Langham said.

Annabelle began to say something, and he wondered if the word might have been 'conscience', but she bit her lip and shook her head. Instead, she said, 'My father can afford it,' and left it at that.

Langham was about to ask her how Monty had come by the injury to his hand, but Maria was saying, 'It must be nice to see your uncle again, after so long? He doesn't often get down here, I understand?'

'He doesn't. Despite the allowance, Monty and my father aren't that close. But I do see Monty quite regularly; in fact, every time he's in London – perhaps three or four times a year. He takes me to the Travellers Club and introduces me to his famous friends.'

'You're close?' Langham said.

Annabelle smiled down at her coffee cup. 'I love Monty,' she said. 'Yes, we're very close. I think I'm the daughter he never had.' She hesitated. 'You see, the accident he had as a child injured more than just his hands. The burns were terrible . . . As a result, he was never able to become a father.'

Maria winced and Langham made the requisite sympathetic noises.

Annabelle smiled brightly. 'So . . . I'm the daughter he never had – and Uncle Monty is the father I wish I had.'

They finished the picnic in silence, and Langham placed an arm behind his head as a pillow and closed his eyes. The women strolled off, their voices a lulling murmur at the edge of his consciousness.

He heard Maria ask, 'What happened?'

'It only lasted a few weeks,' Annabelle replied. 'You know how it is, to begin with. You think the world of him, see in him what you believe is there, but isn't really. And then you come to know the real man, and . . .' She made the sound of an expiring match, '*Phht!* And it's all over.'

'I know what you mean.'

'But, as they say, that's all so much water under the bridge.'

Langham opened his eyes and sat up.

Annabelle was crouching a few yards away, examining sea shells. Maria strolled back to Langham and hauled him to his feet. 'Come on, lazybones, let's explore.'

He laughed. 'If we must.'

They crunched through the shingle, the slipping stones pulling them this way and that. Maria laughed and almost fell over, and Langham caught her arm to keep her upright. They came to the end of the beach, climbed on to a rocky outcropping and admired the enclosing headlands.

Maria said, 'Annabelle told me something interesting, Donald.'

'Go on.'

'She had an affair with Wilson Royce.'

He pulled back his head, surprised. 'No!'

'That's what she said. Just after he took up his position as her father's business manager, last year, he made a play for her and she reciprocated. It went well for a while, and then she saw through him, she said.'

'That's dashed odd. And now she's paying the agency three guineas an hour to find out what he's up to.'

'Perhaps, Donald, she discovered he was up to no good – or suspected something – and it was this that persuaded her to end the relationship.'

'Maybe. But why didn't she tell me what she suspected?' He stared along the beach at Annabelle Connaught; she was striding along the tideline, lost in thought.

'Do you know,' Maria said. 'I could easily become accustomed to living in the country. Donald, let's take up Charles's offer to stay at his place while we're house-hunting,'

'Very well.'

'After all this countryside, I really want to get away from London. A lovely little cottage in the country.'

He looked at her. 'And a dog?'

'Mmm. And a dog.'

'And I'll walk it while you're at work,' he said.

'And I'll take my turn when you're in London.'

'That sounds like a deal,' he said. 'All we have to do now is find a cottage.'

'And a dog.'

'A cat would be easier to look after.'

'A dog and a cat,' she said, resting her head on his shoulder, '*and a baby*.'

He put an arm around her shoulders and kissed the sun-warmed crown of her head.

It was after five by the time they arrived back at the mooring below Threepenny Cottage, climbed the precipitous stairway and thanked Annabelle for a wonderful afternoon. Only as they were taking their leave did she ask Langham how his investigations regarding Wilson Royce were progressing. He told her that his partner in London was chasing certain leads, and that he'd know more when he spoke to him later today or tomorrow. 'As soon as I learn anything more, I'll be in touch.'

'Do that,' Annabelle said as she waved them off.

Langham drove through the village, then took the lane through the forest to Connaught House.

He was aware that Maria was staring at him. 'What?' he asked.

'You haven't said anything,' she said.

'About what?'

'You know.'

He grinned.

She said, 'So?'

He pulled into the side of the lane, turned in his seat and took her hand. 'Is that what you want?'

'More than anything.'

'Boy or girl?'

'I'm not really bothered, just as long as he or she is healthy.'

'If it's a boy, then I'll take him to watch the Arsenal every other week.'

'Mmm. And if it's a girl, I'll dress her in fabulous home-made dresses and teach her how to bake.'

He looked at her. 'I didn't know you baked.'

She laughed. 'I can always learn, Donald.'

'Do you know something, my darling?' he said as he drove off. 'I feel so good at the moment that not even the prospect of dinner this evening with Denbigh Connaught and his motley crew can dampen my spirits.'

'That's the ticket, my boy – as Charles would say.'

'Speaking of whom,' Langham said as they drove through the gates of Connaught House and crunched up the gravel drive, 'I hope he hasn't been brooding all day.'

'He was fine when I said goodbye this morning,' Maria said.

Pandora Jade had evidently spent the afternoon painting beside the house; she was packing up as Langham braked beside her.

'Productive day?' he asked.

She lofted a big canvas, covered in what looked like children's multicoloured building blocks. 'Very. The landscape around here is inspirational. I think I've captured the essence of the place, don't you?'

Langham and Maria stared at the proffered painting. The tumble of cubes represented the approximate shape of the coastline. 'Fascinating,' Langham said.

Maria was more constructive. 'I like it. I think you've caught the wild beauty of the coast.'

'Thank you,' Pandora said. 'Of course, this is just a rough. I'll knock it into shape once I'm back in London.'

They strolled towards the house.

'You don't know how the colonel is today, by any chance?' Langham asked the artist.

'The old fool was up for lunch, and he seemed as right as rain. No mention of yesterday's folderol.'

Langham hesitated, then asked, 'How did your one-to-one go with the Great Man – if you don't mind my asking?'

Pandora paused at the foot of the stairs, staring at him. 'That's my business, Mr Langham – if you don't mind my saying.' And with this she turned on her heel and marched up the staircase.

Langham raised his eyebrows at Maria, who said, 'And that's telling you, *Mr Langham*.'

He smiled. 'It certainly is.'

They made their way to their room, bathed and changed, then rested for half an hour. He watched Maria as she dressed for dinner.

'Oh, before I forget, did you really like Pandora's daub?' he asked.

'Of course. I thought she captured the essence of the place, in a very abstract fashion.' She turned to him and said, 'Zip me up, Donald. You didn't like it?'

He frowned. 'Must admit it spoke in a language I couldn't comprehend.'

She kissed his forehead. 'You old fuddy-duddy,' she laughed. 'Come on, I don't know about you, but I'm ready for a G and T.'

They made their way downstairs to the drawing room.

Lady Cecelia was standing before the French windows, in conversation with Pandora Jade. Charles stood beside the women, nursing a huge brandy glass and smiling at something Wilson Royce was telling him. The young man was dressed rather comically, Langham thought, in golfing tweeds and plus fours.

'Ah,' Royce said as they entered, 'what's your poison?'

They asked for gin and tonics and joined the others.

'Pandora was regaling me,' Lady Cecelia said, 'with the antics of her artistic set in Soho. I must say, it sounds like another world entirely. A far cry from Knightsbridge!'

'Artists,' Pandora pronounced. 'Mad as hatters, the lot of 'em.'

'But surely,' Charles said gallantly, 'you don't include yourself in that sobriquet?'

'I most certainly do, Elder. You see, you've got to be a bit doolally to see the world in the abstract. As my therapist says—'

Charles pressed splayed fingers to his chest. 'You have a therapist?' he exclaimed, aghast at the very notion.

'An artist must know herself,' Pandora said. 'And you can't do that alone, in my opinion.'

'And what,' Charles asked, 'did your therapist say?'

'Didn't beat about the bush. Came straight out with it. Opined that I'm three sheets to the wind. Which, he said, accounts for my unrecognized genius. Or perhaps,' she went on, frowning, 'my unrecognized genius accounts for my madness.'

Everyone laughed at the strange woman's self-deprecation.

'And I take it that you,' Charles said, eyeing Royce's get-up, 'have been tramping the fairway?'

'I have Sunday mornings off, so I try to get in a quick nine holes,'

Royce said. 'Back by noon in case his nibs wants anything. I was so busy this afternoon, attempting to clear the rubbish from his old study, that I didn't have time to change.'

'Once, in my more athletic youth, I was known to flog the India rubber,' Charles said. 'These days I conserve my energy for more sedentary pursuits, like dining.'

Langham glanced at Maria; she was staring at her business partner with a fond twinkle in her eye.

'I have rather fallen in love with the walled garden,' Lady Cecelia said. 'I spent much of the afternoon there, reading Jane Austen and admiring the roses. What better way to spend a Sunday afternoon?'

Maria told the guests about their voyage across the high seas. Langham heard the door open; Colonel Haxby entered, dressed in military-creased trousers, blazer and regimental tie. The old soldier limped across to the bar and helped himself to a Scotch.

Langham noticed that Charles's glass was empty, and that Maria's was almost so. He drained his gin and tonic, asked if anyone else required a top-up and crossed to the bar.

'Colonel, how are you today?'

'Top-hole.' Haxby leaned against the bar and eyed Langham as the latter poured the drinks. 'I think I'm in your debt, young sir.'

'Don't mention it.'

'Chatting to your chum Elder over lunch. Told me you suffered from vertigo. Dashed brave of you to do what you did.'

'Well, I couldn't very well have left you down there.'

'I appreciate it. You're a scholar and a gentleman, sir.'

The colonel took a liberal mouthful of Scotch, swilled it around his gums like mouthwash, then said, 'I hope you don't have me down as a buffoon, Langham.'

'Perish the thought.'

'Only . . . Dammit, spent years serving the King, and then Rommel blows me to bits. On the scrapheap at forty. Hard to take. Army doesn't want cripples. Offered me a desk job, I'll give 'em that. Did I want to spend the rest of me days pen-pushing? Like ruddy hell I did!'

Langham sipped his drink. 'What did you do?'

Colonel Haxby smiled. 'Went into insurance. Ended up pushing a pen. Then last year wangled early retirement on account of the old pin. Or lack of.'

'Well done,' Langham said. He paused, then said, 'About yesterday . . .'

'If you're going to ask me what passed between me and Connaught, Langham, don't bother. Water under the bridge. I want to forget about it. Move on.'

'Understood,' Langham said. He gestured towards the group near the window. 'Shall we join them?'

'Lead the way.'

Charles was in full spate, describing his ineptitude, as a youth, in the Officer Training Corps at Winchester. 'I tried – oh, how I tried – but the knack of keeping in step with the rest of my platoon was quite beyond me – an affliction that has followed me throughout my life, I might say.'

Wilson Royce glanced at his watch. 'Gosh, it's almost six thirty. I wonder what's keeping his nibs?'

'Whatever it is,' the colonel muttered, 'I'm not complaining. Quite pleasant without him, what?'

'Even so, I'd better go and fetch him.' Royce excused himself and slipped out through the French windows.

The colonel sniffed. 'Is it me, or is something on fire?'

'I do detect a certain singed odour in the air,' Charles agreed.

Pandora said, 'That'll be Royce. I saw him burning papers in a brazier round the back this afternoon. Prodding at it with a long stick like a little boy.'

The colonel gestured to everyone's glasses. 'Drink up. That's the spirit. I'll do the honours. Three G and Ts, a sherry for Lady Cee and Scotch for me and Royce.'

'I'll say this for Connaught,' Pandora said, 'he doesn't keep a lock on the drinks cabinet.'

'Well, he can afford to be generous,' the colonel said. 'Those books of his sell in their thousands.' He moved to the bar.

Langham glanced through the French windows. He was surprised to see Wilson Royce standing on the lawn, staring into the drawing room, a hand raised to his forehead. He looked as if he was about to be sick or pass out.

Langham touched Maria's hand and murmured, 'Back in a tick.'

He slipped through the French windows and approached the young man. 'Wilson, what the devil . . .'

Royce looked stricken, his face pale. 'I . . . I think you'd better come.'

'What—'

Behind him, he heard Charles call out, 'Is everything all right, my boy?'

Before Langham could reply, Royce took his arm and almost dragged him away from the house. 'It's Connaught,' he said, his voice cracking.

In silence, the two men hurried across the lawn and around the boxwood hedge.

FIFTEEN

They approached Connaught's study and Royce pointed to the open door. 'In there,' he said needlessly.

Langham stepped inside and looked around. What he expected to see, and didn't, was Denbigh Connaught, and his absence seemed to fill the room.

Langham turned to Royce. 'I don't see . . .'

Wilson Royce was sitting on the step, holding his head in his hands. He almost moaned, 'Behind the piano.'

Then Langham did see Connaught, or rather saw his head, and he wondered how he'd managed to miss it initially.

The novelist lay on his side in the narrow space between the piano and the wall. Something was caught around the man's neck – a thin wire terminating in two loops, where presumably the killer had gripped the wire with such ferocity that Connaught's throat appeared to be sliced through to the spine. His face was horribly white, drained of the life blood which had spilled across the polished parquet in a great crimson slick as if a paint pot had been overturned.

'I say,' Charles called from outside, 'what is it, my boy?'

Langham returned to the entrance. Beside Charles, Maria had her fingertips pressed to her lips, her eyes wide. The colonel frowned, clutching his drink. Pandora Jade was frowning at Royce, who still sat on the step with his head in his hands.

'I'm afraid Connaught is dead,' Langham said. 'Royce, back to the house quick-smart and ring the police, would you?'

Wilson Royce remained frozen on the step, as if deaf to Langham's command.

Maria said, 'I'll go.' She turned and hurried back across the lawn.

'I think the rest of you should return to the drawing room,' Langham said. 'The police will be here shortly and they won't want people milling around.'

'Dead?' Pandora said, staring at him. 'What happened, Langham?'

'Heart attack, I shouldn't wonder,' Colonel Haxby opined. 'The old boy did like the good life, and he could put it away with the best of us.' Suiting action to the words, he drained his glass.

Pandora said, 'But why should the police be called if—'

Charles interrupted, 'I think we should heed Donald's suggestion and repair to the house.' He shepherded Pandora and the colonel away from the study.

Pandora stood firm. 'Just how did he die, Langham?'

Royce looked up at her. 'Connaught was murdered,' he said.

'*What?*' Pandora exclaimed with horror.

'If you'd all kindly return to the house . . .' Langham suggested.

This time Pandora allowed herself to be led away as if in a daze.

'Good God!' the colonel declared, clutching Charles's arm as they moved off. 'I never cared for the fellow, but *murdered?*'

Langham checked his wristwatch, then looked down at Wilson Royce. 'Was the study door locked when you came to summon Connaught – what? – five or six minutes ago?'

'Of course,' Royce said. 'He always keeps it locked. I knocked a few times and called his name. When there was no reply . . . It's most unlike him not to respond – that is, on the few occasions I've had to summon him.'

'So when there was no reply, you unlocked the door?'

'That's right.'

He looked at the young man. 'But I thought you said yesterday that the spare key was kept under the stairs?'

'It is, but it's on the same keyring as his old study key, and as I was clearing out the study this afternoon' – he pulled the keyring from his pocket to show Langham – 'I still had it in my pocket.'

'Look,' Langham said, 'I'd join the others if I were you and fix yourself a stiff drink.'

Royce stirred himself. 'Yes. Yes, of course.'

Langham watched the young man as he stood and wandered off towards the house, clearly in shock.

He turned and surveyed the study. The piano with the corpse lodged behind it was positioned at two o'clock, relative to where he stood at the door; diametrically opposite, at eight o'clock, was a small two-seater settee, two wicker chairs and a coffee table bearing a portable typewriter. A faded, threadbare Persian rug covered the parquet floor.

All the windows were closed, and none appeared to have been forced. The skylight was closed too. The killer could only have entered through the door. So the killer had a copy of the key, or had managed to take it from Wilson Royce's possession and return it without his knowledge. Alternatively, Connaught might have let the killer in himself.

He moved to the piano, knelt and examined the corpse. The gap between the piano and the wall was about two feet wide; there appeared to have been no struggle. Connaught must have been standing behind the piano with his back to his killer when the latter approached, looped the wire over his head, and strangled him. The corpse had not been moved after the attack, as there was no blood in evidence anywhere else on the parquet or the rug.

Connaught's left arm was pinned under his body, his right arm outstretched above his head. His fingertips were unbloodied, which suggested that death or unconsciousness must have been swift, leaving him with little or no time to fight off his attacker.

What was striking was the obvious force with which the killer had committed the deed. This was no mere strangulation, but a severing of the windpipe and jugular. Blood was splashed across the back of the piano and across the timber-board cladding below the window: the killer must have been covered with the stuff, too. Also, he must have worn gloves to ensure that his hands had not been sliced by the looped wire of the garrotte.

He reached out and touched Connaught's cheek and then his brow. The flesh was still warm. He estimated that Connaught had been dead for perhaps two or three hours.

He stood and stared out at the sparkling sea in the distance. He could just make out the muted drone of the electric motor, somewhere beneath the study, which turned the structure as slowly as the hour hand of a clock.

Fifteen minutes later, he heard voices outside and turned to see
Wilson Royce leading a plain-clothes officer and a uniformed
constable across the lawn. The constable stationed himself outside
the study while the officer stepped inside, nodded at Langham, and
examined the body.

He introduced himself as Detective Sergeant Greaves, a small
man in his thirties with a pencil moustache and a trilby perched on
the back of his head. 'And you are?'

Langham displayed his private investigator accreditation. 'I
happen to be a guest at the house,' he explained. 'Nothing's been
touched or disturbed. Wilson Royce, Connaught's business manager,
discovered the body at approximately six thirty. The door was
locked and Royce used his own key to enter when Connaught failed
to reply.'

Greaves nodded. 'A detective inspector's on his way from
Plymouth,' he said. He moved around the back of the piano and stared
down at the corpse. 'Christ, whoever did this certainly meant business.
A man, by the look of it. Damned near took the chap's head off.'

'A strong woman might have done it,' Langham said. 'That's
piano wire.'

'Gone through his flesh as if it were cheese. Lord, you see some
sights in this job.' He shook his head. 'Just wait till the press gets
to hear about this. Have a field day, they will.'

He backed out from behind the piano. 'Right, let's get back to
the house and see what the guests have to say for themselves.'

Everyone was gathered in the drawing room, with a police constable
stationed outside the door. According to Royce, Watkins and the
cook had been given the Sunday off: dinner was to have been a
cold collation, set up by the cook the previous night. Royce himself
had taken a selection of meats and salad from the refrigerator and
larder at five.

He told everyone this as they sat around on armchairs and sofas
before the empty hearth. He was white-faced and shaking, and was
evidently still in shock. Langham moved to the bar and poured
himself a Scotch; Maria joined him.

'Drink?' Langham asked.

'Just a tonic water,' she said. 'Poor Wilson. He's beside himself.
He hasn't stopped talking since we got back here.'

'Shock,' he said.

They returned to the little gathering, where Detective Sergeant Greaves was addressing the group. 'I'd like to get the groundwork done before the big guns get here. There's a library next door, so I'll see you in there one by one.' He consulted his notebook. 'Right, I'll start with Mr Wilson Royce. If you'd kindly follow me.'

Royce rose to his feet like an automaton and the two men left the room.

Lady Cecelia, seated on a sofa beside Charles, stared through the French windows and dabbed at her eyes from time to time with a silk kerchief. She alone was without a drink.

Pandora looked up from her gin and tonic. 'You said he was murdered, Langham?' Her round, powdered face, with its painted lips and mascaraed eyes, looked grotesque.

He stirred himself to reply. 'That's right.'

'But how? I mean, did someone shoot him?'

He looked at the woman. 'I don't think Greaves would thank me if I divulged that.'

'Poor Annabelle!' Pandora said. 'Someone must tell her. I need to go and see her . . .'

'No doubt the police will see to that,' Langham assured her.

The colonel occupied an armchair with his artificial leg stretched out before him. 'Let's face it,' he said, knocking back his whisky, 'we all detested the rogue. I know I did. I admit it. Detested the man.'

'I didn't.' It was the first time that Lady Cecelia had spoken since Langham had entered the room.

She looked at them one by one, smiling bravely. 'Oh, I know Denbigh could be difficult. But one must make allowances, mustn't one? He was a great novelist, a great man despite . . . despite his frequent anger, and he was very generous.' She sighed. 'And now, if you don't mind, I will have a drink. If someone would be so good as to pour me a small sherry . . .'

Langham did the honours, and had just delivered the drink when Sergeant Greaves appeared at the door and called his name.

The interview was over in five minutes. He gave his name, profession and his connection to the dead man: he explained that he'd come down with his wife, a literary agent, here on business. Greaves asked him where he was between the times of one and five that afternoon, and he told the sergeant that he'd been with his wife and Annabelle Connaught, the dead man's daughter, from noon until a little after five o'clock. He confirmed that Wilson Royce had found the body at approximately six thirty and that he, Langham, had been the second person on the scene of the crime. Greaves thanked him and he returned to the drawing room.

The sergeant interviewed everyone in the course of the next half hour, and at seven thirty a black car, accompanied by a police ambulance, drew up beside the house. Langham moved to the French windows and watched as Greaves greeted the new arrivals and led two plain-clothes officers, a police photographer, a doctor and a forensic scientist towards the study.

Maria joined him. 'I don't think they'll get much out of the colonel.'

Langham looked at the old soldier. He was almost horizontal in the armchair, snoring quietly. Someone had taken the empty glass from his loose fingers. Pandora was seated beside Lady Cecelia, doing her best to comfort her. Wilson Royce hunched forward on his chair, hugging himself, his eyes shut.

In due course, Greaves and the two plain-clothes men from Plymouth appeared from behind the hedge and approached the house. The trio entered the drawing room by the French windows and paused, discussing the case as they regarded the suspects. Langham had never felt more like a goldfish.

The detectives crossed to the group and the tallest man introduced himself as Detective Inspector Harper and his deputy as Detective Sergeant Shaw. 'Same procedure as Greaves put you through, I'm afraid. Same order as before, in the library. Mr Royce . . .'

Wilson Royce opened his eyes as if startled, then stood and followed the men from the room.

This round of interviews, as was to be expected, lasted longer than the first; it was twenty minutes before Wilson Royce returned, somewhat dazed, and crossed to the bar. Langham smiled at Maria and left the room.

Detective Inspector Harper was a tired-looking, thin-faced man in his sixties, with a manner that suggested he'd investigated so many murders in his time that one more, even that of a distinguished novelist, left him unmoved.

Langham repeated everything he'd told Greaves about the discovery of the body, and then Harper said, 'And my colleague mentioned that you're a private investigator.'

Langham explained that although he was here to accompany his wife, he was also being employed by Annabelle Connaught to investigate Wilson Royce.

'Royce? What does she suspect him of?' Harper asked with a slight Cornish burr, glancing at his deputy.

'That's the thing – she doesn't know. She merely had the suspicion that, as her father's business manager, Royce was up to something.'

'And what do you think?'

'I've only been on the case a couple of days, and I must admit I've found nothing untoward as of yet.'

Harper nodded and said to Detective Sergeant Shaw, 'I take it that Connaught's daughter has been informed?'

'That's right, sir. The locals saw to that.'

'I'll see her in the morning, find out what she has against Royce.'

Langham said, 'The dead man's brother, Monty Connaught, was staying in the village—'

Harper interrupted, 'Sergeant Greaves was aware of the fact, apparently, and made arrangements for Connaught to be informed.' He closed his notebook. 'Very well, that'll be all for now. Ask Mr Elder if he'd come along, would you?'

Langham slipped from the room, drawing the door behind him but not fully closing it. He heard Harper sigh. 'Do you know what I'm tempted to do, Shaw?' the detective inspector said.

'What's that, sir?'

'We're on a sticky wicket here. Connaught's famous, and if we don't get a result, and soon, Super'll drag us over the ruddy coals. When we're done here tonight, I'll suggest we get in the big guns from the Yard, OK? Dump the lot in their lap.' He yawned. 'Christ, I'm retiring in three weeks and I don't like the idea of falling at the last hurdle.'

The younger man said, 'Feather in your cap if you did wrap it up, though.'

'Shaw, you get to my age and you don't give a tinker's damn for the Super's pat on the back. Give me my pipe and a pint and I'm a happy man. Right-ho . . . Now who's this Elder chappie?'

'Charles Elder,' Shaw said. 'A fruit, according to Greaves. Some kind of literary agent.'

Langham hurried back to the drawing room and gave Charles the nod.

At nine, with everyone interviewed, the world-weary Harper returned to the drawing room and stood before them like a headmaster about to give his end-of-term address.

'Right-ho, the situation is this. As long as the investigation is continuing, I'd be delighted if you'd all remain here at Connaught House. By all means, you can take the time to visit our wonderful Cornish countryside, but don't go scooting off back to the Smoke or elsewhere. That's the ticket. I'll have a couple of men stationed here for the next few days and nights. The chances are that I, or one of my colleagues, will be around tomorrow for another little chat.'

And with that he wished them goodnight and took his leave.

'Droll cove,' Pandora said when they were alone.

'I think the technical term, my dear,' Charles said, 'is that the man is a cynic.'

From the depths of his armchair, Colonel Haxby stirred himself. 'My God, is that the time? I wonder if Connaught would mind if I made a little sortie on the kitchen?'

Pandora grunted, 'I should think, Colonel, that he's past caring much one way or the other.'

'Ah, quite . . . Well, in that case, I might just dash along and make meself a sandwich.'

Charles, Pandora and Lady Cecelia said goodnight and took themselves off to their respective rooms.

Wilson Royce said, 'I don't know about you two, but I need another drink.'

'I'd go easy . . .' Langham said, but Royce ignored him and moved towards the bar.

Maria said to Langham, 'Early night?'

He kissed her fingers. 'Good idea, but first I need to make a quick phone call.'

They said goodnight to Royce, and Langham made a detour to the sitting room. He dialled the operator and was put through to Detective Inspector Jeff Mallory's home number.

'Jeff, sorry to bother you on a Sunday night, but something's cropped up . . .'

Five minutes later, he thanked his friend, rang off, then called Ralph and informed him of Connaught's death.

'Ruddy hell, Don! Murdered? You don't think young Royce had a hand in it?'

'Early days, Ralph. You come up with anything on him?'

'Just a bit. Looks like our young friend *was* getting his hands dirty in the illicit art market, just as we thought.'

Langham listened while Ralph detailed his meeting with a dodgy art dealer called Harker.

'And I got the key cut for Royce's place in Chelsea. I'll pop round there in the morning.'

'Good work, Ralph. I'll be in touch.'

He replaced the receiver and hurried upstairs.

Maria was removing her make-up at the dresser when he entered the bedroom. 'Phoning Ralph?' she asked.

'Yes, and Jeff Mallory.'

He told her what he'd overheard Harper telling his deputy, and went on, 'If the Yard is brought in, then there's no one better I'd like on the case than Jeff.'

'What did he say?'

'He'll have a word with his boss first thing. He thinks he can swing it, as I'm down here and have the inside gen.' He stood beside her and kicked off his shoes. 'And according to Ralph, Wilson Royce has been doing a bit of shady dealing in the art market.' He told her what Ralph had discovered.

She nodded and stared down at her hands.

'Maria?'

She sighed. 'Oh, I'm just wondering who might have . . .' She trailed off, then said, 'In all likelihood, Donald, it was one of the guests, wasn't it?'

He kissed the top of her head and murmured, 'Come to bed.'

SIXTEEN

'Are you ever going to get up, Ralph?' Annie called up the stairs on Monday morning. 'I thought you said you wanted an early start!'

Ryland rose through fathoms of half sleep, rolled over and stared at the cracked ceiling. He rubbed his eyes and peered at the alarm clock. It was almost nine.

He recalled Millwall's one–nil victory against Walsall on Saturday, with Shepherd scoring in the second half. That had set him up nicely for Sunday and the picnic on Hampstead Heath with the boys sailing their toy boats on the pond. The weather had kept fine, and Annie's ham and mustard sandwiches had slipped down a treat.

Then last night Don had called from Cornwall.

So the scribbler Connaught was dead, and Wilson Royce was a suspect . . . Well, he'd go through Royce's place with a nit-comb that morning.

He rolled out of bed, splashed his face with cold water, then dressed and made his way downstairs.

'Toast's ready,' Annie said. 'Marmite or marmalade?'

'Strawberry jam.'

'Kevin's finished it.'

'The little blighter. Marmalade, then.'

He sat at the table with a big mug of strong tea and two slices of toast and marmalade.

Annie sat down with her own tea. 'That business in Cornwall, Ralph. You won't be needing to go down, will you?'

'No fear. Looks like Scotland Yard will be brought in. Inspector Mallory. Good man. He and Don'll get to the bottom of it in no time. No, I'll poke about up here for the next day or so, see if I can find out a bit more about our young Mr Royce.'

'You won't be long this morning, I hope?'

'An hour – two at the most.'

'I want you back by twelve. Don't forget you promised to take me into town for a new coat.'

'I'd better be getting a shuffle on, then.'

'Egg and tomato sandwiches for lunch?'

'Smashing.' He gave her a kiss. 'See you on the dot of twelve.'

'Likely story.' She swiped at him. 'You're never on time for anything, Ralphy.'

When he went out to the car, Terry and Kevin were playing cowboys and Indians with a noisy gang of local kids on the bomb site across the road. He managed to slip in behind the wheel without being targeted by either the cavalry or Comanches, and set off north to Chelsea.

He'd picked up the key from Harry Beckett after the match at five on Saturday, but the promised half pint had turned to three, while the boys had been happy with a bottle of Tizer and a couple of pickled eggs.

'That doesn't smell like a half to me,' Annie had said on his return.

'Kevin, Terry, tell your mum . . .'

Terry, the eldest, had grinned at Ryland and said, all innocence, 'He had three pints, Mum.'

You had to laugh, he thought, as he took the Hammersmith Bridge over the river.

He reached Chelsea by ten thirty, found Saddler's Way and parked at the end of the mews.

Now to see if Harry's key would do the business.

He sauntered up the cobbled mews, as casual as you like, and found number ten. He slipped the key into the door and turned it; it worked like a dream. A second later he was in the front room with the door shut behind him.

He'd heard that these mews houses – Victorian stables converted after the Great War – were small and poky, but this one was bigger than his Lewisham terrace house. It had a medium-sized lounge, a big kitchen and two bedrooms upstairs. He found nothing in the bedrooms, other than an unmade double bed, a pile of well-thumbed Penguin paperbacks, and unwashed clothes strewn across the floor.

Downstairs, a portable typewriter sat on a rickety desk. Royce had started a letter to the blonde: *Dear Beatrice* . . .

He stood in the middle of the room and looked around, then pulled the drawer in the desk all the way out and sat down on a two-seater settee. He went through the contents of the drawer item by item: bills, paid and unpaid, an old ration book, loose stamps and a current Barclay's paying-in book, with a cheque sticking out of it like a bookmark. He pulled out the cheque and studied it.

Now this was interesting . . .

The cheque, dated five days ago, was for two hundred pounds sterling, to be drawn on the account of Denbigh Connaught.

He flipped through the bank book until he came to the most recent deposits, and ran a finger down the list.

Bingo!

Every month, on or around the twentieth, Wilson Royce deposited a cheque for two hundred pounds into his account. He flipped back a few pages and found that the deposits had started just over a year ago.

Two hundred nicker, *every* month?

Very well, Royce worked for the novelist Denbigh Connaught – but surely he wouldn't be pulling in that kind of monthly salary, would he?

He went through the rest of the papers, found nothing of interest, and was about to replace the contents back in the drawer when he caught sight of a letter addressed to Denbigh Connaught.

The envelope had been opened. He pulled out a single sheet of notepaper and read through the short, scrawled letter.

It was addressed simply to 'Connaught' and was from someone called Pandora Jade.

She would be taking up his invitation to come down to Cornwall on the weekend of the eighteenth, but only on the condition that Annabelle would not be present. *The agreement*, she went on, *was that she would not be told about me, and you will appreciate that from my point of view I'd rather not run the risk of bumping into our daughter . . .*

Strange, Ryland thought. What was a letter addressed to Denbigh Connaught doing in Royce's possession? Granted, he was the novelist's business manager, but the letter had nothing to do with business as far as he could make out.

He replaced the letter in the drawer and slipped it back into the desk.

On top of the desk, beside a telephone, was a small black address book. He turned to the back of the book and looked for Venturi's name and address under V, but nothing was listed.

He should have known that tracing Venturi wouldn't be that easy. Last night he'd settled down with the London phone book and found half a dozen entries under Venturi, but not one of them had been a P. Venturi . . .

Just a tick, he thought, staring at the names and addresses in the book. Wilson Royce had entered his contacts under their *first* names . . .

He turned to the letter P in the thumb index and smiled.

No wonder he'd been unable to find a Signor P. Venturi in the London phone book.

Piero Venturi, Rowan Cottage, Church Lane, Smarden, Kent.

No phone number was listed.

Ryland copied the address into his notebook. All things considered, it had been a morning well spent.

Now it was time to get back home before the twelve o'clock deadline, to prove to the trouble and strife that he *could* be punctual.

And tomorrow, he thought, he would take a little drive out into the country.

SEVENTEEN

As they were dressing the next morning, Maria said, 'I had an awful dream, Donald. All about Wilson Royce . . . The police were hauling him off to the gallows, and he was screaming.' She shuddered. 'You don't think Royce could be mixed up in this business, do you?'

Langham considered. 'I honestly don't know. He had the spare key to the study, and he was around all afternoon. And although he isn't exactly Charles Atlas, perhaps he could have strangled Connaught.'

Maria pulled a face. 'It must have been . . .' She didn't finish the sentence.

'Pretty damned awful, my darling,' he said. 'The killer was obviously known to Connaught, as there was no sign of a struggle, and I suspect he had his back to his killer when he was attacked. Against the possibility of Royce being the culprit, what might his motive have been? Why would he murder his employer – the hand that feeds?'

'Also,' she said, 'he seemed very distressed yesterday. Unless he's an excellent actor . . .'

'Mmm.' Langham opened the door and they left the room. 'I'm inclined to look elsewhere, I must admit.'

Charles was the only other person at breakfast when they entered the dining room.

'Wonderful!' he called out. 'I feared, for a space, that I might be eating alone.'

'We're here to spare you that,' Langham said. He helped himself to toast and scrambled egg from the sideboard and sat beside Maria, who was applying butter and raspberry jam to her toast.

'Do you know,' Charles said, 'breakfast, once upon a time, was the loneliest meal of all. I mean to say, one can hardly ring someone at eight in the morning and say, "Come over for breakfast, why not?" All the other meals of the day, one can assuage one's loneliness with the company of friends.'

Maria smiled. '*Was* the loneliest, Charles? But now?'

'Now, my dear, since Albert has moved into my Suffolk abode and taken over the running of the house . . . I rise to the sound of his manly baritone in the kitchen and the scent of bacon and eggs. Did I tell you that he's the most divine cook? I didn't? Well, his breakfasts are heavenly, if he still has a little to learn in the dinner department.'

Charles popped a kidney into his mouth, chewed as if in bliss and said, 'But here I am, describing the delights of cohabitation to newlyweds!'

Maria laughed. 'But *I* don't wake up to Donald cooking me breakfast!' she said, nudging him in the ribs.

'You're such a good cook,' Langham said, 'that in all fairness I couldn't inflict my offerings on you, could I?'

'Perish the thought.'

Charles dabbed his lips with a napkin. He looked from Langham to Maria. 'I couldn't sleep a single wink last night. I couldn't help thinking about Connaught, and that yesterday afternoon, while I lay in bed reading his novel . . . someone was . . . was . . .' He pulled a sour face. 'It's just too ghastly to think about.'

Langham drained his tea and asked Charles, 'You didn't happen to look out of your window yesterday afternoon and see anyone in the grounds?'

'I lunched with Lady Cecelia at twelve thirty, and we had a pleasant little chat about mutual acquaintances in London. I returned to my room at approximately two, and resumed reading the manuscript. I left the house for a breath of fresh air, at perhaps three thirty, and walked along the lane for a hundred yards before exhaustion ensued. I returned, via the drawing room, for a glass of tonic water.'

'What time would that be?' Langham asked.

'Perhaps a little after four,' Charles replied. 'And at what time did the terrible deed occur?'

'It's not certain yet, but at a guess I'd say between two o'clock and four. Did you see anyone when you were in the drawing room?'

Charles frowned in concentration. 'Colonel Haxby was slumped in an armchair, dead to the world. I poured myself a tonic water . . . moved to the French windows . . . admired the view, the sea, the cloudless sky . . . And yes – I saw young Wilson off to the right.'

'What was he doing?'

'Nothing. That is, staring across the lawn. I think he might have been smoking a cigarette.'

'And you saw no one else?'

'A little earlier, on returning from my amble, I saw Pandora composing one of her fearful abstracts on the side lawn. But I fear I saw no one stalking the grounds.' He looked downcast. 'But then I wouldn't have, would I? For the sad and tragic fact of the matter is that poor old Connaught was done to death by someone resident in the house all along.'

Langham wiped his lips with his napkin. 'That's a possibility, Charles, but not a foregone conclusion. Someone from outside could easily have entered the grounds, unseen, and approached the study.'

'I hope so,' Charles murmured. 'I know it's ridiculous, but it would be easier to accept if the perpetrator was not someone with whom one had actually socialized, wouldn't it? Or am I being a silly old fool?'

Maria assured him that he'd expressed exactly what she had been thinking earlier.

A little later they were joined at the table by Pandora Jade and Lady Cecelia.

'Has anyone seen Royce?' Langham asked.

'I saw him a minute ago, taking a cup of tea into his room,' Pandora said. 'He looked somewhat morose and sorry for himself.'

'Sorry for himself?' Lady Cecelia pondered. 'I wonder why?'

'Probably thinks he'll soon be out on his ear,' Pandora said, tucking into her bacon and eggs. 'He was Connaught's business manager, after all. With Connaught gone to meet his maker, there's effectively no business to manage. Ergo: exit Royce.'

Langham found himself studying the hands of each person around the table. Lady Cecelia's were thin, grey and frail – very much like the rest of her – while Pandora's were short and stubby, but in such a way as to suggest effeteness, not strength. Charles's hands were pink and plump, not that Langham for a second entertained the notion that his friend might have strangled the novelist. He recalled Wilson Royce's long, epicene hands and Monty Connaught's damaged claw, and wondered how any one of the group could have summoned the strength to commit the deed.

An outsider, then? Someone who had sneaked unseen into the grounds and bearded Connaught in his study?

He turned to Pandora. 'Yesterday afternoon you were painting from just after lunch until we saw you around five. Were you there all the time?'

She set down her knife and fork very deliberately. 'Playing the amateur detective, Langham? Do you think I did it?'

'Of course not. In fact, I'm pretty sure that no one in the house at the time was responsible. But you might have seen someone – a stranger, perhaps, who entered the grounds at some point yesterday.'

'As I told the inspector last night,' she said, 'I saw no one, and I was there from around twelve thirty until well after five. No one came in through the gates, other than Charles. I also saw Lady Cee briefly, and we chatted.'

'Of course,' Lady Cecelia said, 'the killer might have climbed over the perimeter walls. They are rather high, but where there's a will . . .'

'That's certainly a possibility,' Langham said.

Lady Cecelia placed worried fingers to her mouth. 'Do you think the police are taking that line: that the culprit was an outsider? Or do you think they consider us all as suspects?'

'Face it, Lady Cee,' Pandora said, 'everyone who was anywhere in the vicinity yesterday is on their suspect list. The police have to do their job.'

'But I couldn't strangle a lamb!' Lady Cecelia protested.

'Of course,' Maria said, smiling at the dowager. 'And I'm sure the police know that and have crossed you off their list.'

Lady Cecelia murmured her thanks to Maria. 'But it does make one feel terribly guilty, doesn't it, with all these policemen buzzing about the place?'

'They've more or less packed up now,' Pandora said. 'The ambulance carted the body off last night, and the forensic chap left this morning.'

'Even so,' Lady Cecelia's voice quavered, 'whatever would my friends in London think if they found out that I was *present at the scene of a crime*?'

Pandora shrugged. 'Well, they're bound to find out sooner or later, once the press get wind of the Great Man's murder.'

Lady Cecelia's eyes grew enormous with alarm. 'Do you really think . . .?'

'It's only a matter of time before the gutter press drag all our names through the mire, mark my word. The publicity might even help me shift some paintings. You never know.'

Charles said, 'I think you're being unnecessarily alarmist, Miss Jade.'

But the damage had been done, and Lady Cecelia rose unsteadily from the table, smiled falteringly at the others and stumbled from the room.

To her credit, Pandora had the good grace to look sheepish. 'Put my foot right in it, didn't I?' She flung down her napkin. 'I'd better go and tell her I was speaking through my hat.'

She left the table and hurried after the dowager.

'That woman,' Charles said, 'is either obtuse or uncaring.'

'The latter, I think,' Langham said. 'She doesn't give a fiddler's damn about what anyone thinks about her.'

They finished breakfast and Langham suggested a turn around the garden.

As they were leaving the room, two figures entered the house through the front door, though with the dazzling sunlight filling the aperture it was impossible to make out their identity. Not until they were halfway up the carved oak staircase did Langham recognize Annabelle Connaught and her uncle; Monty Connaught had his arm around her shoulders and was murmuring something to her.

Maria said to Charles, 'That was Annabelle, Connaught's daughter.'

'The poor child,' Charles murmured as they stepped outside.

They strolled past the parked cars and across the sloping lawn to the tussock-fringed cliff edge. In the distance, the skylight on the conical roof of the late novelist's study reflected the morning sunlight.

Langham wondered at the luxury of being able to afford a study that turned to follow the sun: there were, he thought, other things he would indulge in first.

Charles was saying, 'I read a little of Connaught's manuscript yesterday, my dears, and I was struck anew at the fact of his passing. He was a truly talented novelist, and no one deserves to die before their time, and in so horrific a fashion.'

'You were going to forgive him, weren't you, Charles?' Maria said.

'I had resolved to accept his apology, yes – for my own peace of mind, I must say, as much as for his. And that is another tragic aspect of the whole affair: that he died bearing such a burden of guilt, for I am sure he was genuine in his remorse.'

A racing green Humber rolled up the drive and came to a sedate halt beside the Lagonda. Detective Sergeant Greaves climbed from the passenger seat, and from behind the wheel emerged the tall, broad figure of Jeff Mallory. The Scotland Yard man followed Greaves into the house.

'Excellent,' Langham said. 'Jeff swung it with his superiors.'

They strolled along the clifftop; Charles wondered aloud when they might be allowed to leave Connaught House. 'Not that I don't doubt that Molly is holding the fort with aplomb,' he said. 'But I do want to get back behind the desk.'

'It'll be a few days yet,' Langham said. 'Thursday or Friday at the earliest. We'll be grilled a few times yet before we're let off the hook.'

Charles sighed. 'Well, I suppose there are worst places to be stranded.'

The French windows to the drawing room opened, winking in the sunlight, and Jeff Mallory stepped through. He made a beeline for them, raising a hand in greeting.

'Don! Good to see you. Maria, you're looking wonderful. Married life suiting you?'

'Marvellously!'

'I trust you're keeping this reprobate in his place?'

'As if any woman could do that,' she laughed.

Jeff shook hands with Charles. 'We met, briefly, at one of your excellent garden parties,' the detective inspector said.

'I well recall,' Charles said. 'You regaled me with an account of your rugby-playing days in Durban.'

'Long gone and far away, I'm afraid,' the South African said.

Maria linked arms with Charles. 'And now, I suspect, Donald and Jeff wish to talk shop. Shall we leave them to it?'

Langham watched them stroll towards the walled garden and then turned to his friend. 'I'm glad you could make it.'

'I was on the blower to Harper in Plymouth first thing, and he filled me in. I'll be working on the case with the local man, young Greaves. He seems eager enough, unlike Harper. Greaves is rounding up the guests for a session of interviews this afternoon, but I'd like to hear what you know before that.'

Langham indicated a bench looking out over the open sea; they crossed to it and sat down.

He told Mallory about being hired by Annabelle Connaught to

look into the movements of Wilson Royce, whom she suspected was up to no good.

'And what do you think?'

'Ralph's working on that end of things in London. It looks as if Royce might be dealing in stolen paintings.'

'Not linked to this business?'

'Well, not directly, as far as I can make out.'

He described his fellow guests, one by one, and the fact that Denbigh Connaught had known them all many years ago and wished to apologize to them for past misdemeanours.

'Apologize?'

'They're keeping pretty tight-lipped about whatever happened back then. All apart from Charles, that is.' He told Jeff about what had passed between Charles Elder and Connaught while at school.

'Harper interviewed everyone last night,' Mallory said, 'but none of them said a thing about Connaught's wanting to apologize.' He paused, staring out at the brilliant blue sea. 'Not all that surprising, when you come to think about it.'

'There wasn't much love lost between Connaught and his guests,' Langham said, 'at least before he apologized on Saturday. Colonel Haxby is on record as wanting to shoot him, and Pandora Jade made no bones about hating his guts.'

Mallory eyed him. 'Serious?'

'No. All just so much hot air, in my opinion. Oh – I had an encounter with the colonel on Saturday, and he mentioned something about Connaught, back in the thirties: he claimed he'd killed a man, back then. It must be said, though, that Haxby was the worse for drink at the time.'

'He said Connaught had killed a man?'

Langham described the dialogue on the cliff path. 'It's something we need to look into,' he said.

'So . . . it appears that there were a few people present who resented Connaught, to put it mildly?'

'That's right,' Langham said. 'But, to be honest, I doubt that any one of them could have overcome Connaught. He was a big man, and they're all pretty much lightweights.' He paused. 'So my money, for what it's worth, is on an outsider.'

Mallory swore. 'Dammit. And here I was, thinking that with a gallery of captive suspects it'd be an open-and-shut case and I could put my feet up for a day or two and enjoy the scenery.'

'Afraid not, old boy,' Langham laughed, filling his pipe.

'Oh, who was the attractive popsy I saw in the house just now?'

'Daisy the cook? Isn't she a bit old for you, Jeff?'

'The cook? You duffer! No, this girl was tall, auburn-haired, a bit of a stunner.'

Langham smiled. 'Brains and beauty, Jeff. Out of your league, I'm afraid. That's Annabelle, Denbigh Connaught's daughter. A medical doctor.'

'Where was she when . . .?'

'With Maria and me. She took us out in her boat from around noon yesterday until five. So that puts all three of us in the clear.'

Mallory smiled. 'According to Harper, forensics are certain that Connaught died between two o'clock and four.'

Langham nodded. 'That's roughly what I surmised.'

Mallory shielded his eyes from the glare of the sun and squinted across the lawn at the novelist's study. 'So that's where it happened? Should we take a mosey across?'

They were about to set off when Langham saw a figure walk around the box hedge and approach them across the lawn. 'Annabelle,' he said to Mallory.

The two men stood, and Langham suppressed a smile as he noticed Mallory straighten his tie and run a quick hand through his thinning mop of fair hair. Just a month ago, at Langham's wedding, Jeff had been drunkenly bewailing his lack of success on the romance front of late.

'Gentlemen,' Annabelle said, smiling from Langham to Mallory. 'I've just seen Detective Sergeant Greaves, and he tells me Scotland Yard has been drafted in. That's gratifying to know.'

Langham made the introductions; Mallory and Annabelle shook hands. 'I'm terribly sorry . . .' Mallory said.

Annabelle murmured, 'Thank you, Inspector.' She turned to Langham. 'I've decided to stay here for the time being. I couldn't face staying in the cottage by myself. And anyway, I need to go through my father's papers.'

Mallory nodded. 'Wise move.'

She stared out to sea. 'Your colleagues called on me last night, Inspector,' she murmured. 'The odd thing was that, as soon as I saw the car pull up outside, I knew something dreadful had happened. I *knew*. Isn't that odd?' She smiled from Langham to Mallory, then continued, 'So when the constable told me, it didn't come as that much of a shock. It was later, in the early hours when I couldn't sleep, that it really hit me. And then it wasn't so much the shock that my father was dead, but that someone had hated him so much that they were prepared to kill him.' She paused. 'The constable said that my father had been strangled, and I must admit that that was a surprise. For some reason, I assumed the killer would shoot him.'

Mallory said, 'Why was that?'

Annabelle shrugged. 'I don't honestly know. But strangled . . .? My father is a big man . . . *was* a big man. It would take considerable force, I would have thought, to overcome him.'

'Do you know if your father had anything to do with the locals which might have led to this?' Langham asked.

'My father rarely ventured into the village. He kept very much to himself. Other than his dealings with Watkins and Daisy, I doubt he knew anyone in the area.'

Mallory indicated Connaught's study. 'I'll be interviewing everyone a little later,' he said, 'but first I'd like to take a shufty at your father's study. I quite understand if you'd rather not.'

'No.' Annabelle smiled charmingly. 'If it's all the same to you, I'd like to see where it happened. I firmly believe in facing down one's fears.'

'An admirable attitude,' Mallory said. 'After you.'

They strolled across the lawn.

A police constable was stationed before the entrance on the far side of the study. He opened the door and stepped aside as they approached. Mallory led the way inside.

Langham watched Annabelle as she paused just beyond the threshold and took a deep breath. She looked at him. 'Where was my father found, Donald?'

He indicated the piano. 'Just behind there. I suspect he was facing away from the door, perhaps chatting with his . . . with whoever had entered. There was no sign of a struggle.'

She flashed him a look. 'Are you saying that he knew his killer?'

'It would appear so, yes.'

She nodded. 'I don't know whether I find that reassuring or even more . . . horrific.'

Langham was relieved to see that the parquet had been cleaned, though flecks of the sawdust that had been used to soak up the blood still remained. Annabelle moved to a window and stared out in silence.

Mallory knelt, examining the floor. Langham gazed around the study, looking for anything he might have missed on the first occasion. He stepped over to the portable typewriter on the coffee table and examined the sheet of quarto wound into the machine. There were no words typed on the paper: the novelist's archetypal blank page.

Annabelle moved to the door. 'If you don't mind, I'll return to the house.' She smiled at the men. 'I think I need a drink.'

Mallory stood. 'Not at all.'

'I'll be there if you need to interview me,' she said.

'I'll get the others over and done with first,' Mallory said, 'and then we'll just cover the basics with you. I'd like to build up a picture of the kind of man your father was.'

Annabelle hesitated at the door. 'To be perfectly honest, Inspector, my father wasn't a very nice man – as you'll no doubt find out. He didn't like his fellow humans, and didn't expect to be liked in return. I found him a somewhat frightening figure during my childhood. He showed me no affection, and, of course, asked for none in return. I sometimes wonder if he resented me – resented my presence, in lieu of that of my mother.'

'And yet you returned here to start a medical practice,' Langham said.

'As I said the other day, the attraction was the locality, not my father. It's a beautiful part of the world. I missed it, living in London.'

Mallory asked, 'How would you describe your relationship with him more recently?'

Annabelle thought about that. 'We rubbed along. He admired me for what I'd achieved as a GP; it was at his insistence that I trained for the medical profession, after all. I had little say in the matter. Now, if that will be all . . .'

'Of course.'

She gave Mallory a dazzling smile, nodded to Langham, and stepped from the study.

'Well,' Langham said when they were alone, 'I think you've made an impression there.'

Mallory looked dubious. 'You think so?'

'Play your cards right, bag Connaught's killer, and you'll have her eating out of your hand in gratitude.'

'I should cocoa,' Mallory murmured. He moved to the piano and gazed down at where the body had lain. 'So between two and four,' he said, 'the killer comes along and is let in by Connaught, who is sufficiently at his ease to turn his back on whoever it was and walk behind the piano.'

Langham looked at him. 'What for?'

'Come again.'

Langham regarded the space behind the piano. 'It's just occurred to me, Jeff. Why would he walk behind the piano? It's a narrow gap. There's nothing behind it. Why might Connaught have walked between it and the window?'

'Now you come to mention it,' Mallory said, 'it does seem strange. Perhaps he wasn't behind the piano when the killer looped the wire around his neck and throttled him. Perhaps the ensuing struggle took him there.'

'But the wire would have drawn blood pretty damned fast, so there'd be evidence of it somewhere other than where it was, in a great pool around his head. And I found not so much as a splash anywhere else.'

'And nor did the forensic boys,' Mallory said.

'So he must have been standing just behind the piano when the killer struck,' Langham went on. 'But, as I say, *why*?'

'That's one to keep in mind, Don,' Mallory said. He took one last look around the study. 'Right, shall we go and get the interviews out of the way?'

Langham followed him out into the sunlight.

EIGHTEEN

Mallory sank into an armchair and looked around him. 'Well, this is certainly the most sumptuous room I've ever conducted an interview in.'

'Bit different from the cells at Scotland Yard, sir?' Detective Sergeant Greaves said, taking the armchair next to Mallory. Langham thought that Greaves was a little in awe of Mallory. Not that the Scotland Yard man was at all overbearing or made a display of his authority; his manner was deceptively quiet and easy-going.

Langham seated himself on a dining chair before the window, crossed his legs and opened his notebook on his lap.

Greaves said, 'I've had everyone gather in the library, sir.'

'Very good.' Mallory consulted his notebook. 'Let's have Lady Cecelia Albrighton along first, shall we?'

Greaves left the room and closed the door behind him.

'Of everyone Connaught summoned here for the weekend,' Langham said, 'Lady Cee is the only one who didn't seem to bear him any grudge. Apparently, they had an affair during the war, and Connaught wanted to apologize for something.'

'We need to find out what that was, then,' Mallory said, and looked up as Lady Cecelia entered the room, followed by Greaves. The dowager looked even frailer and greyer today; she smiled at the men and lowered herself slowly into the armchair indicated by Mallory.

'I'd like to assure you that this is a mere formality,' he began. 'I'm sure you understand that I must follow a protocol and speak to everyone present at the time of the incident.'

'I understand entirely, Inspector, and I'll do my best to assist you in any way possible.'

She looked across at Langham, clearly puzzled by his presence, and Mallory explained. 'Donald is assisting me in his official capacity as a private investigator, Lady Cecelia.'

She smiled. 'I did wonder at some of your earlier questions, young man,' she said.

Mallory looked down at his notebook. 'Now, I understand that you knew Denbigh Connaught during the war.'

'That is correct,' she said. 'With my husband, I ran an estate in south Lincolnshire, and we gave over a considerable amount of our land to the war effort.'

'And Connaught was drafted in, as a conscientious objector, to work on the land?'

'He and a dozen other men and women.' She paused, looked up and gazed beyond the inspector, her watery grey eyes distant. 'He was a little different from the others: older, for one thing – perhaps forty at the time. And he was very well educated – and by that I mean he was exceptionally well read. He read the Greeks in the original and was a published novelist. If I am to be honest, Inspector, at the time I felt I was somewhat culturally sequestered up there in Lincolnshire. I had been married ten years, and my husband was of a practical mindset. He managed the estate, hunted to hounds and shot pheasant, and that was the extent of his interests. I must admit that the county set bored me terribly.'

'So when Connaught arrived . . .'

She gave a thin smile. 'I would have found Denbigh interesting, whatever the circumstances, but, as it happened, I had recently discovered my husband's infidelity. Denbigh was relatively young, single and handsome, and we shared an interest in literature and the arts.'

'Precisely when was this, Lady Cecelia?'

'We first met in May 1940,' she replied. 'And our affair began later that summer.'

'And lasted for?'

'Almost a year.'

Mallory laboriously wrote that down; buying himself time, Langham thought, in which to formulate his next question. Lady Cecelia sat stiffly upright, indomitable in her posture, yet vulnerable in her frailness.

'I wonder if you might tell me how the affair ended?'

She fixed Mallory with her grey eyes. 'Denbigh walked out on me. He told me he was leaving – he'd requested a posting to a farm in Kent – and departed a day later. I was . . . I don't mind admitting that I was devastated. I loved Denbigh. I . . . I was even thinking of leaving my husband for him. His leaving crushed me, extinguished my dreams. Also . . .' she began, and stopped suddenly, staring down at her wrinkled hands. 'Also, the fact was that Denbigh left me with child.'

Langham looked up from his notebook and stared at Lady Cecelia.

Mallory nodded, smiling compassionately at the woman. 'Was this the reason for Denbigh's leaving you?'

'No . . . He said he was leaving before I told him that I was bearing his child. I begged him to stay, pleaded with him. Then I did tell him about . . .' She shook her head. 'But he was adamant. Our affair was over.' She stared down at her clenched hands, then looked up and went on, 'When my husband discovered that I was pregnant, and obviously not by him, he told me he would be seeking a divorce. A month later I lost my baby. A boy. The effect of this, so soon after Denbigh's desertion . . . I am afraid I suffered a nervous breakdown, and I was hospitalized for quite some time.' She smiled at the men. 'When I was discharged, I found myself a small apartment in London, put the past behind me and started a new life.'

Mallory nodded. 'So, all things considered, you had reasonable grounds for disliking Denbigh Connaught – even hating the man?'

Lady Cecelia returned his smile. 'All things considered, Inspector, one might assume so. However, you would be mistaken. Oh, at the time I resented his desertion, his selfishness – but at the same time I loved the man. Denbigh Connaught is . . . *was* . . . a special person. He was a true artist and incredibly ambitious. I could not find it in me to hate him.'

Gently, Mallory asked, 'Did he say why he was leaving you, Lady Cecelia?'

She stared into space, smiling sadly to herself. At last she looked up. 'Not in so many words, no,' she said. 'Hard though it is to admit, I think he thought I wasn't good enough for him, intellectually. I gave him nothing but my . . . my rather pathetic devotion, and that was not enough. He wanted more . . . something that, I'm afraid – as he remained single for the rest of his life – I think no woman could give him.'

'So when he contacted you a little while ago, inviting you down here for the weekend and offering an apology . . .?'

She regarded Mallory. 'What is your question, Inspector?'

Mallory smiled to himself. 'How did you regard the invitation, Lady Cecelia? Were you minded to refuse?'

'No, young man, I certainly wasn't. I was intrigued. I had, of course, kept abreast of Denbigh's career, and read all his novels as they came out, and devoured the infrequent interviews he consented to give to the broadsheets and literary journals. I wanted to see what kind of man Denbigh Connaught had become, and I suppose – you will think me foolish for this – I suppose a small, romantic, silly part of me did wonder if perhaps now, years later, something of what we shared back then might not be rekindled.' She smiled at the detective inspector. 'But, of course, I was being unrealistic.'

Mallory read from his notes. 'I understand that you spoke with Connaught in his study on Saturday morning? Would you care to tell me what he said?'

'It . . . it was something of a shock to see him again, after so long. Time had not been kind to him, Inspector. He had gone to seed and gained weight. He had been lean and strong, but he'd . . . he had bloated, somewhat. And also, I thought, he had lost some of his passion for life, his intellectual curiosity. He seemed like a sad, defeated man. But as for what he said . . . He spoke fondly of our time together, and said he'd treated me terribly, and that he regretted his behaviour.'

'And that was the extent of your conversation? He apologized—'

'He apologized, yes, and went on to say that he understood – and I have no idea how he knew this – that I was living in what might be described as reduced circumstances. I could not deny the fact. I struggle, in these times of privation, to make ends meet. Denbigh knew this, as I said, and went on to say that he intended to make me a gift, a small measure of atonement, he said, and that he would counter no objection.'

'A gift?' Mallory echoed.

'He had a number of paintings that he'd collected over the years, many of which were quite valuable. He said that I could choose a number, to the value of ten thousand pounds, and that he would arrange everything with his solicitor.'

Greaves whistled, then coloured and apologized quickly.

Mallory asked, 'And you accepted, of course?'

'I refused, at first. I had my pride, Inspector, and I suppose that small romantic part of me that had wanted more from Denbigh Connaught was indignant at the thought of being bought off, as it were, by this gift. However . . . well, Denbigh broke down. He wept like a child, almost begging me to take the paintings. I must admit that I was shocked, saddened at the sight of his distress. When he said that I *must* take them, to save his sanity, I relented and agreed to his offer.'

'Do you know if he had already approached his solicitor with a view to . . .?' Mallory began.

'No, he had not – he said that he would do so, first thing on Monday morning. Of course, now . . .' She looked up. 'Not that I in any way regret the fact that I will not receive the paintings, Inspector. Beside the fact of what happened to poor Denbigh, that is immaterial.'

Mallory nodded and wrote in his notebook for a minute before looking up. 'I must ask you about Sunday afternoon, Lady Cecelia. I wonder if you could tell me something of your whereabouts, and movements, between two and four o'clock?'

'Of course. I finished lunch just before one and spent perhaps two hours in the walled garden with *Mansfield Park* – Austen is such a solace, I find. A little after three, I think it was, I went for a short walk. I spoke to Pandora briefly on the side lawn, then proceeded down the drive and along the lane for a little way, before returning to my room at some point before four.'

'And other than Pandora Jade, did you see anyone in the grounds of the house or in the lane?'

She thought about it, then shook her head. 'No, no one.'

Mallory nodded and finished writing in his notebook. He smiled. 'Thank you for your time, Lady Cecelia. I might need to chat again at some point, but that's all for now.'

Lady Cecelia smiled, inclined her head to each of the men in turn, and left the room.

'Game old bird,' Greaves said.

'I'll say,' Mallory agreed. He looked from Greaves to Langham. 'Any thoughts?'

Langham said, 'Try as I might, I can't see Lady Cee garrotting Connaught. Or, for that matter, hiring someone to do the job. I think she was sincere when she said she no longer resented him. And anyway, what motive might she have had? He was about to give her ten grand worth of paintings, after all.'

Greaves said, 'I agree. She'd be the most unlikely strangler I've ever come across.'

'Right,' Mallory said, regarding his notebook. 'Who's next? Let's have Colonel Haxby, shall we?'

NINETEEN

The old soldier stumped into the room and fell into the armchair, his artificial leg sticking out before him. The reek of alcohol filled the room and his right hand was shaking uncontrollably.

'Don't suppose,' he said as he eyed Mallory with his liquid green gaze, 'that there's any chance of a teensy-weensy drink, is there? Just to steady the old nerves.'

Mallory said, 'Nerves?'

'Manner of speaking,' Haxby said. 'Nip before the battle, as it were.'

The detective inspector considered the request, then nodded to Greaves. 'Just a small one, mind.'

Greaves moved to the bar and poured a finger of Scotch.

'Appreciate it, old boy,' Haxby said as he took the glass. 'Here's mud in your eye.'

Cognizant of the fact that he was unlikely to get a refill, he took a small sip and smacked his lips. 'That's better. Now, how can I help?'

'You knew Denbigh Connaught back in the thirties, I understand?'

'I did indeed. Fast friends. Great chums and all that. Salt of the earth, old Denbigh.'

'When was this, exactly?'

'Met in' – he squinted in recollection – 'in 'thirty-three, I think it was. Savile Club. Great drinker, Denbigh. We hit it off immediately.'

'And then what happened?'

The old soldier blinked. '"Happened", old boy?'

'I understand,' Mallory said, 'that you had a falling-out over something.'

Haxby shifted uncomfortably, scowling. 'Long time ago. Water under the bridge.'

'And yet, according to more than one witness, when you arrived here on Saturday you were prepared to shoot Connaught dead.'

'Was I? By crikey, I don't recall . . .'

'According to my notes,' Mallory said, 'you're on record as saying, "I've come to shoot the yellow belly."'

'I am? I said that? Must've been blotto, is all I can say. Booze talking, don't you know?'

'And then on Saturday, after your meeting with Connaught, you were ready to shoot yourself.'

'Blue funk. Wouldn't really have . . .'

'Why did Connaught want to see you, Colonel? Why did he summon you down here?'

Colonel Haxby raised the glass to his lips, forgot himself and drained it in one go, then frowned into the empty glass.

'Well?' Mallory prompted.

'Old times' sake,' Haxby said. 'He wanted to catch up—'

'Don't talk rot,' Mallory snapped. 'Now tell me, why did Connaught wish to apologize to you?'

'Apologize?' He shook his head. 'Long time ago . . . Can't rightly recall.'

Mallory nodded, sat back and said almost casually, 'Do you have any idea, Colonel, what happens to people who obstruct the police in the course of their duties?'

Haxby stared down at his glass; he looked so forlorn that Langham felt sorry for him.

Mallory went on, 'A few days in the cells, Colonel. And I'm told the only drink you get inside is water and weak tea. Now, in your own time, why did Connaught wish to apologize to you?'

'As I said, long time ago . . . Twenty years. The old memory, y'see . . . a bit vague.'

Mallory turned to Greaves and said, businesslike, 'Detective Sergeant, is that cell at St Austell currently unoccupied?'

'Ready and waiting, sir.'

'What say we continue our little discussion, Colonel, down at the station, with an overnight stay in the cell for afters? Alternatively, I can refill your glass and we can sit here, all nice and cosy, and you can tell me all about what happened back in the thirties.'

For a second, Langham thought that the old soldier would hold out. Then Mallory's threat hit home and, sheepishly, he held out his empty glass.

'And make it a big one, Greaves,' Mallory said. 'I'm sure the colonel has plenty to tell us.'

Greaves filled the glass and passed it to Haxby, who raised it to his lips with a shaking hand and drank.

'So, Colonel . . . Why did you fall out with Connaught back then, and why did he wish to apologize?'

Haxby slumped in his seat, his lips pursed as he stared down at his outstretched leg. 'We'd had an all-day session at some Soho drinking club,' he murmured. 'Must have been eight in the evening when we left. Denbigh had his car. Insisted on driving, even though he was blotto. I was too drunk to object. I lived in Highbury at the time, Denbigh further north somewhere. So off we went.' He fell silent, staring down at the glass clutched in his right hand. 'Off we went . . . I fell asleep, as you do. Warm in the car, a few drinks inside . . . Next thing, screech of brakes and I hit the windscreen. When I come to my senses, Denbigh's dragging me across the front seat, lodging me behind the wheel. I was too kaylied to twig. Next thing, a police car pulls up and two constables pull me out and take me into custody. Thought it odd, at the time – no sign of old Denbigh. Next morning, a sergeant enters the cell and charges me with manslaughter while under the influence. Clipped a fellow in Islington, apparently. Poor chap hit the kerb, died instantly. I protested, of course. Told 'em what'd *really* happened. Days later, before the magistrate, there's Denbigh, claiming he left the club in a taxi but not before giving me the keys to his car because, he said, I'd claimed I was sober enough to drive. He even had the taxi driver to vouch for him. I got off lightly, all things considered. A year in the Scrubs and a fifty-pound fine. I did eight months in the end . . . And who invited me round to his place a few days after I was released, all tears and remorse, and a brown paper envelope full of ten-quid notes?' Haxby stared at his drink, his expression desolate. 'God help the fool I was, I took the money. Five hundred pounds. Connaught wanted to go back to how things were in the old days, good old drinking chums again and no hard feelings. But I was man enough to tell him to go to hell, and I never saw him again from that day till this weekend. Oh, I dreamed of getting even with him, in the months after I got out. I even thought of killing the swine. But good sense, p'raps even cowardice, prevailed . . . Then the war came along. And, y'know, I thought I'd found my calling. Never been happier in my life.' He looked up at Mallory and knocked on his false leg. 'And then a Jerry landmine did for me.'

Greaves reached out, took the old soldier's empty glass and filled it up without a word.

'Much obliged, sir,' Haxby said, and drained half the measure.

Mallory said, 'And when you received the letter from Connaught, inviting you down for the weekend and offering an apology? What made you accept, Colonel?'

Haxby considered the question. 'Curiosity, I think. Wanted to see how the blighter had fared. Wanted to see how he might see fit to apologize, how he *could* possibly apologize for what happened.'

'And? What did he say, when you saw Connaught on Saturday?'

The colonel sighed. 'Must admit I was well cut. Fortified, you might say. Dim recollection of Connaught saying he didn't know what'd come over him that night. He was deeply, truly sorry. And . . . and he said he wanted to make it up to me. Said he'd give me a gift – ten thousand pounds, would you believe? Mine, for what I'd suffered back in 'thirty-four . . .'

'And did you accept?'

'D'you know something, sir? I can't remember. Don't have a ruddy clue. Thing was, seeing him again, him talking about the accident, what he did . . . He brought it all back again. Brought back all my anger at the terrible injustice, brought back how powerless I'd been . . . How powerless I still was, and what a bloody mess I'd made of my life.' He looked from Mallory to Greaves, and then across at Langham. 'And all I wanted to do was to end it all . . .' He laughed, but without humour. 'But thanks to you, Mr Langham, thanks to you, I live to drink another day.' The old soldier lifted his glass in a toast and drank, and Langham was unable to work out whether his gratitude was in any way ironic.

Mallory finished making his notes, then said, 'On Sunday afternoon, Colonel . . . if you could tell me where you were between the times of two o'clock and four.'

The colonel pointed a shaking finger to the chair that Greaves was occupying. 'Right there, sir, in that very chair. From straight after lunch until later, whenever it was that young Royce found the body. Helped myself to a little snifter or two and snoozed on and off all afternoon.'

'I take it you didn't see anyone during those times?'

Haxby closed one eye as he thought back. 'Big chap, the nancy boy. Elder – that's the fellow. Pranced in at one point, I recall. Then later everyone came in and the drink flowed.'

'And you haven't seen any strangers hanging about the place over the weekend?'

He shook his head. 'Not that I recall, no.'

Mallory sighed. 'Right. Well, I think that will be all, Colonel.'

Haxby looked startled. 'What? You're letting me go? Scot-free? You're not arresting me, Inspector?'

Again, Langham was unable to discern if there was a note of irony in the colonel's words, or whether he was truly surprised at his reprieve.

'You're free to go, Colonel.'

The old soldier climbed unsteadily to his feet, swayed, and then snapped a salute at the detective inspector, turned on his heel and weaved his way from the room.

'Well, there we are,' Mallory said as the door closed. 'Someone else with a grudge to bear against Connaught. And a hell of a grudge, at that. I don't know about you, but I can't see the colonel overcoming Connaught and strangling him.'

'How about hiring someone to do his dirty work?' Greaves said.

Langham shook his head. 'Why leave it so long? And if he did arrange a hit man, why would the colonel risk being on the scene at the time? It doesn't add up.'

'I think we all agree on that,' Mallory said. 'I don't know about you, but watching the colonel down his whisky made me thirsty. How about a quick one before we haul Wilson Royce in here?'

They moved to the bar and Greaves poured the Scotch.

TWENTY

Ryland drew up along the lane by Rowan Cottage, Smarden, at one o'clock. Minutes later, a short, grey-haired, dapper man left the cottage with a Jack Russell terrier on a lead and walked towards the village. He couldn't have been going that far, what with the dog, so Ryland lit a cigarette and waited.

Framed in the windscreen, the cottage and its leafy surroundings looked like something from an old painting – which would be entirely appropriate if Ryland's suspicions were correct: that Signor Venturi was the middleman in some dodgy fine art scam.

The cottage was located on the outskirts of the village, surrounded by orchards and hop fields. The area brought back memories. In the twenties, when he'd been a nipper, his ma and pa had come hop picking during the summer holidays. It'd been a right lark for a boy of ten, and he'd loved the countryside then. Now, the country was fine for the occasional holiday – but give him the Smoke any day. He didn't understand Donald and Maria's desire to buy a cottage in the sticks, especially as they had that luxurious pad in Kensington.

Still, as long as Don didn't decide to jack it in at the detective agency, everything would be rosy. Ryland had big plans on that front: they'd been doing well of late, and he'd been mulling over a move from Wandsworth. He'd go over the finances with Annie when he had the chance.

The church bell had just struck one thirty when the little man reappeared at the end of the lane, a folded paper tucked under his arm. He walked up the garden path, unlocked the front door and disappeared inside.

Ryland climbed from the car and approached the cottage.

The way to play it with foreigners, he'd always found, was to be very correct and polite: play the English gentleman and speak clearly, as some of those from abroad didn't have a firm grasp on the lingo.

He walked up the garden path and rapped on the door.

The dog yapped. A shape appeared beyond the stained glass set into the upper half of the door. It opened a fraction and a thin face,

topped with grey hair, peered out. 'Can I help you?' the man said
in excellent English.

Ryland smiled. 'I'm awfully sorry to bother you, Signor Venturi.'
He showed his private investigator's accreditation to the bemused
old man, then went on, 'I'm working on a murder investigation and
I would be grateful if you could assist me with a minute of your
time.'

'A murder investigation?' The man was in his seventies, with sad
eyes and a lined face. Ryland wondered at Venturi's experiences
during the war, and what might have brought him to Britain.

'I understand an acquaintance of yours might have been involved
. . . as a witness. If I could come in?'

'Of course, of course.' Venturi opened the door and Ryland
stepped into a small, neat hallway. The old man spoke to the dog
in what Ryland assumed was Italian, and the dog sat obediently
on its haunches and watched as its owner led Ryland into a cosy
front room hung with an array of watercolours depicting English
country scenes.

'This is most upsetting,' Venturi said. 'Please, take a seat.'

Ryland lowered himself into a chintz-covered armchair, and
Venturi sat on the opposite sofa. Everything about the man, from
his gently retiring manner to his cosy chocolate-box cottage,
suggested that he was far from being the middleman in some
nefarious art racket. But if there was one thing Ryland had learned
over the years, it was that appearances, more often than not, were
deceptive.

'Would you care for a cup of tea, or perhaps coffee?'

'I won't bother you, Signor Venturi, and I won't keep you long.'
He looked around the room. 'A very nice place you've got yourself
here, if I may say so.'

Venturi smiled. 'It is the culmination of my dreams, Mr Ryland.
During the war, when my country was invaded by the Germans,
and I was imprisoned, I dreamed of coming here and living in the
countryside. I studied here in my twenties, in London, and came to
love England.'

'Your country was invaded? But I thought you were Italian.'

Venturi smiled. 'My grandfather was Italian, but he moved to
what later became Yugoslavia in the 1880s. In 1941, when the Nazis
invaded, I worked against them in my little way, forging papers and
documents for the Resistance.' He shook his head. 'And then I was

betrayed in 'forty-four, captured and imprisoned. I would have been executed, I am sure, but the end of the war came just in time.'

'Close shave.'

Venturi smiled. 'As you say, a close shave,' he said. 'The thought of a cottage in the English countryside, Mr Ryland, sustained me throughout those dark days.' He waved all this away, dismissing the past. 'But how might I be of assistance? You said that an acquaintance of mine . . .'

'I understand that you have a business partner, a certain Mr Wilson Royce?'

The man blinked. He looked bemused for a second. 'I know Mr Royce, yes, but I would not call him a business partner.'

'What would you call him, then?' Ryland asked.

'Mr Royce put some work my way – a lot of work, I must say.'

'Work?' The more he listened to Signor Venturi, the more convinced he was that the little foreigner was no criminal.

Venturi gestured around the room, indicating the watercolours that adorned the walls. 'All these, Mr Ryland, are my own work.'

Ryland stood and examined the closest paintings, country scenes depicting open fields, distant villages and church spires.

'All scenes of rural Kent,' Venturi said, 'my adopted home.'

'Very nice. You're very talented.'

'You're too kind. I dabbled in watercolours in Yugoslavia, where I worked as an illustrator for various journals in the thirties. I fled to England after the war, when the Communists came to power. I began painting watercolours again and sold them to a small gallery in London.'

'Let me guess,' Ryland said. 'A gallery owned by a certain William Harker, right?'

Venturi beamed. 'But you know him? Mr Harker was just starting out, in 'forty-seven, and sold contemporary artwork before he began to specialize in fine art of the seventeenth century.'

'I see,' Ryland said. 'And I'm guessing again, but was it Mr Harker who introduced you to Wilson Royce?'

'That is correct, Mr Ryland.'

Ryland frowned. 'And Royce wanted to sell you some paintings?'

'Sell me . . .?' Venturi looked puzzled. 'No, not *sell*. You see, he wanted me to copy certain eighteenth-century painters whom he admired. He was interested principally in the work of John Varley and John Robert Cozens. He would supply me with high-quality art books containing plates of the originals, and he said he would pay me handsomely – five pounds per picture – for copies.' Venturi held up a warning hand. 'And before you say that this could be construed as far from legal, let me assure you that I ensured that I signed the back of each watercolour with my own name, so that they could not be passed off, years down the line, as originals.'

'I see,' Ryland said. 'And how many copies did you produce for Wilson Royce?'

'Perhaps fifty, over the course of the past year.'

'And did Royce tell you what he intended doing with the copies?'

'Why, they were for his own pleasure, Mr Ryland, although he did say that he might give away one or two as presents.'

'When was the last time you made a copy for him?'

'A month ago,' Venturi said. 'I haven't seen him since then.' He hesitated. 'But you mentioned a murder . . .?'

'Wilson Royce worked as the business manager for a writer, Denbigh Connaught, who was murdered at the weekend.' Ryland paused. 'Now, did Royce happen to mention anything about Connaught or his work to you, Signor Venturi?'

The old man shook his head. 'He said very little about himself. He discussed, mainly, his passion for eighteenth-century watercolours. Mr Royce isn't . . . is not in trouble, is he?'

Ryland smiled. 'That remains to be seen,' he said. 'We're eliminating suspects, as the police say.'

'I cannot imagine Mr Royce being involved,' Venturi said. 'He was such a pleasant young man. I felt like a father to him.'

'You did?'

'I could not help myself,' Venturi said. 'And I also felt sorry for him.'

'And why was that?'

'You see, his father died when Mr Royce was just five years old. Such an unpleasant story. He was knocked down in the street by a speeding car, and, what is worse, young Mr Royce saw it all happen, right in front of his eyes. It must have left a terrible mental scar on him.' He smiled sadly. 'We are all haunted by the events of the past, are we not?'

Ryland returned the old man's sad smile and rose to his feet.

'Thank you for your time, Signor Venturi. I'd better be making tracks.'

'Are you sure you wouldn't care for a cup of tea?'

''Fraid not, but thanks all the same. Duty calls, and all that. Appointment back in the Smoke.'

Venturi saw him to the door; Ryland thanked him once again and returned to his car.

He sat there for a while, lost in thought.

'Fishy,' he said to himself. 'Ve–ry fishy.'

Why had Wilson Royce paid Venturi a fiver a time to make copies of old paintings? A passion for eighteenth-century watercolours? Likely story! A desire to help out the old boy with regular commissions? Poppycock. Ryland didn't have Wilson Royce down as a patron of the arts. Far from it . . .

He started the engine and drove back to London.

He thought that another visit to Mr Harker might be in order.

TWENTY-ONE

'So, according to your chappie Ryland,' Mallory said, 'Wilson Royce is up to something shady in the art market? How do you think we should play it during the interview?'

Langham added a touch more soda to his whisky. 'Keep mum on that score, I think. It might not have anything to do with Connaught's murder, and we don't want to tip our hand at this stage. I'll contact Ralph later and see if he's come up with anything further on Royce.'

Mallory nodded. 'Right you are.'

'I've heard all about Royce from people in the village,' Greaves said. 'Fancies himself as a bit of a charmer with the girls. From what I hear, he doesn't get very far.'

'Probably tries too hard,' Mallory said. 'Believe me, the way to play things with the ladies, Greaves, is easy does it.'

'So that's how you're approaching Annabelle Connaught is it, Jeff?' Langham asked.

Mallory winked. 'Just you watch.'

'Now there's a beauty and no mistake,' Greaves said. 'You're setting your sights high there, sir.'

'That's as maybe,' Mallory said. 'What's the village gossip on her, Greaves?'

'Local girl made good,' the younger man said. 'And she likes to let everyone know the fact. She has the reputation of being a bit remote and superior, like.'

Mallory sipped his Scotch and asked casually, 'Do you know if she's seeing anyone?'

'A couple of years ago she was engaged to a local landowner's son, but apparently she broke it off.'

'Do you know why?'

Greaves shrugged. 'Word in the village was that young Peters didn't like her gadding off to London every month and seeing the Chelsea set up there. So she gave him the old heave-ho.'

Langham thought back to what Maria had told him at Kittiwake Cove: that Annabelle had had an affair with Wilson Royce.

He asked Greaves, 'And since then? I heard that she had a fling with Royce when he first came here.'

Mallory looked up. 'With *Royce*?'

Greaves was dubious. 'I haven't heard that, sir. Annabelle Connaught likes men, not boys. She's way out of Royce's league.'

'Where did you hear about him and Annabelle, Don?' Mallory asked.

Langham shrugged. 'It was something she told Maria. Annabelle said that she'd had a brief fling with Royce, before she saw through him.'

Mallory nodded and drained his Scotch. 'Right, shall we get back to it? Toddle along and fetch Royce, would you, Greaves?'

When the sergeant had left the room, Mallory said, 'So . . . what if Connaught didn't like his daughter messing about with Royce, and he warned Royce off?'

Langham frowned. 'You mean, if that were so, then Royce would have a grievance against Connaught?'

'I'm just suggesting the possibility, however remote it might be.'

Langham adjusted his dining chair before the window. 'Something about Royce suggests to me that he wouldn't be cut up that much about being either dumped or warned off. He'd just try his luck on the next available woman.'

The door opened and Wilson Royce entered the room.

He had changed from his golfing tweeds of the other day but, continuing the sporting motif, was wearing cricket whites and a blazer, along with his old school tie. His blond fringe flopped over his eyes, and from time to time he flicked it back into place with a negligent gesture. He gave a wolfish smile, his eye-tooth showing.

Then he saw Langham across the room and his eyes narrowed slightly, as if with suspicion.

Langham wondered, for a second, if Royce had suddenly recognized him from the previous Thursday – or whether he was merely wondering why he was sitting in on the interview.

'I'm sure you'll appreciate that we must speak to everyone who was on the scene yesterday afternoon,' Mallory said. 'Just to build up a comprehensive picture of where people were at the time.'

'Of course.'

Mallory referred to his notebook. 'I understand that from just after lunch until a little before five you were attending to papers in Denbigh Connaught's old study in the west wing?'

'That's right. I was having a clear-out, on Mr Connaught's instructions. Over the years he'd accumulated a lot of papers which he didn't wish to keep.'

'What kind of papers?'

Royce shrugged. 'Old letters from readers going back years. Leaflets and circulars that he'd never thrown away, old magazines and newspapers he'd kept for research purposes.'

'What did you do with them?'

'Burnt them. There's a brazier in the cobbled area at the back of the house where the dustbins are kept, beside the kitchen garden.'

Mallory leafed through his notebook, then leaned forward and said, 'I sketched a map of the house earlier. If you could show me where the kitchen garden is located, and the brazier.'

Royce studied the drawing and pointed with a long finger to an area beyond the west wing. 'Just there.'

Mallory nodded and thanked him. 'So you carried the papers through the front door, around the house, past the French windows here and along the back of the house to the kitchen garden?'

'That's right.'

Mallory studied the map, frowning. 'But surely there's a door in the kitchen, and it'd be quicker for you to have used that from the study in the west wing?'

'It might appear so, sir, but actually there's a back staircase from Mr Connaught's study to the entrance hall; there was not much in it, but the route I took was slightly shorter.'

'Quite. So . . . How many journeys to the brazier would you say you made that afternoon?'

Royce thought about it. 'Perhaps a dozen. In between times I was going through the papers to ensure there was nothing Mr Connaught might have wished to keep. All in all, it took me a good five hours.'

'And I see from the map that going by this route, along the back of the house, you would have passed close to the hedge that shielded Connaught's study.'

'That's right.'

Mallory allowed a silence to develop as he studied his notebook. 'You could, had you so desired, have slipped around the hedge and crossed to the study?'

'If I had so desired, yes, sir.'

'And did you?'

Royce gave another lazy vulpine smile. 'I knew better than to disturb Mr Connaught. It was one of the first things he impressed upon me when I started the job. He was not to be interrupted, for any reason, while he was working.'

'And I take it you saw no one else approach the study, either a guest or a stranger?'

'That's right. As far as I was aware, no one went near it.'

'And yet, manifestly, someone did.'

'Manifestly,' Royce said.

Mallory flipped through his notebook, found what he was looking for and leaned back. 'How did you come by the post of Connaught's business manager, Mr Royce?'

'I wrote to Mr Connaught, offering my services.'

'Wasn't that a rather . . . unconventional approach?'

Royce shrugged lazily. 'Perhaps. But I don't like to be conventional, sir. I find that one must take every opportunity that life affords, and that to go by the book leads one nowhere.'

Langham wondered if there was a faint note of mockery in the young man's words.

'Why specifically Connaught?' Mallory asked. 'Or did you write to many of the great and the good, offering your services?'

'No, just to Mr Connaught,' Royce replied. 'I admired his books. I considered him one of our finest writers. I must admit that I didn't expect him to take up my offer, and I was flattered when he called me down for an interview, and then offered me a modest stipend.'

'And this was a year ago?'

'A little over.'

'And you have been content in the post?'

'Very.'

'And you spend your free time . . .?'

'Quite often in London, seeing friends.'

Mallory nodded, paused while reading his notes and then said, 'Shortly after your arrival here, Mr Royce, I understand you conducted an affair with Connaught's daughter, Annabelle?'

Langham looked from Mallory to Royce as the young man smiled, shifted position and crossed his legs easily. 'Wherever did you hear that?' he asked.

'So you didn't?'

'We had an occasional drink in the Fisherman's in the village,' Royce said. 'Perhaps the locals saw us once or twice, and a rumour spread. But no' – the young man shook his head – 'Annabelle Connaught is not my type.'

Mallory nodded. 'And your relationship with Denbigh Connaught?'

'I would describe it as impersonal and businesslike, sir. Mr Connaught, despite his brilliance as a novelist, was not an easy person to like. He could be . . . prickly, let's say.'

'As his business manager, were you aware of his holding any animosity towards anyone?'

Royce thought about it. 'There were one or two critics he would gladly have poisoned, I think, and a couple of fellow novelists he disliked intensely. But he had little to do with these people; he rarely ventured up to London.'

'And as for what other people felt about Connaught – did he make any enemies in the area?'

'Not as far as I'm aware. He wasn't that sociable, to be honest. Some people describe him as a recluse, but I wouldn't go that far.'

'And so the fact that someone saw fit to brutally murder him?'

'It's shocking, is all I can say. And quite mystifying.'

'Did he mention to you why he had invited the guests down for this weekend?'

'He didn't.'

'He wrote the letters of invitation himself, or was he in the habit of dictating them to you?'

'He wrote them himself,' Royce said. 'I am . . . or rather I *was* . . . his business manager, not his secretary.'

'Did he post the letters himself?'

'No, he gave them to me to post, along with his other correspondence.'

'So you knew the identities of his guests?'

'That's right. In one or two instances, I had to track down their current addresses.'

Mallory looked across at Greaves, then at Langham. 'Any further questions, gentlemen?'

Langham removed his pipe. 'I was wondering at the state of Denbigh Connaught's finances,' he said. 'As his business manager, I take it that you had access to these details?'

Royce looked guarded. 'That's right.'

'And was Connaught a rich man, would you say?'

The young man hesitated. 'He was not as well-off as I'd assumed, on first taking the post. His later books had not sold as well as his earlier ones. Still, he wasn't exactly a pauper.'

'Do you know what he was worth?'

Royce rocked his head back and forth. 'Aside from the house, he had perhaps thirty thousand pounds in the bank. He didn't bother about stocks and shares, or bonds.'

Langham nodded. 'Thank you.'

'Very well,' Mallory said. 'That'll be all for now.'

Royce rose from the armchair, nodded to the detectives and, with a lingering look at Langham, made his way from the room.

'Slippery customer,' Greaves said. 'Can't say I took to him.'

'I come across his type all the time,' Mallory said. 'Come up from Oxbridge and think they own the world, swan into posts at the BBC or the Foreign Office and regard everyone with a proper job as menials.'

'He manages to avoid being arrogant by a whisker,' Langham said, 'but can't stop himself from being superior.'

'Can't see why Annabelle took a shine to him,' Mallory said, frowning. 'But why would Royce lie about their relationship?'

Langham pulled out his pipe and began stuffing it. 'Pride,' he said. 'He's not the type to admit he had an affair and that she ended it.'

Mallory looked at his notebook. 'I'll have Charles Elder in next.' He looked across at Langham. 'I won't bother to question Maria.'

'I'll vouch for her,' Langham said.

Greaves slipped from the rooms and returned with Charles Elder. The interview was over in five minutes. Charles had left his room at around three thirty on Sunday afternoon and had glimpsed Wilson

Royce through the French windows of the drawing room, where Colonel Haxby had been snoozing in an armchair. On a short stroll along the drive, he'd passed a minute or two in conversation with Pandora Jade.

He had last seen Denbigh Connaught at school forty years ago, when they had parted on bad terms – something of an understatement, Langham thought – although he said he'd borne Connaught no ill-will. 'I would have been the last person to wish him dead. You see, he wanted my agency to represent his literary interests.'

When Charles left the room, Langham said, 'And I'll vouch for Charles, too. He hasn't a violent bone in his body.'

'But he's bloody huge,' Greaves said. 'He could easily have overcome Connaught.'

The vision that this conjured in Langham's mind's eye was laughable. 'Believe me, Greaves, Charles didn't do it.'

Mallory said, 'Right, we're almost done. We'll have Pandora Jade in next, and I'll finish off with Monty Connaught and Annabelle.'

Greaves left the room, and Langham drew on his pipe and said, 'Something's just occurred to me, Jeff.'

'Go on.'

'Lady Cee mentioned that Connaught wanted to give her some paintings from his collection. After what Ralph's uncovered in London, it'd be worth going through the collection with Annabelle to see if she thinks there's anything missing.'

'In case Royce decided to help himself?'

'He'd be a damned fool to bite the hand that feeds, but you never know.'

Mallory nodded. 'I'll have a word with Annabelle about the paintings.'

The door opened and Pandora Jade strode into the room.

TWENTY-TWO

She's an odd-looking woman, Langham thought as she settled herself in the armchair. With her white-powdered face, crimson lips and jet-black coal-scuttle hairstyle, she looked as if she were about to take the stage in a pre-war Berlin cabaret. In contrast to the artifice of her make-up, she wore a pair of baggy green corduroy trousers and a man's white shirt splattered with paint.

She glanced across at Langham as she lit a cigarette. 'I had you down as a copper at our very first meeting,' she said.

'Donald is a private investigator, working with me on the case,' Mallory said.

'Is that so?' she said, regarding Langham. 'Kept schtum about that, eh?'

Mallory interrupted. 'Now, it would seem that in common with some of Denbigh Connaught's other guests, he invited you down here so that he might apologize. Also, I understand that you didn't see eye to eye with Connaught.'

Pandora exhaled a plume of smoke and eyed Mallory narrowly through the rising cloud. 'About a fortnight ago I received the first of his letters stating his desire to apologize, yes. And to be perfectly blunt, I despised the man.'

'Would you care to tell me why, Miss Jade?'

'Would you mind if I told you it was none of your business?'

'But the murder of Denbigh Connaught,' Mallory said, '*is* my business.'

'I assure you that his letters, my presence here and what might have passed between us in the past are of no relevance to Connaught's death.'

'I think you should let me be the judge of that.'

Pandora drew on her cigarette. An American phrase popped into Langham's head, which perfectly described the woman: she was a tough cookie.

'Now,' Mallory said, 'why did Connaught wish to apologize to you?'

'By that, Inspector, do you mean what crisis of conscience brought about his desire to atone, or what was the root cause of his remorse?'

'I think you know very well what I mean,' Mallory said shortly. 'What did he do to you, whenever it was, to prompt his apology now?'

Pandora sighed. 'I met Connaught thirty years ago, in the mid-twenties. I was young, stupid and impressionable. Connaught had just published his first novel to great acclaim. He attended the same West End parties and soirées as I did, knew the same arty set. He was handsome, feted and rich. I was just twenty, and considered one of the up and coming artists on the London scene. It was inevitable that our paths should cross.'

'Don't tell me – you fell for him?'

Something smouldered in Pandora's gaze. 'No, Inspector – Connaught fell for me. Head over heels. I think part of the attraction was that he knew that I could take men or leave them. I think he saw me as a challenge. He wasn't my first male lover, but he was certainly my last. At twenty-five, he was even more vain and selfish than he was in later years, judging by his more recent interviews.'

'That begs the question,' Mallory said, 'what did you see in him?'

Pandora considered the end of her cigarette, then replied, 'He was physically attractive, well-off, and he bought me drinks. At that time of my life I was . . . sybaritic, you might say. One of the bright young things Huxley wrote about. A fling with a handsome young novelist was *de rigueur* for a girl of my age.'

'What happened?'

'What do you think, Inspector? The inevitable.' She stopped, looked across at the bar and said, 'I'd like a drink. G and T, if you don't mind.'

'I'm conducting an interview—' Mallory began.

'You were interviewing the colonel, too, and, according to the old boy, you plied him with booze. I find that telling my life story makes me thirsty.'

Mallory nodded to Greaves, and the younger man crossed to the bar and poured a gin and tonic.

Pandora smiled to herself while Mallory scribbled in his notebook. Greaves passed her the drink.

'Where was I?'

'The "inevitable",' Mallory reminded her.

'Ah, yes, the inevitable. I fell pregnant.' She took a drink and went on, 'I had no interest in keeping the kid, and told Connaught as much. He went off the handle. He said that it was his child, and he wouldn't allow me to go through with its . . . "murder".' She gestured with her cigarette. 'I told him that he had no choice in the matter as I'd already made arrangements.' She stopped, and even now, thirty years later, Langham could see her bitterness at the recollection.

'So he blackmailed me. My father was high up in the Stock Exchange, a pillar of the community. Connaught not only threatened to inform him that I was pregnant and seeking an illegal abortion, but said that he'd spill the beans about my "indiscretions" with women. I was close to my father, and I knew that the scandal would hurt him terribly. I was too petrified to call Connaught's bluff, and agreed to have the child, a girl.' She hesitated, then said, 'Annabelle.'

Langham stopped writing and looked up, startled. 'Annabelle?'

Pandora smiled across at him. 'That's right, Langham.'

He wrote in his note book: *Annabelle Connaught – Pandora's daughter!*

He was about to ask if Annabelle knew that Pandora was her mother, but Mallory went on, 'You obviously didn't keep the baby and bring her up yourself – but why not?'

'Perish the thought. By this time Connaught had moved on and was involved with another woman. To my surprise, and disbelief, he claimed he was serious about her, and intended to marry the poor girl. It was arranged that Annabelle should go to Connaught and be raised by him and his new bride.'

'And you gave up your child without a qualm?' Langham asked.

Pandora smiled and fanned smoke away from her face. 'Call me cold,' she said, 'but I felt not the slightest stirrings of any maternal instinct. I could hardly wait to see the back of the kid and start my life again.'

'According to Annabelle Connaught,' Langham said, 'her mother died when she was very young.'

'Well, Connaught's wife died a year after Annabelle was born, so I suppose it was a lie of convenience on his part.'

Mallory wrote something in his notebook. 'So Annabelle has no idea that you're her mother?'

Pandora smiled. 'And I fully intend to keep it that way, gentlemen. I had no maternal feelings for my daughter back then, and I certainly have none now.'

'You don't think you owe it to Annabelle?' Mallory asked.

'What, to waltz up to her out of the blue and announce myself as her long-lost mother?' She laughed without any mirth. 'She has her own life, and I have mine. I certainly don't want any messy emotional complications at my age.'

Langham looked at the woman, attempting to discern any likeness between the artist and Annabelle. Pandora's face was ill-defined, plump and oval, whereas Annabelle's was long and graceful: the only similarity was in the eyes, and the way both women narrowed their gazes when regarding a speaker.

Mallory said, 'So Connaught's apology . . .'

'He wanted to atone for how he treated me thirty years ago, apologize for his blackmail threat.'

'What did he say to you on the Saturday afternoon when you met in his study?'

She smiled. 'He reminisced. Went on at length about those "heady, carefree days". He also said that he'd been a shallow, egotistical fool. I didn't disagree. He blamed his behaviour on his youth, and said that he deeply regretted the threats he made. He claimed that he felt, back then, that he couldn't allow any creation of his to be destroyed – he was so caught up in his own ego that the thought of having his child aborted was tantamount to having one of his books destroyed. At least, that's what he said.'

'What did you say to him?'

'I just smiled and said that, yes, he had been a vain and insufferable egomaniac.'

'You mentioned that he wanted to atone. In what way?'

'He wished to make me a gift of ten thousand pounds, Inspector.'

'And what did you say?'

'I was incredulous. My instinct was to tell him to keep his money.' She shook her head. 'But I managed to restrain my indignity. I've scrimped and saved for long enough; I felt I deserved a little luck. He said he'd arrange the transfer of funds through his solicitor.' She smiled. 'And then he went and got himself murdered before he could make good his promise. So, you see,' she said, looking from Mallory to Greaves, and then to Langham, 'my presence here and what happened all those years ago can have no bearing on Connaught's murder. Do you really think I'd be stupid enough to kill the man before I received the blood money?'

'That depends,' Mallory said, smiling equably at the woman, 'if your claim of poverty is all it seems to be, and if you valued the need for revenge more than the receipt of ten thousand pounds.'

Pandora tipped back her head and laughed. 'If I'd hated him that much, Inspector, then I would have exacted my revenge years ago, not left it until now.'

Mallory jotted something in his notebook. 'On Sunday afternoon you were painting on the side lawn from just after lunch until approximately five o'clock.'

'Approximately. I'm hardly aware of the time while I work.'

'And in that time you saw no one approach Connaught's study, either one of the guests or a stranger?'

'Young Royce was buzzing back and forth, and I spoke briefly
with Mr Elder and saw Lady Cee in the drive. But I noticed no one
go near Connaught's study.'

Mallory finished his notetaking. 'Well . . . that's been very instruc-
tive, Miss Jade. I've no doubt that we'll wish to see you again, but
for the time being you're free to go.'

Pandora Jade finished her drink, placed the empty glass on a side
table, and left the room without another word.

'Well,' Mallory said when the three men were alone again, 'I
didn't see that coming. Who would have thought that she's
Annabelle's mother?'

'What they call a bolt from the blue,' Langham said. 'But I can't
say I'm surprised that she's being so hard-nosed about her relationship – or lack of – with Annabelle.'

Mallory consulted his notebook. 'Right, Greaves, could you go
and fetch Monty Connaught? And then I think another drink will
be in order.'

When Greaves had left the room, Mallory stretched his arms
above his head. 'By Christ,' he said, 'what a situation. Denbigh
Connaught sounds like a bastard of the first water.'

Langham smiled and knocked out his pipe in an ashtray. 'An
egotist who treated people appallingly, and yet could write so
insightfully about the human condition.'

'I wonder how many people he hurt over the years – other than
those present – and whether it was an outsider who did for him?'

'We're looking for someone with the strength of a stevedore and
an abiding grudge,' Langham said. 'I doubt we've spoken to the
murderer today.'

'The thing is, Don, how did a notional stranger enter the grounds
without being seen by Pandora, who was on the side lawn all day,
or by anyone else who was in or around the house?'

Langham was staring through the window as the tall, limping
figure of Colonel Haxby crossed the lawn and disappeared behind
the boxwood hedge. It occurred to him that the old soldier was
about to reprise his suicidal shenanigans of Saturday morning – but
then the colonel emerged from the far end of the hedge and headed
towards the walled garden.

He laughed suddenly. 'Bloody hell, Jeff.'

Mallory looked up. 'What is it?'

'Why didn't I think of it before? What if the killer approached

Connaught's study from the other side – from the steps in the cliff leading down to the jetty?'

Mallory nodded. 'There's a path at the foot of the cliff that leads all the way around the headland to the village. I'll have Greaves check if anyone was seen on the path yesterday afternoon.'

The door opened and both men looked up as Monty Connaught walked in, followed by Greaves.

TWENTY-THREE

Monty Connaught nodded to Langham and Mallory and lowered his big, powerful frame into the armchair, resting his right hand on his lap. Nipped between the thumb and forefinger was an unlighted cigarillo. He lifted it. 'Would you mind terribly if I . . .?'

'Not at all,' Mallory said, leaning forward and offering a light from his Zippo.

'Thank you.' Connaught leaned back and blew smoke into the air.

As he watched the man smoke, Langham realized that the mutilated claw served to point up his quiet strength: he was broad across the shoulders, with a thick, well-muscled neck. Not for the first time, he wondered how Monty Connaught had come by his injury.

Mallory said, 'I won't keep you, Mr Connaught. I know you've accounted for your whereabouts yesterday afternoon to my colleague here' – Mallory indicated Greaves – 'but if you don't mind, I'd like to go over the same ground.'

'I quite understand, Inspector.'

'So you can confirm that between twelve and six yesterday you were in the Fisherman's Arms?'

'Or close by, yes. I spent the morning here, going through some old books, and at noon hitched a lift into the village with Donald and Maria. From then on I was with a few friends. We spent around three hours in the Fisherman's, then went for a wander. I wanted to show them around my ketch in the harbour.'

'And you were with them until . . .?'

'We went back to the Fisherman's at four and had another couple of pints, then they left around six. I had a sandwich in the tap room and chatted with a few locals until about eight. I had an early night, went up to my room in the pub and read for an hour. Constable Hampton woke me at eight this morning with the news.'

'I'm sorry. It must have been something of a shock.'

Connaught pulled on his cigarillo and considered Mallory's words. 'If I'm to be perfectly honest, Inspector, I wasn't that shocked. Saddened, yes, and upset. But, you see, the way my brother treated people, it's little wonder that someone held a grudge and did what they did.'

'We've heard all about his past . . . indiscretions, shall we say.' Mallory hesitated. 'How would you describe your relationship with your brother?'

'I'm not so sure that we had a relationship, as such. I hadn't seen him for about ten years.' He shrugged disarmingly and smiled. 'When we were younger . . . There was a five-year age difference, which didn't help. Denbigh was always dictatorial, somewhat arrogant. He found it hard to relate to people he felt were his inferior, and as he considered most people inferior . . .' He smiled again. 'I fell into that category. I was always more practical than academic, unlike my brother, and I think he resented me for that.'

'As the older brother, he inherited the house, I presume?'

'That's right. When my father died back in 'thirty-eight, the house and its contents went to Denbigh.'

'How did you feel about this?'

Connaught shrugged his broad shoulders. 'It was no more than I'd expected. I've never been materialistic: I didn't want the tie of a big house. My father left me two thousand pounds, which allowed me to buy my first boat, which in turn led to my first book.'

'You didn't resent your brother?'

'For what? His inheritance or his success as a writer?'

'Both.'

Connaught smiled. 'Neither, Inspector. As I said, he was welcome to the house, and the fact that he's lauded as a fine writer doesn't bother me in the slightest. He's a better writer than I am; he deserves . . . deserved . . . the plaudits.'

Mallory referred to his notes. 'I understand that you received a telegram last week. Your brother wished to see you urgently?'

'That's right.'

'About what?'

'That's what I wanted to know. The summons was something of

a surprise. As I said, I hadn't seen my brother for ten years. So why the urgency now?'

'And?'

'And at two o'clock yesterday afternoon, in that ridiculous spinning study of his, he told me he was dying.'

Mallory sat up, staring at the man. 'Dying?'

Langham sat back in his chair, taking this in.

'Apparently, he'd been diagnosed with lung cancer last year,' Connaught went on, 'and just a month ago he was told that it had spread. His specialist gave him a matter of months – three at the most. He wanted to see me about his will. He told me he was leaving me ten thousand pounds.'

'Do you know if he'd already altered his will to that effect?'

Connaught smiled. 'He said he was due to see his solicitor later this week, but had wanted to ensure first that I was satisfied with his bequest.'

'And were you?'

'I considered it very generous, Inspector, and told him so.'

'Do you know the details of his most current will?'

'No, I've no idea. I presume the house will go to Annabelle, which is only right, after all.'

Mallory nodded. 'Very well . . . I think that covers everything for the time being, Mr Connaught. Thank you for your time.'

'Don't mention it.'

Langham watched Monty Connaught lift his rangy frame from the chair and stride from the drawing room.

'Well,' Mallory said as the door clicked shut, 'Denbigh Connaught's illness explains why he summoned those he'd slighted over the years. He wanted to make amends, apologize while he still had the time.'

'I wondered at his uncharacteristic *volte face* on that score,' Langham said.

He considered what Monty Connaught had told them about his brother's promise of ten thousand pounds. To Mallory he said, 'Pandora Jade told me that she'd seen Monty leave the study yesterday with a face like thunder.'

Mallory frowned. 'Jade might have misinterpreted his expression. He was probably brooding over his brother's illness.'

Langham agreed. 'That's certainly possible.'

Mallory looked at Greaves. 'Monty Connaught's alibi for yesterday afternoon – cast iron, is it?'

Greaves nodded. 'I questioned Monty Connaught's friends at the Fisherman's. Connaught was with them all afternoon. The publican backed up his story, too.'

Langham said, 'And anyway, what would his motive be? He stood to inherit ten grand from Denbigh in a few months.'

Mallory sighed. 'Right, let's get this over with. Greaves, run along and fetch Annabelle Connaught, would you?'

Greaves left the room.

'You're not going to tell Annabelle about Pandora being her mother, are you?' Langham asked.

'God, no. I don't see the relevance, at the moment. If we find anything that might lead us to believe otherwise, then I'll think again.'

In due course, the door opened and Greaves ushered Annabelle Connaught into the room.

TWENTY-FOUR

On the way to Belsize Park, Ryland stopped at the office in Wandsworth to pick up his service revolver, but left it unloaded. The mere sight of the shooter would be enough to put the frighteners on Mr Harker.

By the time he pulled up outside the gallery, he had a pretty good idea what kind of scam Wilson Royce might be pulling.

He just needed Mr Harker to confirm his suspicions.

Pamela was doodling in a sketchpad when he entered the gallery.

'Nice,' he said. 'You've got talent. Before you know it, your work'll be hanging next to this lot.'

'You think so?' The girl held up her drawing of an elephant. 'Thing is, it's quiet here and I get bored, so I've got to fill my time doing something. Here, what you said the other day – about that job . . . You weren't kidding me?'

'Scout's honour,' he said. 'I've been thinking about it. As soon as we move premises. I'll be in touch.' He pointed towards the office. 'Harker in?'

She nodded. 'And he'll be pleased to see you.'

'You're joking, right?'

'I'm joking. He was in a right tizz when you left the other day.'

'Well, he'll be in an even bigger tizz when I've finished with him this time.'

She made her lips into the shape of a loose elastic band and crossed her eyes. 'Eek!'

He laughed and crossed to the office door. He knocked, then entered without waiting for a reply.

'Oh,' Harker said, looking up, 'it's you.'

This time, rather than standing up for the interview, Ryland made himself comfortable. He sat down across the desk from Harker. 'Developments,' he said. 'I thought you'd like to know that your chum, Wilson Royce, he's just gone and got himself involved in a murder, he has.'

'As I said on Saturday, I hardly know—'

'Shut it, Harker,' Ryland snapped. 'I had enough of your lies last time. You know Royce well enough – and I know you introduced him to Signor Venturi.'

Harker blanched. 'You've no proof.'

'For Christ's sake,' Ryland muttered to himself. 'You know something, Harker? You're not a good liar. You try, oh, you try so desperately, but the fact is you can't act. You're so full of fear that instead of playing it cool, you're shitting yourself. Don't want to do another spell in the slammer – is that it?'

Harker stared at him. 'What do you want?'

Ryland sat back in his seat, smiling. 'That's better. That's what I like to hear – a little cooperation. Now listen very carefully to me, Harker, because I don't like repeating myself. I'm going to ask you a few questions, and you're going to answer them like a good fellow. Understood?'

'Go on.'

Ryland crossed his legs, shot his cuffs and said, 'Why did Wilson Royce pay Venturi a fiver a pop to make copies of eighteenth-century watercolours?'

Sweat appeared on Harker's bald pate. 'I've no idea. You should ask Royce—'

'Wrong answer. You know very well. Now, I suggest you tell me what I want to know, or I'll get nasty. Do you know what that means, Mr Harker?'

The gallery owner moved his hands from the desktop and hid them on his lap so that Ryland was unable to see them shaking. 'You can't threaten me.'

Ryland sighed. He pulled the revolver from his jacket and laid it on his knee, casually.

Harker regarded the gun, his eyes wide. 'You wouldn't dare . . .'

'What? I wouldn't dare shoot you in your great fat gut? You know something, Harker, you're very right. I wouldn't. I wouldn't be so bloody stupid, would I? But do you know what I would do?'

He nodded across the room to a landscape hanging on the wall. 'Now, I assume you've got that little piece in here because you're fond of it, right? Also, it's probably pretty valuable into the bargain. But it'd lose its value if I were to shoot a hole right through it, agreed?'

'You wouldn't . . .' Harker stammered.

'Oh, I would, Harker. And the story I'd give the boys in blue is this: I confronted you with your wrongdoings, and you lost your rag and attacked me. So in self-defence I fired off a warning shot and, oh deary me, I just happened to perforate a work of effing art.'

He raised the revolver, aimed at the painting, and smiled at Harker.

'Now, this is what I'm going to do. I'm going to ask you a few questions, and you're going to answer truthfully. Get the gist?'

Harker swallowed.

Ryland snapped, 'I said, you get the gist?'

Harker nodded.

'Very good. Now,' Ryland said, resting the revolver on his knee but still directing it at the oil, 'what I think is going on is this. Your chum, this Mr Wilson Royce, is a bit of a wide boy. Fingers-in-every-pie sort of fellow – dirty fingers and *very* dirty pies. Now, he makes enquiries in certain quarters and finds out you're bent, done time for shady dealing and all that, and he comes to you wanting to sell a watercolour, eighteenth century, valuable. You ask him where he got it, and he gives you the old maiden aunt tale. You don't believe a word, but you don't say no, do you? Greed gets the better of you, especially when he tells you there are many more where this one came from. So you make a suggestion. To make sure the theft isn't discovered, you suggest exchanging the original for a copy. And you know just the dupe who can make the copy – poor old Signor Venturi, who sold his watercolours to you back when you were starting out in this lark. And you suggest that Royce goes to Venturi with a colour plate of the watercolour, rather than the original, so's not to arouse his suspicion. So Venturi duly makes the copy, and Royce takes it and swaps it for the original, which he gives you. You sell it for a pretty penny and split the profit with him. He does the same with another fifty or so, and between you both, you make a tidy little sum.' He lifted the revolver and took aim at the painting. 'Now, this is where you nod if I've got the story more or less right, ain't it?'

The art dealer stared at him, sweat beading his brow.

'Well?' Ryland snapped.

After a delay of five seconds, Harker nodded his head minimally.

'Now that wasn't so painful, was it?'

Harker licked his lips, found his voice and said, 'You said . . . you mentioned a murder?'

Ryland slipped the revolver into his pocket. 'Looks like young Mr Royce might've gone and done in a writer chappie called Connaught. I reckon you'll have the rozzers crawling all over this place in a day or so, I do.'

Harker went white and stared at Ryland in silent alarm.

Ryland climbed to his feet and moved to the door. Then he turned and nodded at the painting on the wall. 'You don't really have me down as a desecrater of artworks, do you? Tut-tut, Mr Harker. Be seeing you.'

On the way out, he paused beside Pamela's desk. 'I feel a bit guilty, I do. I reckon Mr Harker will be out of business, once the cops know what he's been up to. Tell you what . . .' He fished a business card from his breast pocket and passed it to the girl. 'Give me a bell when this place goes belly-up, all right?'

Pamela stared at the card. 'Ryland and Langham. Blimey . . . I always wanted to be a private dick.'

Ryland saluted. 'See you later, Pamela.'

He left the gallery and crossed to his car.

All in all, another good day's work.

Now to phone Don with all the sordid details . . .

TWENTY-FIVE

Annabelle Connaught was subdued as she took the armchair opposite Mallory, although she did give the detective a tremulous smile of greeting. Her golden hair and lambent skin seemed to irradiate the room.

'This is just a formality, Doctor Connaught,' Mallory said. 'I'm attempting to build up, as best I can, a comprehensive picture of what happened on Sunday afternoon.'

'Of course.'

Mallory looked down at his notes. 'Now, I understand that your father was ill?'

'That's right. He was diagnosed with lung cancer last year, just before Christmas.'

'And the prognosis?'

'To begin with, it was fairly sanguine. The specialist at Plymouth gave him two or three years. However, a few weeks ago it was discovered that the cancer had metastasized, spread from his lungs to his spine and liver. At that point, the specialist gave him no more than three months.'

Mallory nodded, arranging his features in an appropriately sombre expression. He asked, 'And presumably it was this – the knowledge of his illness – that made him look back on his life and decide to make . . . reparations to certain people?'

Annabelle nodded. 'I think, on reflection, that it might have been.'

'But he made no mention of this decision to you?'

'No, not a word.'

'Do you know if many people, other than your father, you yourself and his doctors, were aware of his illness?'

'He didn't publicize his condition, Inspector. He didn't want the sympathy or the attention it would have engendered. He was stoical in the face of the inevitable, at least to his doctors.'

'And privately, to you?'

Annabelle furrowed her brow. 'He feared death, and feared that he might die in pain, though he tried to protect me from these fears. He was not a man to open up and admit to them. I . . .' She paused, considering. 'I sometimes wonder if his later reserve was assumed in order to protect me, or merely that he did not wish to be seen as weak.'

'And have you come to any conclusion?'

She laughed, but without humour. 'I'd like to think it was the former, Inspector.'

Mallory turned a page in his notebook, then looked up and asked, 'On Wednesday you hired Donald to investigate the activities of your father's business manager, Wilson Royce, but you were rather vague as to your reasons. You told Donald, at the time, that you thought Wilson Royce was corrupt – although you admitted that you were going on nothing more than intuition.'

'That's right.'

'I hope you don't mind my asking if that wasn't a rather flimsy pretext for hiring a private investigator?'

'I think not,' she said. 'I set great store by my intuition.'

'And do you have an intuition regarding Wilson Royce's possible involvement in what happened to your father?'

Annabelle's eyes widened, as if in surprise. 'I . . . I wouldn't put anything past Wilson,' she said, 'though I must admit I'd be hard-pressed to see what motive he might have had.'

Mallory cleared his throat. 'I have one more question, and I hope you don't think it indelicate. I believe that you were at one time romantically involved with Wilson Royce?'

Annabelle coloured suddenly and looked down at her fingers. 'That was a long time ago, Inspector – last year – and I ended it after a few weeks.'

'On the grounds that . . .?'

'That I found I didn't care for the man.'

'Quite,' Mallory said, closing his notebook. 'There is one more thing. I understand your father owned a small collection of paintings.'

'A rather large collection, actually. Over a hundred valuable watercolours, mainly eighteenth century.'

'Where are they kept?'

'In his old study, which is locked for most of the time. My father worked there until he built his outdoor place.'

'I wonder if you could show us the collection?'

'Of course, but why?'

'Would you be able to tell if any individual items were missing?'

'Well, it's a long time since I last took much notice of the collection, but I was familiar with the more valuable items. My father had a passion for the work of Varley and Cozens, among others. He kept a spare key to his old study in the small room beneath the stairs.'

'And the other key?'

'He kept on him at all times.'

Mallory rose, gesturing Annabelle to lead the way. Langham followed them from the room. In the hallway, Greaves said to Mallory, 'I have a couple of men searching the guest rooms, sir. I'll check how they're getting on.'

'Good man,' Mallory said. Annabelle collected the key from the room beneath the staircase and led the way upstairs.

'Along here,' Annabelle said, gesturing to a corridor that led to the west wing.

'Wasn't it a rather large house for just one person?' Mallory asked.

'It's been in the family for a couple of centuries,' she said. 'My father couldn't bear to sell it. He loved the house, and the coast. And, of course, when he moved back from London with my mother and me . . . Well, I suppose the intention was to raise a large family here.'

Annabelle switched on a light to illuminate the corridor; dust sheets covered various items placed in alcoves, and the carpet underfoot was threadbare: the west wing had the appearance of somewhere uninhabited for decades.

'Here we are.'

Annabelle turned the key in the door and led the way into a big, darkened room. She crossed to the damask curtains and tugged them aside, admitting a dazzle of afternoon sunlight.

Langham blinked in the glare, and as his eyes adjusted he made out a room furnished with several chaise longues, heavy early Victorian occasional tables and an ostentatious marble fire-surround, all in keeping with the landscapes that adorned three of the four walls.

Mallory whistled. 'Reminds me of the time I visited the Royal Academy.'

'My father built the collection over many years, and he was proud of his acumen. You see, he began buying them when water-colours were considered less than collectable, and he picked up many at bargain prices. Since then the fashion has changed – watercolours have become popular and often sell for many hundreds of pounds.'

Langham counted forty small paintings on the left wall alone, and wondered at the value of the entire collection, which comprised perhaps a hundred paintings. For the most part they were landscapes, meadowland, valleys, and a few Highland scenes.

Experimentally, he lifted a small painting in a heavy gold frame from the wall, revealing a small square of bright flock wallpaper. He replaced it and examined the other walls, but there was no evidence of any paintings having been removed.

Annabelle stood in the middle of the room and regarded the collection. 'Before the war, my father came in here and sat for an hour or two, just admiring the paintings. I think they were a great consolation, after the death of my mother.'

Mallory asked her if any paintings were missing.

'No,' she said. 'They seem to be all present and correct.'

'Were you aware,' Mallory said, 'that on Saturday morning your father offered Lady Cecelia certain items from his collection?'

Annabelle smiled. 'No. No, I wasn't, and Lady Cecelia is not the kind of person to have mentioned his generosity, in the circumstances.'

Mallory looked around the room. 'Do you intend to sell Connaught House?'

'After everything that has happened here, Inspector, I couldn't bring myself to keep it.'

Langham moved to the window and looked out. The room overlooked the kitchen garden, and beside it a cobblestoned area where two policemen in navy blue boilersuits, supervised by Greaves, were sifting through the charred contents of the brazier. The punctured oil drum lay on its side, debris spilling from it like volcanic ash.

Annabelle asked, 'Just why do you think that items might be missing?'

'Just a routine inquiry,' Mallory said. 'After such an incident, and with such a valuable collection on the premises, it would be remiss not to give it the once-over.'

'Well, as far as I can tell, nothing is missing. Although . . .'

'Yes?'

Langham turned. Annabelle was frowning. She approached the wall beside the fireplace and leaned forward. 'I wonder if my father had some of these restored.'

'What makes you think that?' Mallory asked.

Annabelle shook her head, nipping her bottom lip between her teeth. 'Some of them – this one for example – seem brighter, almost cleaner, than some of the others. I must admit that I don't know much about watercolours, and whether they can be restored or cleaned, like oil paintings.'

Langham turned back to the window. Down below, Greaves was crouching down beside the men in boilersuits; the ash had been spread across the cobbles, and one of the men was prodding at something with an iron rod. The object was too far away for Langham to make out.

Greaves stood and hurried into the house.

Langham said, 'Hello. I think they've found something in the brazier.'

Mallory joined him at the window. The men had isolated the object, which lay on the cobbles before them: a dark scrap about the size of a hand.

A knock sounded at the door, and the butler appeared. 'Detective Sergeant Greaves would like to see you, sir.'

Mallory led the way from the room, along the gloomy corridor and down the staircase. Greaves was pacing the hall. 'Ah, there you are, sir. We've come across something of interest in the brazier.'

They moved through the house, along a stone-flagged corridor to the kitchen and out into the walled yard. Langham held open the door for Annabelle.

Mallory crouched beside the burnt debris. The charred object was the remains of a leather glove, its fingers and thumb burnt to blackened stumps.

'And look,' Greaves said, indicating the glove's seam with the iron rod, 'the maker's tag. And that stain, right there, looks suspiciously like blood.'

'Good work,' Mallory said.

'Do you recognize . . .?' Langham began, looking up to where Annabelle had been standing; she had left the yard and was hurrying away through the kitchen garden.

Mallory stood. 'Right, bag it up and we'll get it to the forensic boys. Might be the break we've been looking for.'

'Very good, sir.'

Mallory stared down at the grey, curled remains of the burnt papers, fluttering in the breeze. 'And go through the rest of it with a fine-tooth comb.' He turned to Langham, 'Right, Don, could you show me the steps in the side of the cliff you mentioned?'

Langham led the way through the kitchen garden and across the lawn.

TWENTY-SIX

Maria sat in an armchair beside the French windows in the library, a copy of *Homes and Gardens* forgotten on her lap. The windows stood open, admitting a warm afternoon breeze freighted with the scent of the climbing roses which grew along the back of the house.

Charles sat in the armchair opposite her – or rather lay in the chair, his legs crossed at the ankles and his colossal midriff rising between the arms of the chair like a waistcoated barrage balloon. His head was tipped back, topped by peaks of snowy hair, and he was snoring gently. Maria smiled at the sight of him, admiring his ability to drift into slumber at the drop of a hat. She had often caught him, in his office, stretched out on his Chesterfield snoring the afternoon away. When challenged, he would claim that he had not been asleep: 'I have the peculiar ability to respire noisily while being wide awake, my child!'

Earlier, before the interview when the library resembled a waiting room full of anxious patients dreading the doctor's summons, Maria had paid particular attention to Annabelle Connaught – or rather to how everyone in the room, in their very different ways, had reacted to the bereaved woman.

Maria herself had limited her condolences to a brief, understanding smile, to which Annabelle had responded in kind. Lady Cecelia had approached her and spoken falteringly, while Colonel Haxby, half-cut, had blurted some garbled commiseration.

It was, surprisingly, Pandora who seemed unfazed at the idea of speaking forthrightly to Annabelle about her loss. She had drawn up a footstool before the young woman's armchair, taken Annabelle's hand in hers and spoken earnestly and at length in tones too low for Maria to catch. Annabelle had responded with smiles and nods, and soon the women were engaged in animated conversation. Before Pandora's summons by Greaves, Maria had heard her say, 'And the next time you're in London, my girl, you *must* call in on me,' and her estimation of the artist had risen by a degree or two.

She looked through the French windows, her attention attracted by movement across the lawn: Wilson Royce was striding towards the house. For a moment, she assumed he would enter the library, and she prepared herself to greet him. However, he paused outside without seeing her, lit a cigarette and sat down on a wrought-iron seat beneath the bountiful roses.

Across from Maria, Charles opened his eyes suddenly and declared, 'I have decided!'

'In your sleep?' she smiled.

'I was not sleeping, child. While giving that impression to the world at large, I was in actual fact cogitating upon a matter of deep moral and ethical significance. And I am pleased to announce that I have arrived at a solution both practical and personally satisfying.'

'I'm all ears, Charles.'

'For the past day,' he said, 'I have been mulling over the probity of accepting Connaught's offer to represent him and take on his latest – his last – novel. I might say that I spent a sleep-less night dwelling upon the matter, and this morning was no nearer a decision.'

'But now you are?'

'Indubitably.'

Maria replaced the magazine on a side table. 'And?'

'And I have come to the decision that in all conscience I cannot accept his offer. While I would have accepted his apology, and done so to his face had he lived long enough, I cannot see how his desire for atonement would be satisfied, posthumously as it were, by my taking on the book.' He sat upright, leaned forward over his gargantuan stomach and went on, 'I will forward the manuscript to Pritchard and Pryce in due course. I hope you understand, my dear?'

'Of course I do. I would have made the same decision, in your situation.'

'Oh, I am relieved that we see eye to eye on this matter. As business partners, we have an equal say in the running of the agency, and I would understand if you demurred. I am gladdened that this is not so, my dear.'

'The fact is, Charles, we're doing very well without Denbigh Connaught on our list. We don't need his novel, and all the pain associated with it.'

Charles beamed across at her. 'When all this terrible business is

over, Maria, I shall take you and Donald out for dinner, and we will
discuss the practicalities of your purchasing a cottage in Suffolk.
That is still your intention, is it not?'
    'Of course. Donald and I cannot wait.'
    Charles smiled to himself, settled back in the armchair, laced
his pudgy fingers across his stomach and within seconds was
respiring noisily.
    London and life in the capital, she mused, seemed very far
away this afternoon. For the last ten years she had lived in
Kensington, shuttling between her apartment and the agency
in Pimlico, going out to the West End from time to time and
never once entertaining the idea of living anywhere else. Since
meeting Donald, however, something had changed: it was as if
she was entering a new phase of life in which London would
play an ever smaller part. She wanted to settle down, find a quiet
place in the country and bring up a family, in combination with
working on a part-time basis at the agency. Was she getting old
and staid, she wondered? If so, she could not complain. The
quiet life was what she craved.
    And it cheered her that Donald had not objected to the idea –
nor to that of their having children. The thought of having a little
Donald running around the garden made something flip wonderfully
in her stomach.
    She looked up as the door opened.
    Annabelle Connaught peered into the room, smiled at Maria
and said, 'I don't suppose you've seen Wilson Royce?'
    Maria pointed through the French windows and silently mouthed,
'*There.*'
    Annabelle crossed the room, smiled her thanks at Maria and
stepped outside. She stood over Royce, her arms folded, until he
edged further along the bench. She sat down and turned to him;
Maria could only see her slim back as she leaned forward and spoke
to Royce in urgent, lowered tones.
    Maria picked up her magazine and flipped through it.
    It was obvious that Annabelle and Royce were arguing, although
she was unable to make out the gist of the conversation. Then
Annabelle, raising her voice, said, 'You're more than despicable!'
    Royce drawled something in lazy response. Then he said, 'And
anyway, what makes you think . . .?'
    Maria, acting on impulse, set aside the magazine, rose and crossed

to the window. She stood with her back to the wall so that she could not be seen from outside.

'You did!' Annabelle whispered.

'You're insane . . .'

'The police have found something, you know? In the brazier. You burnt it, didn't you? But why would you do that?'

'Found what?' Royce affected unconcern.

'A glove. I recognized it. *Your* glove. Why on earth would you burn your—'

'I don't know what the hell you're talking about.'

'You killed him, didn't you?' she hissed.

'Go to hell!' Royce responded. 'I'm taking no more of this.'

Maria hurried back to her seat, crossed her legs and took up the magazine. Through the French windows she saw Annabelle stride off across the lawn, hugging herself, and stop at the edge of the cliff.

Wilson Royce strode into the library and crossed to the door, leaving it ajar as he stormed out. Maria saw him a second later as he climbed the stairs.

She sat very still for the space of half a minute, staring across at Charles who had dozed through the entire encounter. Then she stood and hurried to the door; she must find Donald and tell him what she'd overheard.

She was stepping from the library when Donald himself appeared at the far end of the hall. He hurried to her, smiling. 'There you are. What say a stroll down to the village and a pint at the Fisherman's?' He faltered. 'I say – what's wrong?'

She took his hand, almost tugged him into the library, and eased the door shut behind them.

'I've just heard Annabelle and Wilson Royce. They were outside' – she pointed through the French windows – 'arguing. I heard her say that a glove has been found in a brazier.'

'That's right. I was with Jeff and Greaves—'

'Well,' she interrupted, 'Annabelle recognized it. She said it belonged to him, to Royce. And then she accused him of killing her father.'

'She said that? Royce's glove? My God!' he exclaimed. 'Do you know where Royce is now?'

'He stormed through the library and went upstairs – to his room, presumably.'

'Right,' Donald said, 'stay with Charles. I'll be back in a jiffy.'

'Donald, do be careful.'

'Don't worry.'

The door opened and the butler appeared. 'Mr Langham, a phone call. A Mr Ralph Ryland, from London. He said it's urgent. In the sitting room, sir.'

Donald thanked him and turned to Maria. 'I'd better take that, then go and see what Royce has to say for himself.'

She watched him slip from the room, then returned to her chair beside the window and tried to interest herself in an article about how to grow roses in a cottage garden.

TWENTY-SEVEN

Langham settled himself in the armchair beside the telephone table and picked up the receiver. 'Ralph.'

'Don, good to hear you. It's a clear line – sounds as if you're in the next room. How's things in sunny Cornwall?'

'Barring murder and inscrutable suspects, it's pleasant . . . and sunny.'

'You got your notebook to hand?'

'Ready and waiting,' Langham said, opening it on his lap. 'What have you got?'

'Shed loads,' Ryland said. 'Your man's been up to mischief and no mistake. Tracked down a few of his contacts up here, and for a toff he certainly knew his way around the backstreets. Long and short of it, he was bringing some valuable watercolours up to the Smoke and doing a deal with a gallery owner called William Harker of Belsize Park.'

'Well done, Ralph.'

'That ain't the end of it. This Harker, he put Royce on to a foreign Johnny in Kent, a nice old geezer called Venturi, a dab hand at copying watercolours at a fiver a go. So Royce filched the originals, some fifty in all, and replaced them with the copies so the owner wouldn't get wise.'

Langham laughed. 'And that owner, Ralph, was Denbigh Connaught. He had quite a collection down here. My word, young

Royce had a nice little racket going, stealing the watercolours, one by one. He must have made a mint.'

'There's more. I had a poke around Royce's place yesterday, and what did I find? Just his bank book, is what.'

'Stuffed full of his ill-gotten gains, I'll wager.'

'And some. But the odd thing was, every month Wilson Royce deposited a cheque for two hundred quid, regular as clockwork. And tucked into this bank book I found a cheque, ready to be deposited. And guess who it was from?'

'The gallery owner, right?'

'Wrong. It was from Denbigh Connaught, is who.'

Langham laughed. 'Well, blow me down.'

'Two hundred quid every month?' Ryland said. 'That's a hell of a salary!'

'That was no salary, Ralph. Young Royce was up to something.'

Ryland chuckled. 'He was on to a little gold mine when he went to work for Connaught,' he said. 'What's he like in the flesh, this Wilson Royce? I see him as a pathetic little drip, conning people with his sob story.'

'His sob story?'

'I had this from the old bloke in Kent. Venturi said that Royce told him about how he'd lost his dad when he was a nipper, knocked down in a hit-and-run incident.'

Langham felt his heartbeat quicken. 'What?'

'Royce's pa was killed outright when he was five, run over by a car right outside his house in Islington. Apparently, young Royce witnessed the whole thing.'

'Ruddy hell.'

'I know. Nasty.'

'No, I mean . . . Listen, Denbigh Connaught was involved in a hit and run back in 'thirty-four. He killed a pedestrian but got someone else, a chum at the time, to take the rap. If Royce saw it happen . . .'

'Blimey. You don't think young Royce did Connaught in as payback for his old man?'

'I don't know. I need to think about this. Good work, Ralph.'

'Oh, one more thing. I don't know if it means anything, but I found a letter in Royce's desk. It was addressed to Connaught from a certain Pandora Jade – one of your fellow guests, I take it?'

'That's right. Go on.'

'Well, she wrote that she'd be coming down for the weekend, and asked if her daughter, Annabelle, would be there.'

Langham smiled to himself. 'Right,' he said. 'So . . . Wilson Royce had the letter in his possession, did he?'

'That's right. Seemed a bit odd, so I thought I'd better mention it.'

'You did right,' Langham said, and explained the situation regarding Pandora Jade, Denbigh Connaught and Annabelle. 'Thanks, Ralph.'

'Cheers, Don. Right, that's me for the day. I'm going to get some fish and chips for Annie and the boys, then it's down the boozer for me Monday night darts.'

'Have a good time,' Langham said. He thanked him again and replaced the receiver.

He sat where he was for five minutes, going over what Ryland had told him and piecing together the facts with everything he'd learned at Connaught House.

Then he made his way upstairs and knocked on Wilson Royce's bedroom door.

'Yes?' Royce called out.

'It's Langham. I'd like a word.'

The door opened and Royce stared at him. The young man's hair was dishevelled and he looked more than a little flustered. 'Look, can't it wait? I was just about to take a bath.'

'I think it's your bath that can wait,' Langham said, and eased past Royce. The room was a mess, with clothes scattered over the bed and old laundry piled in one corner. The odour of Royce's eau de cologne filled the air.

Langham walked to the window and stared out.

'Well,' Royce demanded, 'what is it?'

On the clifftop lawn, far below, Lady Cecelia and Colonel Haxby strolled side by side in the late-afternoon sunlight; it struck Langham as an unlikely pairing.

He turned to face the young man. 'I'd like to know why you wrote to Denbigh Connaught, last year, requesting a job.'

Wilson Royce leaned against the door; he was sweating. In order to hide the fact that his hands were shaking, he placed them behind his back. 'I don't see by what authority . . .' he began. 'And for that matter, why were you sitting in on the interviews?'

Langham crossed the room, pulling his accreditation from an inside pocket. He hung it before Royce's frightened gaze, then moved to an armchair and sat down. He indicated a second chair beside a small fireplace.

'Take a seat,' he invited.

Royce remained leaning against the door. He was staring at Langham in an odd way, as if something had suddenly struck him.

'That first morning,' Royce said, 'when you arrived here . . . I was sure I'd seen you before.'

Langham nodded. 'That's very observant of you. Sit down.'

'The public house in Pimlico . . . You drove me home!' He stopped. 'That bitch Annabelle put you up to this, didn't she?'

Langham indicated the chair. 'I said, *sit down.*'

'I don't see why I—'

'It's really no skin off my nose, either way. Either you answer a few questions now, or Detective Inspector Mallory takes you to Plymouth for a nice overnight stay. Now, what is it to be?'

Resentfully, Royce pushed himself from the door and sat down across from Langham.

'Now, why did you want to work for Connaught?'

Royce swallowed. He balled his hands into fists to stop their shaking. His eyes avoiding Langham's, he said, 'As I mentioned before, I admired his work.'

'Don't talk rot, Royce. You hated the man.'

'I . . .' He shook his head. 'What makes you think—'

'Let me tell you why I think you wrote to Connaught,' Langham said. 'It was quite simple: you wanted revenge. You wanted to pay Connaught back for what he did over twenty years ago, when you were five.'

Royce clenched his teeth, his face white. 'I don't know what you're talking about.'

'You witnessed the accident in which your father was killed,' Langham said. 'I can't imagine how terrible it must have been.'

Royce looked up. 'That's right, Langham, you can't begin to imagine. You have no conception.'

Langham murmured, 'What happened?'

Royce gazed into space. 'To have the man you worship taken away so . . . so brutally and arbitrarily. I still have nightmares.' He took a long breath. 'The day after it happened, I was packed off to the country to stay with an uncle and aunt. Before that I was questioned by the police . . . But I was only five. I didn't understand what I'd seen. When I became distressed, my mother called a halt to the questioning.'

'What did you see, exactly?'

Royce stared down at his fists. 'I was at my bedroom window. I saw my father coming home from work at the Stock Exchange, crossing the road. It was late – perhaps eight or nine – and dark. A car came careering around the corner and . . . and it struck my father, sent him flying. The car stopped and I saw someone climb out from behind the wheel – a big man with very fair hair. He approached my father, lying there in the gutter, examined him and then, instead of summoning help, he returned to the car and dragged the passenger across the seat and behind the wheel. Then . . . then he slammed the car door and ran off.'

Langham leaned forward. 'Did you tell this to the police?'

'I . . . I honestly can't recall. I can't have done, or . . . or Connaught would never have got away with what he did. But I was incoherent, according to my mother. Hysterical. I stayed with my aunt and uncle for a time, and when I returned to London, the trial was over and my mother had sold the family house and moved to be closer to her sister in Bromsgrove. It was only years later that I read about the trial, and discovered the name of the man who supposedly killed my father. I read a transcript of the proceedings and discovered that the accused, James Haxby, claimed that Denbigh Connaught had been driving the car. The jury disbelieved him and Haxby was found guilty – but, of course, I knew that it was Connaught who'd killed my father.'

'So you planned to come down here and exact revenge?'

Royce was silent for a while, staring down at the carpet. 'Do you know something? I wasn't sure what I intended when I wrote to Connaught. A part of me was curious. What kind of man was it who had run down my father, and then so cold-bloodedly arranged for someone else – and a friend at that – to take the blame? That was despicable, and I wanted to know how anyone could live with that on their conscience.'

'And did you find out?'

Royce looked up at Langham. 'I discovered that Denbigh Connaught was a monster, an unconscionable, egotistical monster who thought only of his own needs and gratification, and everyone else could go hang.'

'And did that make blackmailing him all that easier?' Langham asked.

Royce flinched. 'What makes you think . . .?'

'Don't take me for a fool, Royce. You demanded two hundred a month, and he paid up in order to keep you quiet.'

The young man shook his head. 'When I came down for the interview, I casually mentioned the trial, and he said it was a time he had no desire to revisit. Oh, the shock on his face when I told him who I was and what I had seen that evening. I could see he was thinking of the scandal it would bring down on him if I made my knowledge public. Even if I wasn't believed, and he managed to wriggle out of the charge yet again, he didn't want that kind of publicity tarnishing his reputation. I demanded that he employ me and pay me a healthy monthly salary.'

'Of two hundred pounds.'

'A small price to pay, I thought, for the crimes of his past.'

The two men sat in silence for a while in the warm, scented room; beyond the window, sparrows chirped in the wisteria. Langham thought of Maria and Charles in the library, and wished he were with them now.

'And then, Royce, you decided that the price Connaught was paying for your silence was not enough. You decided to steal his prized watercolours, and in such a devious manner that he might never discover your deception.'

'What makes you think—'

'I know all about the gallery owner in Belsize Park, one William Harker.'

Langham saw, in the young man's face, the impulse to deny the charge – then he realized the futility of it. He said quietly, 'Connaught rarely visited the west wing and his collection. He'd never have been any the wiser if . . .' Royce shrugged. 'I had a contact in London, a dealer who knew someone who could make passable copies.'

'How many paintings have you stolen, Royce?'

The young man could not help but smile with pride. 'Well over fifty.'

'And what were you paid for each one, on average?'

'Between a hundred and two hundred pounds.'

Langham whistled. 'A nice little earner. You must have lived it up on your weekends in the Smoke.'

That prideful grin again, the eye-tooth showing. 'I was harming no one, Langham. Connaught could afford the two hundred a month. And the copies of the watercolours were locked in a darkened room, admired by no one.'

Langham stared at Royce, calculating his next words. At last he said, 'And then what happened?'

Royce looked up. 'What do you mean?'

'Let me hazard a guess,' Langham said. 'Connaught approached you about this little weekend, told you about the various guests he was inviting, and perhaps even why. When he mentioned that he planned to make a gift of some of his watercolours to Lady Cecelia, you saw the writing on the wall. Your little scam would be rumbled when she took possession of the watercolours and had them valued. So Denbigh Connaught had to die.'

Royce stared at him. He said something, but it was too low for Langham to make out.

'I didn't quite catch that.'

'I said, I didn't kill him.'

Royce sat with his elbows resting on his knees and his head hanging. His blond fringe flopped forward, obscuring his wolfish face. 'I didn't kill him,' he repeated.

Langham said, 'Your glove was discovered in the brazier, where you were burning papers on Sunday afternoon. You had ample time, as you passed back and forth, to make a detour to Connaught's study, and you had the spare key.'

Royce shook his head, still not looking up. 'No . . . You've got it wrong. Oh, I don't deny that there were times when I would gladly have killed him. And then, when I found him dead on Sunday . . . yes, a part of me exulted.' He looked up and stared at Langham. 'But I swear I didn't kill him.'

Langham sighed, pressed down on his knees and stood up. 'Well, it'll soon be in the hands of the police, so we'll see how they handle it, shall we?'

'You're going to inform Inspector Mallory?'

'Of course I am.'

He moved past Royce and approached the door. 'Oh, one more thing. A letter from Pandora Jade to Connaught was discovered at your London place. She asked if her daughter, Annabelle, would be present this weekend. What were you planning to do with that piece of information, Royce?'

'I . . .' Royce shook his head. 'I must have picked up the letter by mistake, along with other paperwork.'

Langham snorted. 'Likely story, but that's something else that Mallory can look into.'

The young man stood suddenly and faced him. 'Do you know something, Langham?' he said desperately. 'I really don't fear hanging, even if it is for a crime I didn't commit. The thought that my father is finally avenged . . . that's worth far, far more than my futile life.'

Unable to find a suitable response, Langham nodded and left the room.

He found Watkins in the hall and asked after the whereabouts of Inspector Mallory.

'I understand that he took Miss Annabelle into the village, sir. You might try the Fisherman's Arms.'

Langham thanked him and crossed to the library.

Maria stood and hurried to him. 'Donald! What happened?'

'How about a quick one at the Fisherman's?' he asked. 'I'll tell you all about it on the way.'

'Very well, but what about . . .?' She gestured at Charles, who was fast asleep in an armchair.

He tore a page from his notebook. 'Leave him a note saying we'll be back in time for dinner.'

Her tongue-tip showing, she took the paper and wrote: *Charles, we had to dash – see you for dinner. Maria.*

She crossed to the sleeping man, inserted the folded note between his fingers laced across his stomach, and tiptoed from the room.

'What did Ralph say?' she asked as they crossed the drive to the car.

Langham opened the passenger door for her, then slipped in behind the wheel. As he drove from the grounds, he relayed what Ralph had told him and described his confrontation with Wilson Royce.

'My word, but . . .'

'He denied the murder, of course.'

'But do you think he is guilty, Donald?'

'I honestly don't know. He certainly had the motive, and the opportunity. Oh,' he went on, 'there's something else. We learned while interviewing Pandora that she's Annabelle Connaught's mother.'

He turned to watch Maria's reaction to the news, and he wasn't disappointed. 'What?' She made her eyes huge and her mouth hung open. '*Sacré bleu!* That is incredible!'

'Pandora and Connaught had a fling in the twenties, and Connaught gained custody of the child.'

'But Annabelle doesn't know about this?'

'No, and Pandora has no desire to tell her.'

Maria bit her bottom lip. 'Do you know . . . earlier, in the library, Pandora was very good with Annabelle. I was thinking how considerate she was in her commiserations. Now I think I understand.'

'Perhaps Pandora is softening in her middle age,' Langham said, and slowed down as they approached the cobbled harbour. 'There's Jeff's Humber,' he went on, pulling up behind it.

Mallory and Annabelle were seated at a table outside the public house; an almost empty pint glass sat before the inspector, and Annabelle was finishing her drink.

'They seem to be getting on well,' Maria said. 'I wonder if he's interviewing her in the line of duty.'

They left the car and crossed the cobbles to the Fisherman's Arms.

Annabelle lodged her sunglasses in her hair and gave Maria a dazzling smile.

'Just in time,' Mallory said, draining his glass. 'I'll get them in.'

Langham followed the detective inspector into the pub. 'Developments,' he said at the bar, and summarized what Ralph had told him over the phone. 'I confronted Wilson Royce, and he admitted blackmailing Connaught and filching the watercolours.'

'And killing Connaught?'

Langham shook his head. 'Claimed innocence.'

Mallory ordered the drinks. When the barmaid moved off to the pumps, he said, 'We have a damned strong case against him.'

'I don't deny that,' Langham said.

'I sense a "but" coming.'

'But my cavil all along – it needed a hell of a lot of strength to have caused Connaught that injury. And Wilson Royce isn't exactly Charles Atlas.'

'I've been thinking about that,' Mallory said, picking up his pint and taking a mouthful. 'How about this? Connaught wasn't strangled to death – his throat was cut with a knife. That'd explain the severity of the injury—'

Langham interrupted, 'But why would the killer go to the lengths of slitting his throat and then making it look as though he'd been garrotted?'

Mallory said, 'Precisely to make us think that someone built like a wrestler was responsible – to deflect attention from the fact that the killer wasn't that big and strong.'

'So . . . Wilson Royce would fit the bill?'

'It's a working hypothesis.'

Langham shook his head. 'Won't wash. Presumably, Connaught had his back to the killer, who comes up behind him with a damned big knife and slits his throat . . . In that case, where was all the blood? Crikey, it would've spouted like a geyser. It'd be all over the place.'

'OK, so the killer struck him on the head, causing him to fall to the floor, and then slit his throat. I'll have the surgeon check for head wounds.'

Langham thought about it. 'But why would the killer then drag the body behind the piano?'

'Perhaps,' Mallory said, 'Connaught was standing at one end of the piano when the killer clobbered him. It's entirely feasible that he'd stagger forward a few paces, behind the piano, before falling to the floor.'

Langham nodded. 'I'll give you that, yes.'

'So that's the line I'll take when I haul young Royce over the coals.'

Langham was about to leave the bar with the drinks. 'Oh,' he said, 'Maria asked if you were interviewing Annabelle in the line of duty. I think you're smitten, Jeff.'

'Well, she is one heck of an attractive woman,' the detective inspector allowed. 'She has a place in London, and comes up from time to time. I'm going to suggest I take her out for dinner at some point.'

'Good luck,' Langham said, leading the way outside.

They joined the women and sat down at the table. Mallory said to Annabelle, 'You're looking pensive.'

She looked up and smiled sadly. 'The brazier, the ashes and the glove . . . They brought back a lot of unpleasant memories.'

Mallory looked at her. 'Of what?'

Annabelle sighed. 'Well . . . it might have been the first of my father's . . . the first of his – I don't really know what you'd call them – cruel, unthinking acts?'

Langham glanced at Maria, bemused. 'What might?'

'Annabelle?' Mallory said, reaching across the table and touching her hand.

'Uncle Monty told me this years ago,' she said. 'He was in London, just back from Africa. He'd never before told me exactly how he received his injuries, but he'd had a few to drink and he opened up.'

Langham murmured, 'What happened?'

'Monty was nine or ten at the time. One weekend during the summer his father built him a ramshackle tree house in the oak behind the house. He was understandably proud of it, and wouldn't let my father anywhere near it. They'd just had one of their many arguments . . . Then one night my father decided to take revenge. He stole a canister of petrol from the garage, doused the creepers at the base of the oak, and set it alight.'

Langham glanced at Maria, who was wincing in anticipation of what was to come.

Annabelle went on quietly, 'What my father didn't know was that Monty had decided to spend that night in the tree house. Or . . . or perhaps he *did* know. At any rate, the fire engulfed the tree house and Monty was lucky to escape with his life, but he suffered horrendous injuries.' She shook her head. 'He was in hospital for months, undergoing a series of operations and skin grafts. My grandfather hushed it up, put it around that it had been a terrible accident. My father was beside himself with remorse, according to Monty.'

'And Monty himself?' Mallory asked.

Annabelle smiled. 'My uncle is a good man,' she said. 'He told me he hated Denbigh at the time, but that over the years he'd come to terms with what had happened – and he even claimed that it had made him the man he was. It would have destroyed many people, but not my Uncle Monty.'

She paused, regarding her drink, and then looked up with tears in her eyes. 'But, you see . . . the sight of the brazier and the ashes . . . and that glove, lying there like a burnt hand – it made me think. You see, I can't help but ask myself if my father did it intentionally, knowing that Monty *was* in the tree house – and if that was the first indication that there was something . . . something malicious, even psychotic, in my father's make-up that manifested itself in his various acts of unkindness down the years.'

She took a sip of her gin and tonic. At last she said, 'About the brazier, Jeff. I was about to tell you about the glove before Donald and Maria arrived.'

He said, 'You recognized it as belonging to Wilson Royce?'

She looked surprised. 'But how did you know?'

Mallory glanced at Langham and said, 'There've been certain developments on that front. I'll be questioning Royce when I get back.'

'Do you think . . .?' Annabelle began.

He hesitated. 'Were you aware that Wilson Royce was black-mailing your father?'

She opened her mouth, for a moment lost for words. 'Blackmailing? No, I never . . . But why?'

Mallory told her about the accident in Islington back in 1934 that had killed Wilson Royce's father, and Connaught's subsequent ruse to place the blame on Haxby.

Annabelle reached into a pocket, pulled out a handkerchief and pressed it to her eyes. She shook her head. 'I never knew.'

Mallory murmured, 'I'm sorry.'

Bemused, Annabelle said, 'But why would Royce kill my father if he was blackmailing him? It . . . it doesn't make sense.'

Mallory said, 'You didn't know that Royce was stealing your father's watercolours and replacing them with copies?'

She looked shocked. 'God, no.'

'Your father promised Lady Cee her pick of the collection, and we presume Royce learned of this and feared the thefts would soon be discovered.'

She stared at the detective inspector. 'So he . . .'

Maria reached out and touched her arm.

Annabelle smiled. 'I'm fine. It's just . . . I knew there was something not quite right about Wilson Royce, but I never guessed . . .'

They drank in silence for a minute, then Mallory drained his glass. 'I'll drive you back to the house, Annabelle. Then I'll find Greaves and we'll question Royce.'

Annabelle gathered her handbag, slipped her sunglasses down

from their perch in her hair and murmured goodbye to Langham and Maria.

Langham watched them cross to the Humber and drive away from the quayside.

Maria said, 'Poor Annabelle . . .'

He nodded. 'Drink up,' he said, indicating her glass. 'I think there's time for a quick one before dinner.'

TWENTY-EIGHT

Maria glanced across at Donald as they climbed into the car and drove back to Connaught House. 'You're quiet.'

'Just thinking,' he murmured.

She'd seen him like this before, when working out the twists and turns of his latest thriller. He would sit in his study with his empty pipe jutting from his mouth, a frown creasing his forehead. On other occasions he'd fall into an impenetrable silence, while at dinner or reading the paper, and stare into space. She knew, then, to leave him well alone and he'd return to his normal self in time.

As they drove through the woods, he said, 'Dash it all, there's something very wrong.'

'What?' she coaxed.

'I don't buy it for a single minute,' he said. 'Everything about the murder is just plain *wrong*.'

'Wrong?' she said. 'In what way?'

He gripped the apex of the steering wheel, his pipe clenched in his jaw. 'Maria, when we get back to the house, will you come for a walk with me?'

'Of course,' she said, surprised.

'I need to think, and talk . . . and I think best either when I'm in the bath or walking. And as I don't feel like taking a bath right now . . .'

She laughed. 'I don't know . . . I could scrub your back.'

'No, I need to stretch my legs,' he said, and the fact that he'd taken her seriously indicated how abstracted he was.

He steered through the gates and up the drive, braking beside Mallory's car.

Maria climbed out and followed him around the side of the house and across the lawn. She slipped an arm through his and matched his stride. As they passed the drawing room, she noticed Mallory and Greaves through the French windows. Wilson Royce was seated in an armchair, staring at the detectives like a frightened rabbit. Mallory strode back and forth, firing questions at the young man.

Donald led her past Connaught's study and the constable still stationed outside.

Up ahead, Monty Connaught was striding towards the cliff path that led down to the jetty, his rucksack slung over his right shoulder.

Donald called out, and Connaught turned and lifted a hand in greeting. He came towards them, smiling. 'I'm about to push off in the next hour or two. I would have come to find you and say goodbye. Inspector Mallory gave me the all-clear.' He gestured towards the cliff. 'I had Sam and Ginger bring the ketch around to the jetty – Morocco, here I come.'

'We never did have that drink,' Donald said.

'No, I'm sorry to say we didn't, did we?'

'Maybe some other time.'

'Look here,' Connaught said. 'I'll be back in Blighty for Christmas, staying at my club, the Travellers on Pall Mall, from the twentieth. You're in London, aren't you? What say we meet up and go out for dinner? I'll tell you all about my North African adventures.'

Donald nodded. 'That sounds like a good idea. I'll be in touch.'

Connaught lifted his claw in a farewell salute. 'Till then,' he said, and moved towards the cliff path.

'What a nice man,' Maria said, 'compared with his brother.'

'Yes,' said Donald, 'isn't he?'

They continued across the lawn and came to the walled garden. Donald pushed through the timber door and led the way along the gravelled path. He seemed miles away.

'Donald?'

'Mmm?'

'A penny for them?'

He smiled at her. 'Oh, I've been thinking about the way Denbigh Connaught was murdered. To cut through flesh like that, to inflict such a severe injury . . . it'd take quite some strength. Jeff came up with a working theory back in the pub: he wondered if the killer

had first cut Connaught's throat, and then arranged the piano wire
to make it appear that he'd been garrotted.'

'But why would anyone do that?'

Donald shrugged. 'To make it seem as though someone with
phenomenal strength had killed him? I know; I don't buy that, either.
I think the forensic bods will discount the possibility pretty damned
quick.'

'Also,' she pointed out, 'if he was attacked with a knife, then
surely there would have been signs of a struggle, and lots of spilled
blood.'

'You'd make a good detective,' he said. 'That's exactly what I
told Jeff.'

'So it's back to square one,' she said. 'Connaught *was* strangled
with piano wire.'

He shook his head, frowning. 'So the killer enters the study and
chats with him. There was no sign of a struggle, so the chances are
that Connaught knew his killer. He turned his back on whoever it
was, and the killer takes his opportunity and loops the wire around
his neck. But Connaught was a big man. He'd put up one heck of
a struggle, fight like an enraged bull. However, there was no sign
of a struggle in the study itself, or on Connaught's person: no bruises
on his hands or face, or cuts to his fingers – nothing to indicate that
he'd put up the slightest resistance. And there was also the fact of
where he was when he died.'

'Behind the piano?'

He came to a halt. 'But why was he *there*, Maria?'

She frowned at him, then tugged his arm and set him walking
again. 'Well . . . he had to be somewhere—'

'But dash it all, girl, the gap between the piano and the window
was about two feet wide. A big man like Connaught wouldn't choose
to walk behind the piano. It was almost as if he'd been *placed* there.'

'But why would the killer have put him there of all places?'

'That's the blasted question I've been asking myself ever since
I saw the body. Why was it *behind* the piano like that?'

She pursed her lips, contemplating the riddle. 'Donald . . . how
was the body positioned?'

He looked at her. 'On its side.'

'Facing the piano,' she asked, 'or the wall?'

'Facing the wall, lying with its back hard up against the back of
the piano.'

'And the head? Was it projecting a little way from the end of the piano?'

'Ye–es . . . Yes, it was. What are you driving at?'

She turned, gravel crunching underfoot, and looked at him. 'I don't know,' she said slowly. 'Perhaps the killer attacked Connaught elsewhere in the study, asphyxiating him before he had time to struggle, rendering him unconscious. And then he placed the body behind the piano, with his head projecting, and exerted the necessary force to cut through the flesh, with the piano acting as a kind of counterweight?'

'Still, the force needed to exert the requisite pressure . . .' He stopped, staring at her aghast.

His expression alarmed her. 'Donald?'

'You genius,' he whispered. 'But if you're right . . .'

As she stared at him, she could almost see the thoughts ticking over in his head, one by one, as he reached an awful conclusion.

'Donald?' she repeated.

'Let's take another look at the study,' he said suddenly, taking her hand and almost dragging her along the path.

'Donald,' she laughed, 'what have I said?'

'If you're right, Maria, and the killer placed the body behind the piano deliberately . . . My word, but that's terrible.'

They crossed the lawn to the study. Donald was withdrawing his accreditation to show the constable, but the young man waved him on. 'That's quite all right, Mr Langham. Inspector Mallory said you're working on the case.'

Donald pushed open the study door and they stepped inside.

Denbigh Connaught's presence seemed to haunt the place. He had been larger than life while alive, and now, in death, he exerted a strange and powerful influence. Maria felt, irrationally, that he was watching them as they attempted to piece together the conundrum of his final minutes.

Donald crossed to the piano, knelt and examined the parquet floor just in front of the piano's small brass wheels. She crouched beside him.

He pointed. 'Look.'

A small indentation showed in the polished wood directly in front of the left-hand wheel. He indicated the wheel on the right. 'And there's another.'

She shook her head. 'What?'

'Dents made by the wedges,' he said, 'placed there to prevent the piano from moving.'

He stood and stared down at the rug in the centre of the floor. 'Now, if I'm right,' he said, 'there should be a trapdoor concealed beneath the rug.'

He knelt before the settee and made to roll up the rug. Belatedly realizing that she was in the way, she stepped back off it and watched as he took the tasselled edge and folded the rug over little by little.

'And what do we have here?' he said, rolling the rug the rest of the way and revealing the outline of a trapdoor in the parquet flooring.

He knelt beside the trapdoor, pulled a handkerchief from his trouser pocket, then stopped. He pointed to the coffee table before the settee. 'Pass me that paper knife, would you? I don't want to risk smudging any fingerprints.'

She passed him the knife and he slipped it in the gap between the boards and the trapdoor and levered. He created a gap, then inserted his fingers and opened the trapdoor the rest of the way.

He peered into the hole; Maria joined him.

He pointed. 'Look,' he said. 'The study sits on an X-shaped crossbeam or chassis. See that girder, there?'

She lowered her head and peered into the shadows at the girder.

'And do you see those markings on the rust?' he asked.

In the shadows, she made out two sets of silver lines, nine inches apart, on the facing plane of the girder. 'Yes. But what does it mean?'

Donald stood up and pointed to the frame of the trapdoor. 'Note the cuts in the edge of the wood, parallel with the left-hand side of the piano.'

She nodded, peering at the double lines scored in the timber, perhaps a quarter of an inch deep. 'Yes, but—'

He sat down suddenly on the settee. She noted, with alarm, that his hands were trembling. He shook his head and swore quietly to himself.

She felt a moment's panic. 'Donald, I don't understand.'

He said, very quietly, 'This answers everything, old girl. Or almost everything.'

'But how? How does it, Donald?'

He stared at the piano, then at the trapdoor, shaking his head.

She sat beside him and gripped his hand. 'Donald?'

He smiled at her bleakly and found his voice at last. 'The killer came here in the morning, Maria, as casual as you like, and engaged

Denbigh Connaught in conversation. Then he rendered Connaught unconscious – I'm not at all sure how, maybe drugged him – and manoeuvred him behind the piano with his head projecting, wedging chocks under the wheels to ensure the piano didn't move when pressure was exerted. Then the killer slipped a length of piano wire around the unconscious man's neck, led it across the study and through the trapdoor, and climbed down to attach the ends of the wire to the girder. Then the killer left the scene of the crime-to-be, locked the door and crept away.'

Maria squeezed his hand as a terrible understanding swept over her. 'And then . . .'

'And then,' Donald went on, 'a few hours elapsed, and the revolving study turned, and little by little, as the study moved slowly around, the piano wire tightened and gradually sliced through Denbigh Connaught's throat – and cut into the frame of the trapdoor as it did so – eventually severing his jugular and killing him.'

'But,' Maria began, her mouth very dry, 'why . . . why would someone arrange such an elaborate method of murdering him?'

'This was set up in the morning,' he said, 'and the wire eventually sliced through his throat and killed him *hours* later, in the afternoon, between two and four o'clock – just as the killer had planned. And between two and four, the killer was a long way away, doing something else with witnesses who could testify to his whereabouts. All this,' he finished, indicating the piano and the trapdoor, 'was a very elaborate means of setting the killer up with a cast-iron alibi.'

He rose suddenly, pulled open the door and stepped from the study.

TWENTY-NINE

Langham crossed the lawn to the edge of the cliff and peered over, a tide of vertigo pressing against his chest and compelling him to lie down.

'Donald?' Maria sounded alarmed.

Down beside the jetty, its sails furled, Monty Connaught's fifty-foot two-master rode a slight swell. Its skipper stood on the deck, speaking to someone in the cabin.

Maria joined Langham and gripped his elbow. 'Donald . . .'

Langham waved down to Connaught. 'Monty! I'd like a word before you go.'

Connaught raised his maimed hand to his brow, shading his eyes from the glare of the sun, and peered up the cliff face. 'Langham?'

'A quick word . . .'

Connaught nodded. 'Very well.'

He stepped from the deck of the boat on to the jetty, and for a second Langham assumed he was about to ascend the precipitous stairway. His stomach turned as he watched Connaught sit down on the capstan and light a cigarillo.

'Donald,' Maria said, 'you're not going down there!'

'I'll be fine,' he said, wishing it was true.

'But you said—'

He turned to her, smiling. 'As I recall, I gave you my word that I'd never again attempt to rescue a suicidal, drunken, one-legged man from halfway down the side of a cliff. Well, Connaught hardly falls into that category.'

Temper flashed in her eyes. 'But—'

He touched her cheek. 'I'll be fine,' he said. He turned, took a breath and approached the first step.

Behind him, he heard Maria muttering something in French.

He took the descent slowly, telling himself that the ascent would be easy this time with no drunken old soldier to impede his progress. He just had to take it easy, be sure of his footing and not gaze down to his right at the hundred-foot drop . . . In fact, best not even consider the rocks far below.

Which was easier said than done.

He stared down at Monty Connaught, casually smoking on the jetty, and rehearsed what he was about to say.

He came to the halfway point, where on Saturday afternoon Colonel Haxby had sat. He stopped and stared down at the concrete that had crumbled away to nothing, his gorge rising. His heartbeat increased as he gripped the rock to his left and negotiated the perished step without mishap.

Monty Connaught smiled as Langham reached the jetty and sat down on the bottom step, his legs trembling. Langham looked up, saw Maria's tiny head far above and lifted a hand; her relieved wave cheered him inordinately.

'How can I help, Donald?' Monty asked.

Langham mopped his sweating brow with his handkerchief, replaced it and looked at the smiling travel writer. 'I've been thinking over what happened on Sunday afternoon.'

Monty nodded. 'That's all I've been able to think about, too.'

'Only,' Langham went on, 'I don't think the killer struck in the afternoon, despite all the evidence. It really happened that morning, well before midday.'

Monty's sun-browned face creased into a frown. 'It did? I don't follow . . .'

'You see, whoever killed your brother first rendered him unconscious, then looped a length of piano wire around his neck . . .'

And he went on to describe, in detail, how the killer had supplied himself with a foolproof alibi. 'Or an almost foolproof alibi,' he finished.

'I see,' Monty said. 'Ingenious.'

Langham nodded towards the man's maimed hand. 'You never told me how you came by your injuries.'

Monty smiled. 'In all fairness, you never asked.'

'You must have harboured a terrible resentment towards your brother.'

'You know?'

'Annabelle mentioned it.'

Monty sighed. 'You cannot imagine, Donald, how it affected me, at first. And, if I'm honest with you, for years afterwards. I was good at cricket, and I wanted to sail, explore the world. But how could I do that with this?' He lifted his claw. 'My brother's thoughtless – malicious – act of vandalism brought an end to all my dreams. Of course I resented him.' He made a sound halfway between a laugh and a grunt. 'More, I hated him.'

'I can understand that—' Langham began.

Monty swept on, 'But I matured. It came to me, at around the age of fifteen, that I could go on hating Denbigh and pitying myself, or I could move on and prove to Denbigh and to the world that I wouldn't allow my injuries to impede my ambitions. The only person I would be harming by sinking into self-pity, by sitting at home and regretting what might have been, was myself. So I learned how to sail, one-man dinghies and small boats, and did my best with larger ones . . . With the really big brutes like this one, I admitted my restrictions and sought help. I always craved adventure and dreamed of writing about my exploits, and I can safely say that I achieved my dreams.'

'Nevertheless, you must have resented your brother for the many things his actions prevented you doing.'

Monty closed one eye, tipped his head and regarded Langham. 'And you think that resentment reached such a stage, years later, that I felt compelled to murder my brother in an act of revenge – render him unconscious, arrange the piano wire around his neck, tie it to the girder' – he raised the claw of his right hand – '*with this?*'

Langham sighed. 'No, Monty. I don't. Oh, for a time back there in the study I did wonder if it was you.' He paused. 'No, I came down here to reassure myself that it *wasn't* you. You see, I think I know who killed him.'

Monty stared at him. 'I can give you that reassurance,' he said, and pulled his left hand from the pocket of his blue linen jacket. Langham saw that the hand, its fingers artificial-looking and stiffened, was encased in a leather glove.

As he watched, Monty pushed up the sleeve of his jacket with his claw, revealing a strap bound around the left wrist. With his claw, he took hold of his gloved hand . . . and twisted.

As if watching an optical illusion, Langham saw the gloved hand come away from the arm to reveal the rounded end of a scarred stump.

'There, Donald. I couldn't have done what you described in order to kill my brother, with just one finger and a thumb, and a useless stump.'

Langham looked up from the stump and met Monty's steady gaze. 'Of course not,' he said. 'I surmised, when you never used your left hand . . .'

Monty held his gaze. 'So,' he said, 'who do you think did kill him?'

For the next five minutes Langham outlined his theory, and Monty sat very still and listened.

When Langham had finished, the other nodded and said quietly, 'In that case, I think I ought to stay around here for a while, in case I'm needed.'

'I think that might be wise,' Langham said. He stepped forward, held out his hand and said, 'I'm so sorry.'

Monty proffered the claw of his right hand and they shook.

Langham turned to the steps and climbed.

As he did so, he was overcome with a nausea that had nothing to do with the thought of the drop to his left or the state of the crumbling steps.

He reached the top, and Maria clutched his arm and dragged him from the edge of the cliff. 'Donald?'

'He didn't do it, Maria.'

She stared at him. 'He didn't? But if *he* didn't, then who did?'

He took Maria's hand and indicated the bench overlooking the sea. 'Let's sit down,' he said, 'and I'll tell you.'

THIRTY

The guests had gathered in the drawing room for drinks before dinner.

Langham paused outside the French windows and murmured, 'Are you sure you're all right?'

Maria nodded, still looking ashen in response to what he'd told her. 'I'll be fine.' She smiled at him. 'But I'll feel even better when all this is over.'

'You and me both.'

He led the way into the room.

Colonel Haxby was at the bar, refilling glasses. 'Ah, Donald, Maria . . . What'll it be?'

'Whisky and soda for me,' Langham said. 'A big one.'

'I'll have just a tonic water, please,' Maria said.

'Coming up,' the old soldier said. 'I say, bit of shocker about young Royce, what?'

The others drifted over to the bar.

Charles said, 'But is it true, Donald? Has Wilson been arrested?' He looked shocked, and his plump fingers pulled at his bow-tie in consternation.

Langham took his drink from the colonel. 'As far as I know, he's just been taken in for further questioning.'

'But I saw him being hauled off,' Pandora said, 'and he was kicking up a hell of a din.' Her owlish face scanned the group. 'And he was wailing that he didn't do it, that he was innocent. I must say, he looked scared to death.'

Lady Cecelia regarded her sherry. 'He always did strike me as a . . . a somewhat shifty character,' she said. 'I know that it is wrong to pre-judge in such matters, but it wouldn't surprise me if he were found to be guilty.'

'But why the ruddy hell did he do it?' Colonel Haxby wanted to know. 'I mean, I had no love for the man – Connaught, that is. Thought of bumping him off once or twice meself, in idle moments. But what did young Royce have to gain from killing his employer?'

'Who knows what goes on in the mind of someone driven to these terrible acts?' Charles said.

Pandora asked, 'Has anyone seen Annabelle?'

'Bumped into her upstairs five minutes ago,' the colonel said. 'She told me she'd be down presently for dinner.'

The artist sighed. 'It's strange, but in a way I'm relieved that the murderer wasn't one of us – if Royce is proven guilty, that is. I mean, I've been wondering who might have wanted the old reprobate dead, and it occurred to me that none of us much liked the man. Any one of us might have—'

Lady Cecelia said, 'I must object to that, Pandora. Denbigh might not have been perfect, but do you know something, I did feel sorry for him. He was someone so wrapped up in his own concerns that he was unable to apprehend the feelings of others.'

'And this made you sympathetic towards him?' Pandora grunted. 'All the more reason to detest the chap, in my opinion.'

'I know one shouldn't speak ill of the dead,' Colonel Haxby declared, 'but as far as I was concerned, Connaught was a rogue. None of us are perfect, mind, but there was something nasty about the chap. He liked to control the situation, manipulate those around him.'

Langham looked at the old soldier, surprised by his insight.

'Be that as it may,' Lady Cecelia said, 'I think he did see the error of his ways, before the end. He did apologize, after all, and bestow generous gifts on those he'd wronged.'

Colonel Haxby grunted, 'Fat chance of our getting anything now,' then realized his *faux pas* and turned hurriedly to the bar for a refill.

Conversation ceased suddenly as the door at the far end of the room opened and Annabelle Connaught appeared.

'Ah,' Colonel Haxby said, 'can I get you a drink, my dear?'

'I'll have a dry sherry, please, Colonel.'

'Coming up.'

She joined the group and took her drink. Pandora smiled at the young woman. 'We'll soon be out of your hair, Annabelle. Can't be any fun, having a houseful of strangers in such circumstances.'

Annabelle smiled and sipped her drink. 'Oh, I don't know. In a way, your being here has been a welcome distraction.'

'What will you do now, my dear?' Charles asked, 'if that's not too impertinent a question.'

'Not at all. Well, I intend to sell this place and perhaps move from the village. My practice is in St Austell, so it would make sense to relocate there. Threepenny Cottage, with its views across the bay to this place . . .' She shook her head. 'No, I couldn't stay there.'

'Of course not,' Charles agreed.

Pandora said, 'We really should meet up from time to time when you're in London. And you *must* come to my next exhibition.'

Annabelle smiled. 'I'd like that.'

The door opened and Watkins appeared. 'If you'd care to come through for dinner, ladies and gentlemen.'

The others moved off, but Langham touched Annabelle's arm and murmured, 'I wonder if I might have a word?'

'Why, of course.'

On the pretext of fixing more drinks, Langham remained at the bar. He poured Annabelle another sherry, and Maria a tonic water, then said, 'Perhaps you'd care to sit down?'

'Is this about Wilson Royce?' Annabelle asked, taking a seat.

Langham sat opposite her on the settee, Maria beside him. 'Indirectly,' he said.

'But you do think he's guilty?' she said.

He looked up from his whisky. 'Of killing your father?' he said. 'No, I don't. I don't think he's the guilty party at all. In fact, I think he's the innocent dupe in all this.'

'Innocent?' Annabelle sat back in her seat as if pushed forcibly. 'But . . . but what on earth do you mean?'

'Old Colonel Haxby put his finger on the matter just before you came in,' Langham went on. 'He said that your father liked to control situations and manipulate people.' He paused. 'There are two types of writer – and I'm speaking very broadly here – those who understand other people, and those who understand only themselves. Your father was of the latter stripe. He was an egotist who understood only himself, who cared nothing for anyone unless he could gain something from them. That was why, throughout his life, he used people, manipulated them to his own devious ends.'

She stared down at her glass, and he thought it significant that she did not contradict his assessment of her father.

'It's ironic,' he said, 'that his terminal illness should have brought about in him a change of heart, a reassessment of his past and the acknowledgement of how badly he'd treated certain people. Ironic – because it was this change of heart that spelled his premature death sentence.'

She shook her head. 'I don't see . . .' she began.

'In a way, Annabelle, I feel sorry for you. I can only imagine what hell it was for you to have had a father like Denbigh Connaught. You were really as much a victim of his ego as were the many other people he manipulated down the years. Except, growing up in his shadow, you couldn't escape his influence; he even dictated your choice of profession. And you could have practised anywhere in Britain, but his hold over you was so great that you were compelled to return to Cornwall, to the very village where your father lived. Because, mixed up with your hatred was also, I think, a strange love for the man.'

He took a drink, then went on, 'It must have occurred to you that only his death could free you from his grip. And when he told you that he was dying, you must have seen an end to your psychological slavery.'

Annabelle stared down at her glass and spoke slowly. 'You can have no conception of what it was like to be controlled by him, to have every facet of my life influenced by someone as domineering as my father. I hated him' – she shook her head – 'but you're right: a small part of me craved his affection, his love. And I hated myself for this dependence, this need.'

He said quietly, 'But it was not this hatred of him that pushed you, finally, to kill your father, was it? It was his change of heart towards those he'd wronged that drove you.'

She looked at him, startled. 'What makes you think—'

'Do you deny killing your father, Annabelle?'

'But . . . but I was with you when . . .' She looked desperately from Langham to Maria.

'I know how you did it,' he said. 'I know how you made it appear that you were nowhere near the study when he was supposed to have been killed.'

She opened her mouth to argue, then saw the futility of it.

She murmured, 'I thought, when he told me he was dying . . . I thought I would be free of him. I wonder if he realized this and gained some perverted satisfaction in telling me that he planned to give away so much of his wealth. Almost everything, in fact. He even planned to sell the house and give the money to others he judged he'd wronged, leaving me with just ten thousand pounds.'

'And so you planned, before he could do that, to kill him. You were very clever in your method, ingeniously clever – and more so because you planned to kill, as it were, two birds with one stone.'

She stared at him, and Langham detected something of Denbigh Connaught's ego in her: even *in extremis* she could not help but interpret his words as praise.

'At first,' he said, 'I thought that your motive for wanting Wilson Royce out of the way, for ensuring he hanged for your father's murder, was that you'd learned he was blackmailing him and stealing the watercolours.' He shook his head. 'But that, to me, didn't seem sufficient a reason for implicating Royce. I assumed that as you had to implicate *someone* in the killing, then Royce was the obvious candidate – but then my partner in London discovered a letter in Royce's possession, from a . . . a woman to your father, in which she asked him whether "her daughter", Annabelle, would be present this weekend. Wilson Royce was probably in the habit of opening all your father's mail, on the off-chance that he might come across information he could use . . . and in this case he struck lucky.' He stared across at the woman as she hung her head, her eyes closed. 'My guess, Annabelle, is that in some way he used this information against you.'

She drew a deep breath, lifted her head and regarded him without emotion. 'A week ago,' she said in a voice so soft he could hardly make out the words, 'Royce told me he had certain information about the identity of my mother – my *real* mother, he said. He told me that my father had lied to me about my mother's death, that my real mother was not who my father always claimed she was, but someone else, someone still living. And he had a letter to prove it.'

'And . . .?'

'He said that I could have the letter if . . . if I paid him five hundred pounds.'

'And, of course, you refused.'

'Of course!' She said it with venom. 'Wilson Royce is vile – a nasty, unscrupulous criminal. He deserves . . .'

'He deserves to hang for your father's murder?' Langham finished. He looked down at his drink, took a mouthful, then went on, 'I thought it odd, from the very start, that you should hire me to keep tabs on Wilson Royce for no reason other than you had an "intuition" about him. But that was part of your plan, wasn't it? You found out that Royce was stealing the watercolours, but you didn't want to implicate him outright. You merely wanted me to discover Royce's theft, which, when I learned of your father's promise of the paintings to Lady Cee, would lead me to assume a motive for Royce's murder of his employer. No . . .' He shook his head. 'It just didn't ring true. And then there was the murder itself. That didn't ring true, either: the odd location of your father's body behind the piano, and the strength required to cut his flesh to the bone . . .' He smiled. 'So let me tell you how I think it happened, on Sunday morning.'

He stared at her, and she looked back at him, her gaze forthright, cold and expressionless.

'At some point that morning,' Langham said, 'you crossed the bay in your boat and moored at the jetty below Connaught House, then made your way up the cliff steps to your father's study. I'm surmising here, but I suspect that from time to time you administered a sedative or painkiller to your father, and this was one of these occasions. You gave him an injection – a dose sufficient to render him unconscious for hours. Then you dragged your father to his final resting place behind the piano, placed chocks beneath the piano's wheels to ensure it didn't move, rolled up the rug and opened the trapdoor. You then looped a length of piano wire around your father's neck, led it through the trapdoor and secured it to a girder so that, when the study turned and the wire tightened, the wire would sever your father's throat and he would die at some point later that afternoon.'

He took a draught of Scotch. 'You left the study, locking it behind you with a copy of your father's key, returned to Threepenny Cottage and met Maria and me there around noon. Although, had we been unable to accept your invitation, no doubt you would have established an alibi by being seen, at the time your father was "murdered", in St Austell or elsewhere. After dropping us back at your cottage around five o'clock, you set off across the bay to the jetty, ascended to the study, let yourself in and cut the wire leading through the trapdoor, leaving just a short garrotte with loops at each end. You removed the chocks, rolled back the rug to cover the trapdoor and left the study, locking it behind you and hurrying back down to your boat.'

He finished his whisky and stared at the empty glass for a while, then went on, 'At some point you planted Wilson Royce's glove in the brazier and allowed the investigation to take its course, knowing that the chances were we'd discover Royce's theft and his black-mailing of your father. You would then have taken great satisfaction in seeing Royce hanged for the crime *you* committed.'

In a faltering voice, Annabelle said, 'Do you have any idea, Langham, what it was like for me . . . to have been controlled all my life by someone like my father – and then to find myself in the clutches of a worthless, scheming petty criminal like Royce?' She shook her head. 'He deserved,' she finished in a whisper, '*everything* that was coming to him—'

She was interrupted by the sound of a car engine and the crunch of its wheels on the gravel. Langham looked up to see Jeff Mallory's Humber pull up in the drive and its owner climb out.

Annabelle hung her head, her fists clenched in her lap, as the door opened and Mallory appeared on the threshold.

The detective inspector took in the scene and Annabelle's posture, and his expression crumpled. 'Don?'

Bracing himself, Langham stood and crossed the room to his friend.

EPILOGUE

The weather was kind to Charles Elder's annual garden party. The sun shone from a cloudless sky and forty guests milled around the lawned garden of his Pimlico agency, enjoying drinks and nibbles and the kind of eclectic conversation generated by gathering together the great and the good of the London literary world – and, Langham thought, the not so great and good. He'd spotted at least half a dozen spongers along for the booze, writers down on their luck whom Charles, being the kind-hearted man he was, could not bring himself to eject. 'The more the merrier!' he'd trilled when Albert pointed out that a couple of hacks had been seen dipping pint glasses into the punchbowl.

Langham sat in the shade of the summer house and watched Jeff Mallory at the far end of the lawn, absorbed in conversation with their actress friend, Caroline Dequincy.

'They seem to be getting along very well,' Maria commented, sipping her drink.

'I thought it'd be a good idea to introduce them,' he said. 'In my humble opinion, they're made for each other.'

'Well, let's see what happens.'

He sighed. 'Do you know something, old girl, I can't help thinking about Annabelle Connaught.'

She regarded him. 'I thought you've been rather quiet. What is it?'

'Well . . . that last conversation with her in the drawing room at Connaught House. Do you know, I expected her to claim that she killed her father out of compassion, but I don't think that sentiment ever entered into her reasoning. She was her father's daughter, all right, in that she inherited his egotism – she saw a way of killing two birds with one stone, and nothing was going to stop her. The thing is . . .'

He lapsed into silence, and Maria touched his shoe with the toe of her high-heel. 'Go on. The thing is?'

'The thing is, I had her down, in my naivety, as a decent type. Perhaps I was blinded by her beauty, and the fact that she was a doctor.'

Maria smiled at him. 'Do you know, Mr Langham, you *are* a little naive, but that's because you're also a good person.'

He looked up. 'What did *you* think of her?'

She hunched her shoulders, considering. 'I liked her, but even so – and this isn't the wisdom of hindsight – I thought that there was more to her than she was giving away. It struck me that she'd been damaged by her father.'

He shook his head. 'What a terrible legacy he left behind, Maria. I wonder how many people he hurt down the years?'

'My guess is many, my love, but no one more so than Annabelle.'

In a bid to change the subject, Langham pointed across the garden to Charles. 'It's lovely to see him so happy, isn't it?'

'He's like a child on Christmas day,' Maria said.

Charles looked across at Albert, who paused in the act of pouring wine for a guest. The young man caught Charles's eye and gave a dazzling smile.

'And it's nice to see that Albert's settled in so well,' he said.

A little later Charles and Albert retreated to the summer house and joined Langham and Maria.

'That's all the food and drink out,' Albert said, 'and now I can put me feet up. Blimey, but your friends can't half put it away, Charles. I thought the regulars at the Boy and Barrel could sup, but this lot'd win a drinking contest hands down.'

'There is something about the literary mentality,' said Charles, 'which predisposes it to alcohol.'

'In other words, scribblers like their booze!' Albert laughed. 'And look, Don's glass is empty. Can I get you a refill, Donald?'

'Do you know, I think I'll pace myself. The afternoon's yet young.'

Jeff Mallory joined them, pint glass in hand. He was beaming from ear to ear.

'I think you made a hit there, old boy,' Langham said.

'She's a corker, Don. Thanks for the intro. She had to dash off – meeting a director at the Ritz. Did you know that she's started acting again?'

'That's news to me,' Langham said. 'Did you get her number before she flew?'

'Even better, I'm taking her out to dinner next week.'

'Attaboy.'

'You certainly don't waste any time,' Maria laughed.